In Memory of My lifelong friend
John Cornelius Bocskay
Criminal Investigator for the New York, Westchester County,
District Attorney's office

Rest in Peace

PROLOGUE

The most recent rash of murders was not just a day at police headquarters for Johnny Vero. He would orchestrate each homicide like he played each of the four strings on his cello. His childhood dream was to play with the New York Philharmonic Orchestra, traveling the world being the conductor's principal cellist. He was an accomplished musician and earned a partial scholarship to the Manhattan College of Music, a well-known music school located on Perry Street, New York City.

Each of the strings to his cello is tuned in perfect fifths giving the listener a euphoric high. Each crime Johnny Vero solved gave him that same rapturous feeling.

Time and an unforeseen occurrence changed his life from his childhood dream to one of the most decorated detectives in New York City.

There was something Johnny Vero could have never known. How things would turn out the way they did. Events that made him addicted to solving murders, and nothing, absolutely nothing... was going to change it.

CHAPTER 1

After high school and his short term with the Manhattan College of Music which is a major music conservatory located on the upper west side in the Morningside Heights section of New York City, Johnny joined the Navy. His original voluntary enlistment, turned into a four year commitment. During his tenure, he served on two different ships, The USS Monrovia which sailed the Mediterranean as a transport assault ship and the USS Keith known for it being a hunter-killer escort destroyer patrolling the waters of the Atlantic escorting convoys from 'mid-ocean points' to ports around the world, participating in the assault on Saipan. After the battle of the Philippine Sea, she sailed for Guam to continue assaults and then to Pearl Harbor.

In 1899 the United States Naval Board issued a report on the results of investigations of the Marconi system of wireless telegraphy. The report noted that the system was well adapted for use in squadron signaling, under conditions of rain, fog, darkness and motion of speed although dampness affected the performance. They also noted that when two stations were transmitting simultaneously both would be received and that the system had the potential to affect the compass. They reported ranges of from 85 miles for large ships with tall masts to 7 miles for smaller boats. The board recommended that the system be given a trial by the US Navy. Johnny was a quick student absorbing all the data the navy was willing to throw at him. He was chosen to study this system and became a master cryptographer.

Much of his training as a cellist would be applied to the training of electronic devices such as telegraphy, cryptography, and wire taps. Johnny applied the words of his classical music professor that he could hear over and over in his mind saying in a deep thick German accent; *Johan, Johan, Johan, set da strings to vibrate by eeda plucking dem, like a harp, strumming dem, like a guitar or draw da sound out mit a bow. Come, now, Johan, let me hear you do dis. Pretend cello is beautiful woman you vant to caress. You vant to become one mit her, like it feels to be inside her, feeling her warmth and the sensation you get.* He learned that the vibrations of the strings are transferred through a wooden pathway into the body of the instrument, which serves as an amplifier. The air inside of the body vibrates and produces a warm, full, tone just like the professor said. What a perfect metaphor...*just like being deep inside the woman you're caressing, feeling her warmth and smoothness all around you.* Applying this knowledge, Johnny helped develop a simpler device that would siphon current from a telephone converting it to voice patterns. This earned him three stripes with the classification of Petty Officer 2nd Class. It earned the Navy full ownership of the patent. Little did Johnny know this knowledge would serve him in later years as a homicide detective?

CHAPTER 2

Johnny's father was a cop who walked a beat on the lower east side of Manhattan in a tough neighborhood known as "Hell's Kitchen." This is an area which generally runs from Thirty Seventh to Fifty Seventh Streets, West of Eighth Avenue and East to the Hudson River. It was a bastion of poor working class Irish Americans. An early use of the phrase, "Hell's Kitchen", was used by Davy Crockett in 1835 when he said, "In my part of the country, when you meet an Irishman, you find a first-rate gentleman; but these are worse than savages; they are too mean to swab hell's kitchen." He was referring to another section of Manhattan known as the Five Points where multiple murders would often take place, putting the residents in a class as savages. The similarities of ethnicity and crime in both neighborhoods became such that there had to be a distinction from one another. So, the area from Thirty Seventh to Fifty Seventh Streets became known as the infamous "Hell's Kitchen" and the area known as the five points remained as the five points.

CHAPTER 3

Officer John Vero, Sr., would walk his same beat every day while on duty twirling his nightstick with the rhythm of a drum major leading a parade band. In his everyday routine, he would check doors and alleyways and help the residents and shop owners cope with their daily anxieties of the petty crimes and domestic disputes. Occasionally he would use the call in box on the corner for the purpose of contacting the precinct having to say; "Send the paddy wagon over. We have a few drunks."

On this particular day, Officer Vero walked into the First American Savings and Loan Bank on Eight Avenue and Thirty Seventh Street. In his usual manner, Officer Vero would greet the manager who sat at a front desk when you first entered through the doors. This day and only this day Officer Vero who walked into the same bank countless times walked into what looked like, in is mind, a Broadway *show*.

The manager, assistant manager and secretary were standing on their desks with their hands in the air as if they were about to choreograph a singing and dancing segment in a big stage production. People were lying on the floor and the bank tellers were all standing on top of the counters. What Officer Vero didn't know was that he walked into an unsuspected robbery in progress, realizing *this is not a Broadway show*. In the moment he realized what was happening and before he was able to draw his weapon, yelling, "Mother Mary of God," he was shot and killed by the two bullets that pierced into his chest.

Countless lives changed within these few seconds.

CHAPTER 4

Johnny Vero's addiction was born.

CHAPTER 5

Petty Officer 2nd Class Johnny Vero had to end his naval career early, due to his mother's now hardship, and return home helping his mother, Norma, arrange a different life that she was accustomed to.

Johnny was hired by New York Power and Light Company as a telephone pole trouble shooter due to his electronic and wiring expertise the Navy taught him. His job was to find hot spots before they would occur and cause a blackout.

He grew to hate his job, constantly thinking of how his father was ruthlessly gunned down. Now this punk shit head is serving a life sentence in Sing Sing Correctional Facility, a maximum security prison located on the east bank of the Hudson River in the town of Ossining, New York. *This doesn't seem equitable*, he often thought.

Johnny would constantly look in The Chief-Leader, (the weekly newspaper known for in-depth coverage for Firefighters, Police, Sanitation Workers, Teachers and other public servants as well as job openings and exams) scouring for when the police exam would be.

The moment Johnny got word he passed the police exam and was accepted into the police academy, without hesitation, quit his job with New York Power and Light Company. He knew then and there, all he wanted going forward was to get the scum off the streets like the scum that murdered his father. He endeavored to strive to become addicted to solving homicides which came to Johnny as easily as doing the Sunday newspaper crossword puzzle, in ink.

He would read 'True Detective,' a popular periodical magazine featuring homicides and how the detectives came to solving the murders.

Quickly, within a few years, he earned his gold badge as a detective.

CHAPTER 6

It's been quite a few years since his divorce from Simone. Now, Johnny Vero lives alone in a one bedroom apartment in an upscale building located in the northernmost part of Manhattan known as Marble Hill.

Marble Hill is politically part of Manhattan. The Army Corp of engineers designed a needed project to re-route ships between the Harlem and Hudson Rivers through the Harlem Shipping Canal. This endeavor now connected these two areas making Marble Hill part of the Bronx. It confused everyone, including the post office.

Johnny's daughter, Angie, went away to college and would come to stay with her father on some week-ends unannounced. This of course irritated Johnny and would result in many arguments really pissing Johnny off not knowing what situation Angie would walk into, like having a woman guest he might be going at 'it' with.

Angie was a beautiful young girl with auburn hair that helped show off her beautiful bluish green eyes and incredible perfect tits which she herself affectionately named, Irma and FiFi.

Johnny sees how beautiful she has always been with top model quality. He would often start conversations with Angie about men saying, "The only thing men really want is to get into your pants. Don't get caught up with what you think is love and is only infatuation and sex. You have to finish school and think about your career." Angie would listen knowing her father only wanted the best for her.

"Thanks Dad. I always listen to your advice. I will finish school and concentrate on a career." She also knew he had plenty of experience in that arena with many women. Although this was not the reason for Johnny's divorce, it was used against him during their long separation. After her parents divorced and Angie matured, she realized this was not what caused their split.

Angie would look at her father and understand why women couldn't keep away from him. He stood six feet one inch with the same coloring eyes she inherited from him. His build was that of a lifeguard at one of the beaches on Long Island and he carried a badge and a gun. How could any women not like what she saw?

CHAPTER 7

As a homicide detective, there are no 9 to 5 hours, Monday through Friday with week-ends off particularly with the case load Johnny carried.

Being exhausted some days or nights to get home for some sleep, he would park his unmarked police car anywhere he would find a space. Not caring if he parked in front of a fire hydrant or if alternate side of the street parking was in effect that day. He thought, *these giant street cleaning trucks could wash and sweep around his car. After all I'm entitled to just flip down the sun visor with all the pertinent police identification. We're a team, the police, the fire and the sanitation union... I think.*

CHAPTER 8

It's one am. Johnny collects a few days' worth of mail from the lobby mail box skimming through it on the elevator ride taking him to the fifth floor.

Bullshit, bullshit, more bullshit mail. Ah, my pay check is here. Oh shit another paycheck. I'd better get these to the bank before I get notices that I'm bouncing checks.

Being wound up and keyed from the two double shifts this week, Johnny was looking forward to some quiet time and a day off. Once inside his bachelor's decorated apartment with a view from the balcony looking out toward the Harlem River, he kicked off his shoes, took off his tie and suit jacket, laying his gun, badge, police radio, the stack of mail and his wallet on the kitchen table. It all seemed to be in one fell swoop since it was a regular practice.

Grabbing the bottle of his favorite whiskey, Old Crow bourbon, he'd pour himself a double; throws in two ice cubes with a splash of water as he did many times as he walked in the door no matter what time of day or night. In his world of a twenty four hour job, day is night and night is day, so it didn't matter. He savored each sip as if it were the last drop he would ever imbibe.

Thinking; *if this is good enough for Mark Twain, Ulysses S. Grant and for President Lincoln wanting to send every General in the field of battle a bottle of Old Crow, then it's good enough for this old crow.*

CHAPTER 9

Johnny's favorite thing to do while sipping on his whiskey... put on his set of head phones connected to his stereophonic equipment with a long wire. He would listen to Johann Sebastian Bach's Suite number five for the unaccompanied cello in C minor. Lying on the floor in complete darkness, eyes closed, absorbing the wonderful sounds that would swirl into his ears was at times for him, almost, as good as having sex.

Johnny, being so absorbed in his ritual, never knew Angie had come home to spend the week-end. Angie had marked this week-end on her calendar as the week-end her father was going to Florida to visit his mother. Norma relocated to Miami Beach within a year after the tragic death of her husband.

Angie was in her father's bedroom with her boyfriend, Freddy. He was deep inside her pumping as hard as a farm hand trying to pump water from a dry well. Angie is sighing with each thrust, totally enthralled with his manhood as she simultaneously massaged her own clit. Trying to get a better rhythm with Freddy, Angie would pull down on Freddy's back lifting herself into his chest. This gave her a tighter grip so she could get as much of him inside her, she so loved. It also allowed her to see over Freddy's shoulder through the bedroom door that was ajar.

Angie's eyes widened as she noticed a small red light illuminating from the living room. In a panic she started pushing Freddy from her gorgeous body covering his mouth whispering, "Shit, be quiet, stop, my father's home, shit."

"What the fuck are you talking about? You said he was visiting your grandmother," Freddy answers nervously feeling his heart pounding ready to explode. "He'll shoot me! Shit!

"Be fucking quiet." Angie stammers in a whisper. "Get dressed quickly and don't take that rubber off. Leave it on and take it with you and the wrapper. Shit! In a few minutes my father will fall asleep. He has his headphones on. He probably has a glass of 'Old Crow' he likes. It helps relax him. I can see the red light. He's listening to his music. Don't talk. Freddy stumbled filling Angie's request by putting on his underwear first. He wanted to please Angie and did as she commanded. "Keep getting dressed and be ready to leave when I tell you. My father will fall asleep soon. I'll help sneak you out. Shh!"

CHAPTER 10

It was in the first years of the 1940's that the FCC issued a radio License to N.Y.P.D. It was for a 1000-watt transmitter on a high frequency band. It was so successful over the next few years that the N.Y.P.D. had to seek funding to equip a few hundred cars which were approved by the City Council in 1943. However, the budget didn't allow for purchasing new radios, so New York City Mayor Philip Bernhard put a request to the Radio Technical Division to build their own transmitter sets. Police Chief, Patrick O'Brian, in turn, sought out Johnny Vero for his inventive electronic and wiring experience. O'Brian was aware of Johnny's expertise since his naval records were part of his New York City police personnel file.

Everyone was in a quandary where to build the transmitters, trying to find space adequate to house police personnel, equipment and not be disturbed with outside distractions. Johnny Vero suggests using the basement of Gracie Mansion being the official residence for the Mayor of the City of New York.

"This would be a perfect setting." He reasoned saying, "Since the Mayor is the chief executive of the New York City government, and there would be no bullshit that could or would stop the cadence necessary to achieve what the Mayor himself put into motion."

CHAPTER 11

Operation "Radio Mansion" dubbed by Mayor Bernhard himself was so successful within a few months since inception, it was publicly celebrated with a ceremony to give those N.Y.P.D. officers the recognition they deserve. Bernhard himself chose in his own words, "The perfect setting... there could be no better place than the lawn of Gracie Mansion."

Mayor Bernhard was a jovial short round man who was known for giving anyone who deserved their due, their due. He often included giving the devil himself his due by always cursing him to eternal hell.

The recognition ceremony for "Radio Mansion" was held just as planned on the lawn of Gracie Mansion. Mayor Bernhard addresses the audience which included Police Chief O'Brian, soon to retire District Attorney Martin Bernstein, the Police Commissioner, many judges, policemen and their families as well as the press.

"'Operation Radio Mansion' has been very special to me and the City of New York. So it gives me great pleasure to present this medal for meritorious police duty. A medal awarded for an act of intelligent and valuable police service that demonstrates special faithfulness and creditable acts of police service. I present this medal to detective Johnny Vero. Detective Vero performed admirably serving the City of New York and the New York City Police Department with his dedication, technical expertise, work ethic and professionalism to build award winning radio transmitters. These will be used in all of the N.Y.P.D.'s vehicles. And where did he say he was going to do this...in my basement."

The crowd howled with laughter and applause.

"Detective Vero, it is an honor to present this medal to you," handing it to Johnny's daughter. "Angie, please do the honors," as Mayor Bernhard instructs her. The medal was lying in a black velvet box..

Angie was shaking. She carefully removed the medal and proudly pinned it on her father's dress blue uniform. Reaching on her tip toes to give him a kiss said, "I love you Dad." She knew; *this was not his first medal or will it be his last.*

Viewing all the medals on her father's uniform, Angie would always remember a particular medal that was her favorite. It stood out from the rest with its colors of green, white and blue housing a gold star in the middle. It was there for his heroic acts when she was only a week old. A story she heard a thousand times and was just as proud from the first to the thousand times hearing it as she reminisces in her mind...

It rain stormed for days. Newspapers reported the second comings of Noah's Ark. Streets were flooding and so were the river banks and lakes. Hurrying home to be with his new born baby girl, Johnny drove the same route hundreds of times, the Hutcheson River Parkway. Catching a figure from his peripheral vision was a man and his wife screaming from their car window as their vehicle was encompassed in water. Johnny pulled over, took off his shoes and gun throwing them in the trunk of his car to jump into the torrent current with rain still pouring to save these strangers.

For his act of bravery, Johnny received the Exceptional Merit Medal for performing an involved personal risk to life. This was on his uniform with others as Angie placed this new Meritorious Medal proudly to the uniform.

Johnny responded in like, "I love you too Angie. You mean everything to me."

Everyone stood and applauded.

"Let's applaud everyone on this stage that has been recognized today," shouts Mayor Bernhard. "Congratulations to all of you. Please, let's go to the tent for food and drinks."

The applause and cheers subsided as everyone dispersed to the tent.

CHAPTER 12

Waiting for Johnny at New York Municipal Airport was his partner, Detective Billy Bradshaw. At one time in his life, before joining the Navy, something he and Johnny had in common, Billy was destined to play major league baseball with the New York Giants. Playing for their minor league, the Jersey City Giants, which is one step below Major League baseball, Billy had to quit due to a rotator cuff tear on his left shoulder sliding with outstretched arms into home plate. Of course this was his pitching arm that ended his career instantly. During his short stint playing ball, he was known as 'Billy the Kid.' Now he is part of the New York City Police Department in the squad headed by Detective Sergeant, Johnny Vero.

"Johnny, over here," Billy shouts holding his hand up so Johnny can see him as he exits the plane through the passenger gates.

"Thanks Billy for picking me up. Walk me down to the baggage claim. My mom sent a box for Angie and I have to get my luggage," giving Billy instructions as he gives instructions to his squad.

"How is Norma doing?" Billy asks.

"She's a strong woman and I'm glad for that. She's made a lot of new friends. As a matter of fact, there are some friends from the old neighborhood close by who introduced her to Florida. She loves it. There doesn't seem to be a whole lot she doesn't like. It's great weather all the time. She swims, has a tan and is enjoying what she deserves. She wishes my Dad was with her. I like the in and out visit. Three days is plenty. You know, she wants to show me off to her friends who have daughters looking to get hitched," Johnny explains.

Waiting for the luggage and gift box for Angie, Billy eyes a woman who is approaching with a look of pure, polished sophistication and flawless. She's wearing a fitted dress which has small white polka dots that sizzled against the licorice black cotton material. Around her waist is a black sash tied in a bow, accentuating her hour glass figure. Looking up and down her sultry legs were fishnets stockings. Her entire ensemble was complete carrying a purse to match her shoes. For a moment, Billy thought, *I may want to bring her home to meet Mom.*

"Hi, there, you look very familiar. Are you in the movies?" She asks running her index finger across Billy's lips.

"I was a baseball player," Billy answers.

Johnny looks at Billy saying; "Really Billy, really?

"You both look like you belong in the movies," she continues.

"What are your names?"

It took a minute for Billy to absorb Johnny's comment.

"I'm detective Bradshaw and this is detective Vero," Billy says deepening his voice to be more authoritative opening his suit jacket to show his badge.

"Oh! Shit. Two dicks", (slang used for detectives) claims the lady that Billy now clearly knew in his mind, *wasn't coming home with him to meet Mom.*

"Listen," claims Johnny. "We're in a hurry. As much as I like what I see, it would be against the law for us to be with you. And what you're doing is against the law. Now be a nice hooker and go work the bar in the main terminal and we won't put you in handcuffs."

"Thanks handsome," quickly turning to walk away picking up her pace as she twists her head saying; "Maybe next time we can use those handcuffs for something else besides putting me under arrest. I won't even charge you. I know some things the law uses, you know, quid pro quo." Now being exposed as a prostitute, she completely stops, turns slowly and blows a kiss with her hand from her lips to them both.

CHAPTER 13

Housekeeper, Greta, works at The Budapest Hotel on West Forty Third Street between Seventh and Eighth Avenues. The Budapest was pure swank and class. The outside facade was quite ornate with gargoyles in the form of grotesque faces or creatures projecting from roof gutter. This, of course gave the appearance of old world mystic charm.

The desk clerks wore tuxedos. Bell hops wore uniforms complete with epaulets and square hats that stayed in place by a chin strap. The lobby embraced old world European style décor. The walls were lined with original oil paintings under constant scrutiny such as; Claude Lorrains' oil, 'Villa in the Roman Campagna and Franz von Stuck's, 'The Kiss of the Sphinx.' Each of the paintings is worth thousands of dollars unbeknown to the worldly patrons who would scurry to fulfill their itineraries. The carpets are so plush; you felt you were not even walking on them. The marble pillars were enormous giving the lobby direction of separating the hallways that lead to the elevators, cocktail lounge and dining room. Huge leather chairs and couches both faced the fireplace. Guests could enjoy their morning coffee and newspaper or just be mesmerized by the gentle flames and aroma of the pine scent logs.

Starting her day with regular rounds to the rooms she was assigned, changing linens, towels, and performing her general cleaning, housekeeper Greta never dreamed of ever walking into a situation you read about. The room Greta walked into was like most of the other sixty nine rooms with the exception of the presidential suites, which there were 6. The Budapest Hotel was frequented by many dignitaries from around the world and had to accommodate a few at a time.

Opening the door with her pass key, Greta finds a women sitting upright on the bed looking right at her. She lie there naked, legs wide open with a nylon stocking around her neck. Her eyes bulged staring at Greta. The shrill of her scream was heard as it echoed through the hallways. The hotel house detective, hearing this awful howl ran up the stairs huffing and puffing, loosening his tie and unbuttoning the top button of his shirt trying to catch his breath. Finally reaching the stairwell door to the floor where the screams were still emanating, house detective Riley calms Greta and asks, "Did you touch anything? I mean anything?"

"No, not-ting. I just walk in and I stand here. My legs and feet freeze. I haven't moved." Greta answered through her sobbing and shaking.

"Give me your name and employee number. Just turn around and walk out. *DO NOT TOUCH ANYTHING ON YOUR WAY OUT!*" The house detective emphasizes. "Go immediately to the front desk and tell them I'm in room eighteen and to call police."

CHAPTER 14

District Attorney, Amollia Penett, known as Molly was hovering over the body the housekeeper found. Molly graduated top of her law school class from Fordham University and was the third woman in the United States to ever to hold the elected position of District Attorney, soon after the retirement of District Attorney Martin Bernstein.

Along with Molly were uniformed police to cordon off the doorway and to stand guard. Police Chief O'Brian enters, while one of the police officers continues to take picture after picture as fast as he could change the flash bulbs.

"Officer, call the precinct. I want Detective Vero here as soon as possible." Demands Molly. "I hope this doesn't turn out to be what I think it is."

"Good idea," states Chief O'Brian. "I'll pull Vero off his case load and let his squad handle those files."

Molly Penett won the election with the promise of being a 'hands on' District Attorney, not just sitting behind a desk. She wanted crime off her city streets is determined to make that happen.

CHAPTER 15

Detective's Vero and Bradshaw approach the door to room eighteen passing the uniformed policeman entering with an immediate greeting, "Good to see you Molly, Chief O'Brian. Who found her?"

"A housekeeper named Greta," answers Molly, "followed by the house detective."

"Billy, get them both up here," directs Johnny.

"Detective, I want you exclusively on this homicide. I'll re-assign and distribute your case load to your squad," orders Chief O'Brian indicating this is his idea throwing Molly's request to the wind. "I'll leave you with Miss Penett to finish up."

"Chief, can you have the coroner come through the service entrance and use that elevator so the reporters won't get hold of what's going on, at least for now," Johnny asks? As usual, he always let the Chief think it was his idea. Johnny continues to direct the police photographer, known as 'Flash'; "I want you to take pictures of every inch of this place, including the bathroom. Not randomly. Start over at this door and go to your right until you're back at the door you started from. Then do the same in the bathroom. Keep them separate from the other photographs you already took, understand," calling to mind reading this technique in a 'True Crime' magazine story?

"Got it," replies, Flash."

"Ah, here he is the finger print specialist. Good to see you Kevin," says detective Vero. "I heard you just got back from the Los Angeles crime lab. I understand they're teaching all police departments some new techniques."

"Yeah Johnny, great stuff," replies fingerprint specialist, Kevin Kowalski immediately setting up to start his process of dusting for prints.

"Do your magic here. Probably one thousand prints. You know, being a hotel room," detective Bradshaw adds.

"Kevin, what do you have in your bag, do you have a... no Molly, you, probably have a tweezers in your pocket book. Can you hand it to me please," requests Johnny.

"Billy, shine your flashlight on her muff," directs Johnny.

"That's what you want to look at detective, her muff?" Molly snaps.

Ignoring Molly's comment, slowly detective Vero pulls something from the young woman's vagina.

"Well, will you look at that," Vero says holding it up to the light clasped in the tweezers. "Billy, put this in a cellophane evidence bag."

"The housekeeper and house detective are on their way up," Billy interjects.

"Molly, here is your tweezers back," Johnny says as everyone gave a quick laugh.

"Fuck you Johnny. You're going to buy me a new one. Stop at Woolworths on your way home tonight," Molly answers sarcastically. "Be sure to include those tweezers you just used in separate evidence bag too. Over here too, get these personal items and clothes in separate bags."

CHAPTER 16

The New York Borough Coroner Office Report.
DATE and HOUR AUTOPSY PERFORMED:
April 1, 1947 8:04 A.M

Howard Sneider, M.D.
555 Canal Street
New York, New York
Assistant, Antoine Chavrolet, M.D.
Full Autopsy Performed April 9, 1947 8:04 A.M

Name: Victoria Morrow	Date of Birth:08/03/1922
Race: White	Sex: Female
Date of Death: 03/31/1947-04/01/1947	Body Identified by: Federal Security Agency War Production Training Card with one finger print.
Case #: 00388-32A-1947	Investigative Agency: New York City Police, Homicide Division

EVIDENCE OF TREATMENT:
N/A

EXTERNAL EXAMINATION:
The autopsy is begun at 8:04 A.M. on April 1, 1947. The body is presented in a black body sack. When first viewed, the deceased is naked. The hands are preserved for possible evidence. No jewelry was included. The body is that of a normally developed white female measuring 62 inches, weighing 120 pounds and appearing generally consistent with the stated age of 24-25 years. Lividity is fixed and unblanching on the posterior surface of the body.

The eyes are open with petechiae in the skin (pinpoint hemorrhages) conjunctiva of the eyes. The irises are brown. The corneas are cloudy. The scleras are clear. The pupils measure 0.45 cm. The hair is black, straight and approximately 14 inches in length. The posterior region of the neck has a deep circular ligature of approximately 0.5cm in diameter.

The removal of the larynx includes the hyoid bone (fractured). The musculature is consistent with contusion hemorrhage. The chest; abdomen and back are symmetrical and intact. The external genitalia are that of an adult female and there is evidence of injury to the inner thigh areas. There is evidence of semen. Limbs are equal, symmetrically developed and intact. Fingernails are present and painted red with no evidence of struggle. There are no residual scars, markings or tattoos.

INTERNAL EXAMINATION:
HEAD--CENTRAL NERVOUS SYSTEM: Subsequent autopsy shows the neck was choked to asphyxiation. The brain weighs 1,325 grams and within normal limits.
SKELETAL SYSTEM No injury to the brain is present.
RESPIRATORY SYSTEM--THROAT STRUCTURES: The oral cavity shows no lesions. The mucosa is intact and there are no injuries to the lips, teeth or gums. There is no obstruction of the airway. The mucosa of the epiglottis, glottis, piriform sinuses, trachea and major bronchi are anatomic. No injuries are seen and there are no mucosal lesions. The hyoid bone, the thyroid, and the cricoid cartilages are intact. Lungs: The lungs weigh: right, 350 grams; left 360 grams. The lungs are unremarkable.
CARDIOVASCULAR SYSTEM: The heart weighs 249 grams, and has a normal size and configuration. No evidence of atherosclerosis is present.
GASTROINTESTINAL SYSTEM: The mucosa and wall of the esophagus are intact and gray-pink, with lesions and injuries. The gastric mucosa is intact and pink with injury. Approximately 67 ml of partially digested food is found in the stomach. The mucosa of the duodenum, jejunum, ileum, colon and rectum are intact.
URINARY SYSTEM: The kidneys weigh: Left, 120 grams; right, 115 grams. The kidneys are anatomic in size, shape and location and are without lesions.
FEMALE GENITAL SYSTEM: The structures are within normal limits. The deceased has not given birth in the past. There are signs of recent sexual activity including seminal fluid.

LABORATORY DATA:
Culture: No growth after 72 hours
Cerebrospinal fluid bacterial antigens:
Urine screen {Immunoassay} was NEGATIVE. Ethanol: 0 gm/dl, Blood (Heart) Ethanol: 0 gm/dl, Vitreous

EVIDENCE COLLECTED:
1. One (1) women's nylon stocking, size 6.
2. Ten (10) samples collected from under the deceased's fingernails.
3. Samples of Blood (type A+), Bile, and Tissue (heart, lung, brain, kidney, liver, spleen).
4. Nine autopsy photographs.

Manner of Death: Homicide
Immediate Cause of Death: Asphyxiation due to strangulation with a women's nylon stocking.

CHAPTER 17

"Detective Vero, homicide," Johnny answers in his usual matter of fact tone of voice speaking into the telephone.

"Did you get new tweezers you owe me" asks the voice on the other end of the phone?

"Yes I did. I have them right here Molly. I even had it gift wrapped."

"Good. Bring them with you and get over to my office, we have the autopsy report from the Budapest Hotel murder I want to go over with you," orders Molly.

Click.

CHAPTER 18

Detective Vero arrives to Molly's office located in the court house at Federal Plaza. As always, he parked his police car flipping down the sun visor that identified it as a N.Y.C. Police vehicle on official business.

Johnny was quite known within the hallways of the justice building being greeted with every step and turn.

"Go right up detective, Miss Penett is expecting you," recites the lobby receptionist as Johnny scurries to the elevator.

"Here you go Molly, I didn't forget," handing her the neatly wrapped tweezers he promised her.

"I'm sorry Miss Penett. I was away from my desk before I could buzz you stating Detective Vero is here," Louise announces in her high pitched voice trailing right behind Johnny, just as infatuated with him as if she saw him for the first time.

"It's O.K. Louise. Hold all my calls."

Smiling, she sets the box on her desk continuing handing Johnny a folder. "Take a quick look at the autopsy report then we'll chat."

Johnny is moving his lips mumbling the words as he's reading through the report. "O.K., I see she's identified with name, age, one finger print through the Federal Security Agency I.D. card found in her purse. This is going to save us a lot of time. Oh! She had recent sexual activity."

"Remember what you pulled out from her vagina with my tweezers, Molly asks?

"Every time you use it you'll think of me," Johnny replies, with a wide grin undressing her with his eyes.

"The boys in the lab were able to clean it up enough for you to follow up with. Here, look," Molly instructs Johnny. "I've got to get this back to the evidence room today."

Holding the sealed bag, he answers, "They sure did. Well look at that. Our Victoria Morrow was a taxi dancer getting paid on a dance to dance basis for a short three minute dance floor spin at the Flamingo Room. Her killer put the ticket he gave her right up…

"Yes, we know where he put it Johnny," interrupts Molly.

"This is going to take a lot of gum shoe, Molly. But this information will put us ahead by weeks."

"Well, why are you still seating here," Molly asks? "Thanks for the tweezers."

CHAPTER 19

Angie always came home on spring break from school looking forward to spending time with her father. Most of the other students went to Ft. Lauderdale, Florida to party during this break and then home for Christmas.

As she awakens from the Castro convertible couch in her dad's living room (which duplicates as a pull out bed folding back into a couch) tip toes to his bedroom door that's ajar to see if he's awake.

"Come on in Angie. I saw you last night when I came in and didn't want to wake you," Johnny says greeting her.

Flopping down next to Johnny, Angie goes on to say, "Remember how I used to crawl into bed with you and Mom and you would read to me?"

"Of course I do. I still have some of those books. Want me to read to you now?" Johnny asks smiling.

"Do you think Mom is happy living in Europe?" asking with no thought to what Johnny said...that is, *if she wanted him to read her a story not knowing or thinking if he was kidding.*

"She always wanted to live there. You know... her art. She never let you out of her sight," Johnny re-insuring Angie of her mother's love for her.

"Dad, thanks for taking whatever time off you can get. I'm glad of whatever time we can spend together," giving Johnny a kiss dismissing the conversation about her mother. "What are you working on; I mean what kind of homicide?" Angie asks. "Who knows, maybe I can offer some help from my psychology classes. I'm going to put up some coffee. I remember how you take it, black, two sugars."

CHAPTER 20

The Flamingo Room is considered the home of refined dancing as the advertisements read. The bouncers were called housemen keeping order in case the patrons thought they could cause a disturbance due to wanting a certain taxi dancer while she danced with someone else.

Big bands, society orchestras, would broadcast live radio shows from the stage that held thirty to forty musicians with a male and female singer.

The floors were highly polished marble that allowed a huge area for dancing. At times, there would be dancing showgirls along with a burlesque show. Around the sides of the main floor were the areas where patrons would sit, dine and drink at tables clothed in fine white linens and plush carpeting. Men would wear either tuxedos or suits.

The cigarette girls dressed with short skirts to draw attention to them-selves wearing uniforms with bright colors and fish-net stockings. Their trays that hung from their neck were filled with cigarettes, cigars, flowers, candy and gum. They would earn commission on what they sold and would use their wit and charm for tips.

CHAPTER 21

Detective Vero identifies himself and Billy to one of the housemen of the Flamingo Room who points to the owner sitting at the end of the bar sipping a whiskey.

"Mr. Cohen, we're homicide detectives Vero and Bradshaw, New York City Police. One of your 'dime-a-dance gals', Victoria Morrow was murdered. Can we talk here?" Johnny explains.

"Sure," says the burly man named Irving Cohen owner of the Flamingo Room. Irving is a Jew who emigrated from Poland. "Call me Poco. I'm originally from Poland and my name Cohen is mixed to Poco. This is horrible. We're all upset here. Did you find who did this?"

Johnny goes on, "Did Miss Morrow have any regular dance partners or anyone your housemen had to handle that might have been giving her too much attention?"

"You know detective, it's hard to keep my eye on every taxi dancer in the joint. We get real crowded. It's an inexpensive way a gentleman can spend an evening," Poco answers.

"We need to ask you your where-a-bouts between Friday, March 31st and Saturday, April 1st," Johnny asks Poco?

"Look around detective. I'm here every fucking night with at least one hundred to two hundred patrons and employees that can vouch for me," he says.

"Polite society is convinced these ballrooms are merely covers for prostitution," claims Detective Bradshaw.

"You're right detective," Cohen answers in-between sipping his whiskey. "The parallels of buying female company may be undeniable. That's why I carefully control the ratio of blondes, brunettes and redheads, and colored girls that are available for the gentlemen. However, that doesn't constitute I'm running a whore house. I provide a service. This is a sociable meeting place where love and or marriage could happen. My girls can earn over forty dollars per week, more than working in a factory or waiting tables. We've had 2 weddings right here between customers and the girls. We have doctors, lawyers and a mix of men, even policemen at times. You both are welcome anytime. I'll even give you a line of free tickets. It's a terrible thing that happened to Vickie. She was a nice girl. I hope you grab the son-of-a-bitch and cut off his balls! Be my guest and ask around. Just remember that time cost these girls money."

CHAPTER 22

Johnny is in Molly's office waiting for her to return from the court room where she is prosecuting an armed robbery, involving a shooting. The way she added her touch to the décor was simply charming. There's a little sitting area at the far end of the room for casual meetings. It has a table and four French Art Deco leather club chairs to serve coffee or tea. Everyone who had the opportunity to sit never wanted to get up to leave. The richness of the dark brown leather chairs contrasted the dynamite walnut frames with pictures that worked together in perfect harmony, just as Molly herself did and looked every day. There were two more of the same chairs in front of her desk for more formal discussions. Across from the sitting area was a door with textured glass you could not see through. It led to a shared conference room. This room was for the entire staff of the third floor. The walls were mahogany, housing book shelves lined with law and history books with a leather couch that was as long as a caboose on the train to no-where.

Molly had an American Flag folded in the traditional triangle under glass and framed, reminding us of the soldiers who served preserving the rights to our freedom. This flag was used to drape the casket at her father's funeral. It hung behind her directly in eye's view of who ever sat facing her.

Molly was so proud of her father. He came a long way from Italy to become a United States citizen, continuing his servitude in the United States Marine Corp from 1903-1907 protecting American diplomats in Abyssinia. At one point, he was assigned to Tangier, helping to resolve the kidnapping of a U.S. Ambassador and his wife from their home by marauders. This made national headlines arousing international conflict.

Upon his honorable discharge, he continued his service with the New York City Police Department until his injury. Having to leave the force, he then continued as a Bailiff in the same court room Molly enters most days until his untimely death at age fifty one. Scattered throughout were family photos giving a warm view of the District Attorney's office and to all those entering her domain.

CHAPTER 23

"Oh, Detective Vero," caught off guard muttering with surprise entering her office. Not missing a step, she forged forward as the leader of a brigade, arms filled with file folders, thinking... *I see Louise let you in. I'm going to speak to her about this.* "This is attorney Richard Lewis. He's Irving Cohen and The Flamingo Room's attorney."

"Glad to meet you detective. Have you got any details of the murder of Miss Morrow," he asks?

"I'm not at liberty to divulge any information, Mr. Lewis. I'll ask you the question. Does Mr. Cohen or The Flamingo Room need to be represented by an attorney?"

"Mr. Lewis is just here to introduce himself as the representative for both Mr. Cohen and the Flamingo Room and to be a buffer of sorts as he explained to me on our way in," states Molly.

"If you need to question Mr. Cohen detective, you will have our full co-operation. It will be, going forward, with me present at all times. You never know. There may be some questions that can be misleading and ambiguous. Don't you agree detective?" Mr. Lewis asks directing himself to Johnny.

"Molly, we have some police business to discuss here," Johnny said looking directly at Mr. Lewis with a cold calculating stare.

"I'll see my way out. Good to meet you detective. Thanks for your time Miss Penett," Mr. Lewis responds.

CHAPTER 24

"What's with the hostility?" Molly asks Johnny.

"Molly, don't you think it strange that Mr. Cohen's attorney would come without an appointment to see you. Seems it is an intimidation method he gets away with," questions Johnny?

"Don't you think I get tested every time I step into that court room," Molly asks rhetorically, almost offended. "What do you have for me?"

Johnny begins by viewing his notes:

"Victoria Morrow was a twenty two year old originally from Maine on a stopover in New York before heading to Hollywood. She was an aspiring actress who did some summer theater. She was an attractive girl and would have gotten noticed in Hollywood. According to her friend and roommate, Susan Fleming, who also is a dime-a-dance- girl. She said Vickie was a smart girl and knew her looks alone wouldn't get her to Hollywood. Miss Fleming said Vickie would use her time to make as many new acquaintances at the Flamingo Room to use to her advantage figuring she would eventually meet the important people she would need to get her to Hollywood."

"O.K." states Molly. "Is there more?"

"Yeah. The check –in- record indicates Miss Morrow checked in on Friday, March 31st at 9 A.M. Miss Fleming said Vicky was a schmoozer and knew how to get men to spend their money on alcohol and got good tips knowing how to manipulate their conversations to let them think she really cared about their lives. It seems she honed her people skills to her advantage where she wouldn't have to do as many dances as the other girls and made more money than the others."

"Good information. We could also have a jealous taxi dancer on our hands. It is very competitive. Having Vickie off the scene, her regular customers would look for other girls to become friendly with," Molly goes on to say.

"It's a thought," Johnny mentions. "But going to a hotel room with another woman would mean either she was lured there with an opportunity to finally meet her Hollywood connection or she was a dyke. I don't think from my experience it was more than one person. Remember, semen was found. She had sex with a man. We have to use our wits, instinct and logic."

"Alright, I'll go with you, it was one person and a man," Molly agreeing. "Where do you go from here?"

"I'm going to the Yankee game and see the "Yankee Clipper" with Angie. She's home on school break.

"Oh, yes, I know the famous Yankee player, Joe DiMaggio. I know some baseball. My dad used to take me to some games," Molly mentions, giving a slight glance at the framed flag. "We also used to go the opera and ballet. Have a good time and tell Angie I said hello."

"Louise, get in here now!"

CHAPTER 25

The seventh inning stretch came pretty quick. The Yankees are pounding the Washington Senators 11-3.

Both Johnny and Angie welcomed the interruption as they headed to the restrooms and grab a couple of beers and hot dogs. Bringing them back to their seats, they heard the crowd singing 'Take me out to the ball game,' as they both chimed in to sing along.

"That was a great double play by Rizzuto, don't you think so Dad, Angie asks in between bites of her hog dog? Too bad DiMaggio hurt his elbow and isn't playing today. I know you wanted to see him play."

"Oh yeah, Rizzuto! The Scooter is a great short stop. He got that nick name when he was in the minors you know. The manager said of Rizzuto's short legs 'he ain't runnin', he's scootin.' Angie, I might take you up on your offer of picking your brain. I have a gut feeling this homicide I'm working on is not going to be the last by this killer. Maybe I can write some stuff down for you to bring up in one of your psychology classes. You know, present it as a hypothetical situation. Maybe your professor will chime in. I can't release certain information. What do you think, Johnny presenting his thoughts?

"I'd love to Dad. Thank you. Thank you for asking me," Angie responds.

CHAPTER 26

"Billy, I don't know how many more people we can interview. They are all saying pretty much the same thing. Vickie Morrow was determined to make it to Hollywood and would not stop at anything or anyone getting there," Johnny mentions.

"I've done some calculations. Take a pencil and paper." Billy tells Johnny. Miss Morrow made more than most of the dancers. Poco said; about forty bucks a week. Susan Fleming said she made most on tips and hustling drinks her customers would buy. Let's say she does this; twenty five bucks in tips and fifteen in dances. Vickie's cut on each dance in six cents. So to make fifteen bucks at six cents a dance calculates that she would have to have two hundred fifty dances per week working seven days making her dance card having thirty five dances per night. How the fuck are we going to interview these people and how do we know they are regulars? They could come to dance and never go back."

"Good thing she wasn't turning tricks at that rate. Having that much sex each night alone would have killed her," Johnny answers.

"Johnny, what if she was prostituting herself for some customers for the extra cash and a promise to get her to Hollywood," Billy interjects?

"You know Billy; it very well may be that. Let's go back to speak with the hotel workers and see if we can jog their memories that they saw something. Get your hat, let's go," Johnny orders.

CHAPTER 27

Detectives Vero and Bradshaw returned to the Budapest Hotel for re-interviews. They were seeking the people who were on duty and to track down the guests that occupied the rooms to the left, number seventeen and the room to the right, number nineteen.

Both desk clerks on duty said; they *don't recall anyone that stood out of the ordinary.* A review of the check–in-record indicates Miss Morrow checked in on Friday, March 31st at 9 A.M. as was told to Molly.

Housekeeper Greta again repeats her statement; "I opened da door, walk in. My legs froze and I scream. I'm having nightmares now."

The hotel detective, Chester Riley saw nothing that was suspicious as he made his rounds as is stated in his report.

Once they obtained the records for rooms seventeen and nineteen, they were able to track down and contact those occupants. However, their findings did not reveal much...

...Room seventeen was a young soldier home on leave and never left the room for two days with his new bride volunteering their statements said; "We were busy, you know, making love...a lot! The outside world was not there. We didn't hear anything. We never left the room. All our meals were room service. My wife's parents help to pay since this was our honeymoon and I'm being shipped out."

...Room nineteen also was occupied Friday, March 31st by a tourist, now back in England. Saturday, April 1st occupant was a young woman fresh in town for a job interview on Monday morning who spent most of her time both Saturday and Sunday sight-seeing and had nothing to report.

CHAPTER 28

Johnny reflected for a moment on his way to the station house to this past week-end he and Audrey spent together. They never left his apartment or the bedroom. The only time they left the bed was to shower, eat, and drink, not necessarily in that order. In his mind; *it was as the soldier he interviewed in room seventeen at the Budapest Hotel, spending his time with his new bride in a sex fest.* Both Johnny and Audrey always knew that this relationship was nothing more than a warm friendship to fulfill their sexual needs, thinking...

Audrey's platinum blonde hair certainly didn't match her pussy and that was o.k. Audrey's tits were really too big for Johnny's liking, but that was o.k. too. Their sex was uninhibited, whether Audrey was on top bringing to mind how they would role play with their sexual escapes, one time pretending to be western film stars, Roy Rogers and Dale Evans since they liked their movie, San Fernando Valley. Audrey was on top riding Johnny hard as 'Butter Cup'. Her tits were smacking him in the face. Johnny, grabs one of her breasts, brings it to his ear and says....Hello, hello, both laughing hysterically, stopping the on going numbness of their lust whether in the missionary position, on the edge of the bed, or satisfying each other orally. He was also o.k. with the eight inch scar resembling railroad tracks that ran across her abdomen from her hysterectomy surgery. Remembering; *Audrey always felt good when Johnny would comment on how sexy the scar was each time he kissed it or when he ran his penis across it as she was handcuffed to the headboard. The best part they enjoyed of course was Johnny going 'bare back', not using any condoms because of her surgery. What they both liked was simple. Johnny and Audrey knew that one day they would grow apart due to one getting involved in a serious relationship.* But for now, it is whenever either felt the need for a sexual vagary.

Getting back on track, Johnny is questioning himself *as to what he has to do in order to get this Budapest Hotel murderer apprehended. How can he stop the dreaded bad press?*

CHAPTER 29

'Tschhhhhhhhhhhhhhhh...' is the first sound detective Vero hears on his police car radio caused by thermal electronic interference and from the receiver input circuits that are picked up by the receiver's own antenna. A noise Johnny is well familiar with that proceeds with a voice message; "Detective Vero, this is South Central dispatch. I have District Attorney Penett on the wire. Shall I patch you through, over?"

Johnny without hesitation, picks the microphone from the radio and answers, "Yes, 10-4, over."

"Stand by, detective, over," the mystery voice responds.

"Miss Penett, are you there, over?"

"I'm here," responds Molly.

"Go ahead detective."

"Detective I need to meet you at the Budapest Hotel. We have another homicide. Do you understand?" Molly asks.

"I'm on my way Molly," Johnny said, switching on the emergency red lights and siren and pressing the transmit switch on his radio. "Detective Vero, I.D. 4225, to dispatch, over."

"Go ahead detective, over."

"Patch me through to detective Bradshaw immediately, over."

"Oh shit!" Johnny exclaims out loud.

"Did you say something detective, over," asks the mystery voice?

"Huh? No, I'm sorry. I was just thinking out loud."

"May I remind you, detective, we are transmitting on the open airwaves, over?"

"Thank you for the reminder. "

With a sounding swoosh of each passing car and giant iron pillar holding the elevated trains above the street like a Greek Adonis holding up their gods, his foot pushed on the accelerator increasing his adrenaline. His mind racing, keeping pace with the speedometer, thinking...*how am I going to get my ass handed to me and not on a silver platter, knowing the press, and now, the Commissioner, Mayor Bernhard, Chief O'Brian, and Captain Sullivan were all going to pounce on my back.*

CHAPTER 30

Upon arrival, Johnny meets Billy at the entrance to the hotel lobby.

"This is not looking good, Billy. The commissioner is all over Molly because we're not making headway with the Morrow murder. And now here's another homicide in the same hotel. Molly said, the commissioner is going to want us to jump off the roof if we don't come up with something fast," is Johnny's welcoming statement to Billy.

"That's fucking funny Johnny having us jump off the roof thing. Remember Ronnie Ramer from East Harlem?" Billy asks.

"Yeah, of course I do. We used to call him 'birdman.' How many times were we called to the roof where he always stood on the ledge threatening to jump until we talked him down? What's that got to do with the commissioner wanting us to jump off a roof," Johnny asks confused?

"Well as many times we were called to talk him down and drive him over to Bellevue Hospital's physco ward, two patrolmen responded to call.

"And?"

"They told him that N.Y.P.D. is tired coming once a month sitting around waiting until he decides to come off the ledge to drive to the hospital. They said we need to resolve this, Ronnie. He jumped."

"No fucking way," Johnny responds.

"Yep! He jumped. That's one fucked up individual!" Billy answers as he chuckles. "You know what the medical examiner told me when I was on the beat? This lady was always complaining that her husband never took her anywhere. They were always home. She did nothing except cook, clean, iron, shop for her husband and all he wanted to do when he got home was drink and watch T.V. In his confession, he said; *He was tired of hearing her nag, nag, nag about never going out. She wanted to put on a nice dress and go out somewhere.* So, he says; *I told her to put on a nice dress, so I can take her out. After she got all dolled up, I opened the window, picked her up and threw out. You see, she got her wish. She went out!* "Five stories."

"So, you started to say what the M.E. said..."

"Oh, yeah. He said"...*It's not the fall that kills you, it's the sudden stop.* "Then he would roar with laughter."

"Billy, that's a few fucked up people, including the M.E. How fucked up is this killer we need to find?"

"Beyond fucked up Johnny. Way beyond fucked up. Sick fucked up, really sick."

CHAPTER 31

Entering room number forty, both Billy and Johnny saw the same scenario as with Vickie Morrow. Almost one month to the day.

This young woman was in the same position as Miss Morrow, sitting upright on the bed. She was nude with her legs spread open, facing the door with a nylon stocking around her neck. All her belongings were neatly arranged on the night table and her clothes neatly hanging in the closet. Unlike Vickie Morrows' whose clothes were on the floor.

Molly and Chief O'Brian were already there with police photographer and finger print specialist, Kevin Kowalski.

"Hey Johnny, I know how you want the photographs," says Flash, greeting Johnny. I hope you like the last set from room eighteen. They came out pretty good, don't you think," he asks?

"They came out great, Flash. I'm able to pin them on the board and it looks like I'm viewing the entire room. Maybe they can win you the Police Gazette award. What's the prize, these days, Johnny questions?

"That would be a feather in my cap. I think it's a thousand dollar prize. A real nice vacation for me and the Mrs.," 'Flash responds.

"I think I know what you want me to focus my flashlight on," announces detective Bradshaw.

Molly quickly answers, "You had better have brought your own tweeters this time Johnny."

"I didn't, God damn it!

"Don't worry, detective. I've got you covered. Right here in my finger prints kit. You gave me the idea from the last one we did here. I have a few."

"Here we go again. Look, the same thing I'm pulling from her vagina, a dance ticket from the Flamingo Room. Billy, grab two envelopes. I hope I don't have to buy these tweezers by the box," Johnny responds quieting the room.

"The commissioner is on the war path," reports Molly. "The press is going to have a field day with this."

Johnny thinks for a moment then comments, "Who claimed the body of Vickie Morrow?"

"Her mother came from Maine to claim her body. She was able to have her buried in Hollywood Park Cemetery since her wish was to live, work and act in Hollywood," Claims Chief O'Brian. "I don't care about your and Bradshaw's overtime. Get some fucking answers?"

"Billy, Make a note of that cemetery and how it was paid and by whom," Johnny directs Billy.

"O.K. Where and who is the person that discovered *this* body" Johnny asks?

"Another housekeeper who went directly to the hotel detective's office. You remember Chester Riley? He secured the room, called us and has the housekeeper still there, O'Brian filling Johnny in.

Johnny replies, "Let's go and talk to them there, not here this time."

CHAPTER 32

Johnny and Billy entered the office of Chester Riley, the house detective. As directed, the housekeeper who found the body was waiting, slightly fidgeting.

"Tell me, I'm sorry, what's your name," Johnny asks the housekeeper,

"Halina Elzbeta."

"You don't seem to shaken, Miss Elzbeta," Billy comments.

"It's, Mrs., Mrs. Elzbeta," she claims. "I've seen worse tings happen from my country dat I escape from. The devil is all over, not just Europe. Vat you see is same how I see her. I turn and valk out, lock door and put cleaning cart to block door and run right to Mr. Riley office. I see nutting more. Can I go? I have lot of rooms to clean."

"Go ahead," Johnny says. We'll be in touch if we need to talk to you. Thank you for your co-operation."

"I have the registration card detective", claims Chester, handing to Johnny. "I knew you'd want to see it."

"Thank you, what's your name, I don't remember yours either?" Johnny asks.

"It's Chester Riley, detective. Here's my private investigators license," reaching for the framed license on the wall, removing it to show Detective Vero.

CHAPTER 33

Molly stops in Chester Riley's office on her way out to tell Johnny; "Come to my office as soon as you're through here. We have to put together what we have and get a release to the press ready. The commissioner...."

"Yes, I know. He wants me and Billy to be ready to jump off the roof," Johnny answers smiling.

"What the hell is so funny? Molly asks.

"It's a long story Molly," answers Billy, also smiling. "I'll go back to the station and start the background on the name used on the registration, Ruth Silvan."

"I'm sure between the two of you there is a story in there somewhere, Billy. The boys are finishing up in room forty and the coroner is on the way," Molly said.

"Molly, let me get some more information together before I get to you. I'll need a day or two," Johnny answers, hoping she will accept his demand.

"Well, alright. Two days max. I'll expect you then. I'll clear my calendar."

CHAPTER 34

Molly is wheeling a large blackboard from the conference room as Johnny is walking in her office and offers, "Let me help you with that Molly. Where do you want it?

Let's get to work here. Do you want coffee? Molly states as she directs her secretary.

"Sure, black, two sugars. Please don't make the chalk squeal on the board. I hate that sound," Johnny requests of Molly.

"A strong strapping handsome detective is bothered by a little sound? Detective Vero, I'm surprised," Molly says teasingly.

"O.K., you found me out, Molly. Now tell me something strange about you," Johnny questions in a flirting manner?

"No!" Molly sternly answers. "Get your notes. I'm ready to write on the board."

"Here's the info we have and you probably already know."

Victim #1
- Victoria Morrow, Date of Birth, August 3, 1922, age 22.
- Roommate, Susan Fleming.
- I.D. found Federal Security Agency War Production Training Card.
- Mother claims body, buried in Hollywood Park Cemetery, California. We're checking who paid for this.
- Irving Cohen, owner of the Flamingo Room is clear on first victim.

"We have to speak with him for number two since she was also a dime-a-dance girl. We have to speak with him with his attorney present, remember."

- Victim 1 checked in herself on Friday, March 31st at 9 A.M.
- No finger prints in room eighteen.
- Clothes on floor.
- Found dance ticket in her vagina.
- Had recent sex.
- Long strands of thread found on the bed.

Victim #2:
- Ruth Silvan
- Date of birth and death unknown as of now.

"I'm going to say Ruth Silvan is around same age and the coroner will find semen to report she had recent sex as with victim #1."

- Found dance ticket in her vagina, same as victim#1.
- Clothes hanging in closet, not on floor as with victim#1.

- All belongings were on night table, same as victim #1.
- Long strand of thread found on bed.
- Originally from New Jersey making both victims out-of- towners.

"Good," Molly says. "So, far, and you probably will be correct, that there will be a lot of similarities with these two girls. We probably won't find any fingerprints here either. Why did he hang her clothes in the closet, or maybe she did herself in anticipation to her customers arrival? Both victims checked in the hotel with their own names about the same time in the morning. I'm beginning to think, as you mentioned to me, that they may be prostituting themselves for the extra money."

"You know, they could have been. We have a lot more digging to do. This is what I came up with for the press release and should say something like this," Johnny suggests.

"Two women found murdered at Budapest Hotel. Both women worked at the Flaming Room. The District Attorney's office has information that cannot be released at this time."

"If we mention the Budapest Hotel and the Flaming Room, it will put pressure on both to tighten up security and hire more people who can be sharp and detect something before it happens," Johnny suggests. "What do you think?"

"Sounds promising. I like it and we'll use it," Molly agrees.

CHAPTER 35

Barely hearing the ring of the telephone because Johnny always rolled the ring-tone dial to low, Billy comments, "telephone," without looking up.

With a slight tilt of his head, giving Billy a quick stare, as he answers the telephone in an annoyed tone; "Hello, Detective Vero, homicide."

"It's Molly. We need to put the squeeze on people Johnny. Did you see the morning paper?"

"I only saw the Daily Mirror. I'm assuming they're all going to be the same trash."

"Well they're saying completely opposite of my statement, saying; *we're not telling the truth about what we found because we really didn't find anything. They're questioning the connection between the Flamingo Room and the Budapest Hotel and their owners since both emigrated from the same country,* which is not true at all."

"You know as well as I, Molly, that the papers write for sensationalism and are biased to hype the reader to increase newspaper sales," Johnny encourages Molly. "I need you to call the Maine State Police and have them contact victim number one's mother, Victoria Morrow, which you have all the data on her. We need to find the info of who paid for the funeral and burial at Hollywood Park Cemetery. We missed interviewing her. She came here to claim Victoria's body and quickly returned home."

"My office contacted the cemetery's administrator that stated two older women showed up and the one who made the arrangements insisting on remaining anonymous and paid cash for the burial. He said the woman claimed to be Vickie's aunt, her mother's estranged sister. They didn't want a receipt and signed the entry form to accept the body with an 'X' which is legal since the 'X' was witnessed by the administrator himself and notarized. My office will contact him to see if she has additional information," Molly replies.

"O.K., the more information we have, the more pieces we can fit together," Johnny assures Molly.

"Now, I need you to go interview the mother of victim number two," Molly continues. "The medical examiner's office got a confirmation on our recent victim from her dental records and the hotel registration card. Her mother is coming in from the Jersey shore today. Here's the information. Are you ready to take it?"

"Go ahead, shoot."

"Victim number two is Ruth Silvan. Her mother is Margaret Matthews. I spoke briefly with her over the telephone. She'll be staying with her cousin up in Yonkers."

"Yonkers!" Johnny exclaims with a loud burst. "That's a"...

"Yeah, Johnny. It will be a nice ride in the country for you and Detective Bradshaw. Now, as I was saying; Here's the address; 109 Dunston Avenue. She sounds like a real character with a deep raspy voice. I don't care what methods you use to twist people to get information detective, just get it. Victim number two did have semen and the medical examiner's report says there was recent sexual activity. Get back with me as soon as possible." - Click.

CHAPTER 36

Angie came home for a three day week-end school break, un-announced as usual. Unlocking the door, opens it slightly, poking her head in with a yell.....”Dad, I'm here. Dad, are you home?” Since there was no answer and Johnny's bedroom door was wide open, Angie realized *he was still at work*. After getting her week-end bag unpacked in her dresser drawers, she continued entering the bedroom, made the bed, and tidied up his bathroom. Going into the kitchen, washed the dishes in the sink and opened the refrigerator to see what was to eat, nothing. She eyed some Rheingold beer, grabbed it, opened the drawer for an opener and dug it into the top of the can and started slugging it down. *Ah!* Opening the cabinet, *there is spaghetti. I'll wait for Dad before I cook.* Going to the balcony to sip her beer and view the river, she thought, *I could win the 'Miss Rheingold' pageant but then it might not be on the up and up. I don't want to deal with that bullshit.*”

CHAPTER 37

Evening started to fall and Angie on her third beer hears keys jingling and the door opening, gives a yell, "Dad, I'm here on the balcony."

CHAPTER 38

Angie's up early making breakfast for her and her father since he came home with groceries last night. The smell of bacon and eggs with toast, butter and coffee stirs Johnny from his sleep to get up and go to the bathroom to relieve the night's fill of beer, wash his hands and face to wake up a little. Angie hears him calling out, "almost ready Dad, are you?"

"Be right in."

"Good mornin' honey. This looks and smells so good. Thank you."

"Oh, you're welcome Dad."

Johnny asks, "Is there something on your mind Angie you want to talk to me about?"

"Here you go Dad, coffee, black, and two sugars. I understand why you're a detective. Yes there is. I was thinking that you could meet Freddy and".....

"Freddy is a new boyfriend that you actually want me to meet?" Johnny Interrupts.

"Yes, and I don't want you to do what you've always done to my other boyfriends"

"And that would be?" Johnny snickers.

"You know, you toss them one of your .38 bullets and when they catch it they're confused and they say; 'What's this for Mr. Vero? And you always answer and embarrass me with; 'If Angie is ever mistreated, you won't be able to catch the next one.'"

"It sounds to me like he's different. I'll behave, I promise if it's important to you. Maybe we can all go to a ballgame," Johnny suggests.

"Thanks Dad. That would be wonderful. I love you," Angie answers.

CHAPTER 39

"C'mon, Billy. We have to get over to Molly's office and get as much of this information together and fit the pieces. This is a huge puzzle. Just let me get the morning briefing started in the spaghetti room and go over with the Captain what I have the squad working on."

"You got it Sarge. I'm right behind you."

CHAPTER 40

Detectives Vero and Bradshaw enter Molly's conference room seeing it set up with the blackboard and papers taped to the wall next to the board with information about each victim. As they both were reviewing the information, Molly's Gal Friday Louise, as Molly's general assistant, enters holding a tray with coffee. Staring at Johnny, not looking as to where she is going almost stumbling.

"Careful Louise," Billy directs as the sound of the spoons rattled between the cup and saucer.

"I guess we're going to be here awhile mumbles Billy."

"Relax detective," snorts Molly.

"We need to work smarter than this son-of-a-bitch...we don't want to be disturbed Louise. Close the door on your way out...he can't beat us. There's one of him and how many of us to use our smarts? The Commissioner wants an arrest toot sweet."

"Yeah, and I would like a girlfriend named Lola," Johnny interjects.

"We can't arrest someone because they just look guilty. C'mon, Molly, we're working with what evidence we found," comments Detective Bradshaw.

"We hope there's only one of him. What do we have from the State Police in Maine interviewing victim one's mother?" Johnny asks.

"Here are copies for you to look at while I put more information on the board," Molly states.

"Mmmm, Interesting with similarities. Victim one, Victoria Morrow's mother, Mary Webb, originally from London gave birth out of wedlock. Vickie left home by sixteen to be out on her own. Mary told the Maine State Police Victoria changed her name to Morrow legally to fit in with her Hollywood image. Victoria would come to visit once a year and only stay a couple of days. The report says Miss Morrow never would see anyone while she visited her mother and would just hang around the house. Her mother said she found her daughter to be introverted and not very social. The report goes on to say that many visits wound up with arguing and Victoria leaving never letting her mother knows that she left. Mary Webb never saw or spoke with the person who paid for the burial out in Hollywood. She was just told it was paid for and was glad it was not her burden."

"And what do you have on victim number two?" Molly asks.

"I interviewed victim two's mother, Margaret Matthews. She came in from Jersey and was up in Yonkers with cousins. It's like you said Molly, what a character. She lite up cigarette after cigarette and was always asking for a cup of coffee. She had mercurochrome dyed hair, orange color, pulled tight and tied in a bun. She owns and operates a tourist shop on the boardwalk and sells souvenirs, trinkets, tchotchkes, candies and post cards. It looks like she was dressed to go dancing and was humming that song by Fats Waller, 'I'm Going to Sit Right Down and Write Myself a Letter,' every time we took a break. There was so much smoking she should have been called Stinky. She, like victim ones mother gave birth out of wedlock. She stated that Ruth didn't like the boyfriends she chose. Ruth claimed they tried to have sex with her and ran off around the same age as Victim one, around sixteen." Finishing with his notes, Johnny looks up at Molly.

"From what you've described, it's a wonder her daughter didn't run off at twelve," Molly adds.

"There's the similarity," Billy interjects. "Both early run-a-ways from out of state and most likely turned to prostitution to survive. Who frequents the Flaming Room looking for a hooker?"

"Which man there isn't looking to get laid? Molly asks.

"Victim two, Ruth Silvan, used her father's name and did not want to use her mother's name of Matthews. Interesting that both used names not associated with their mothers," Billy continues.

"So, this is good information detective. It gives us a prospective to one of the reasons the killer chooses his victims. They both didn't want to be associated with whatever family they knew, being their mothers, even to the point of not using their mother's names. Since there is no father on the scene, the killer finds this out and hypothesis's that they won't be missed or they are in pain mentally and feels he is doing them a favor. From the interviews with the mothers, he seems to be correct. I wonder how many of the taxi dancers have chosen the same with their lives, leaving home, leaving their names and leaving all the past behind."

"You're probably right Molly. There may be many. Many you know, too many to find out. We could never go through all the dancers and you know the Flamingo Room's records are not going to be correct, that is if they keep records of their dancers. What they can't run from or leave behind is they themselves. As the saying goes; 'you can run but you can't hide,'" Johnny says philosophizing.

"Apparently, the girls must be telling their life story to the killer if what you say is correct, Molly. How else would he be able to know such private information since we all agree the Flamingo Room doesn't keep that kind of detailed information?" Billy chimes in.

"Alright, why are you both sitting here?" Molly asks. "Get going and find out who the dancers are telling their life story too."

CHAPTER 41

Attorney Lewis and Irving Cohen arrive at South Central police station and are escorted into the Captain's office.

"Captain, this isn't good for business," claims Mr. Lewis. "There's been a drop off of customers which doesn't make as much money for the dancers or Mr. Cohen."

"The press and their bullshit stories are out of my control," Captain Sullivan blurts out. "The Commissioner and Mayor have approved more plain clothes policemen to be around as your customers. You or your dancers will not know who they are, but they will be there every night. We've also got approval for men to be at the Budapest Hotel as well not knowing who they are. You know, Mr. Cohen, you have a responsibility here too. You can hire more housemen particularly if they have some sort of formal training looking for suspicious people. It's your responsibility to check their backgrounds."

"Captain, these housemen are nothing more than thugs and bouncers. Many of them are washed up prize fighters that know how to handle a loud mouth or someone looking for a fight," relates Mr. Cohen.

"Alright, I understand," states O'Brian.

Detective Vero instructs Mr. Cohen, "Have each of the housemen wear a white artificial boutonniere in the lapel of their tuxedos."

"I want my men to be able to identify them as part of your staff. Let them dance with the girls as my men will. The best thing is for you to give them a string of tickets and you will have to drop some here to distribute to my detectives whom you will not know," as captain O'Brian said.

"Your dancers need to know it's for their own protection. Have your housemen ask questions about how the dancers feel about some of the customers. We have a special team assigned only to these homicides. We want this bastard caught just as much as you both do," concludes O'Brian.

CHAPTER 42

"Billy!"

"I'm right here Johnny. What instant thought just popped into your mind? Because I know that look."

"Let's go. We've got to go the evidence room and pull all the clothes that were hanging in the closet for victim two Ruth Silvan. It doesn't make sense."

"What doesn't make sense Johnny?"

"I'll tell you when I find out," he answers.

"Now you're not making any sense," Billy states.

CHAPTER 43

Entering the door to the evidence room which took the entire fifth floor of the police building, there, behind a locked gate in eye's view, were rows of shelving. Carefully arranged on those shelves were boxes filled with evidence that would be needed for future court appearances as to the case they were assigned.

Johnny and Billy enter and are greeted by the property clerk known as Sarge saying; "Detectives please sign the log and be sure to put the case number of what you want to review along with your badge numbers. Please hold up your I.D. so I can see it. If you break a sealed item, I have to be present to initial the log."

"Understood, Sarge," answers Billy as he turns the log book to face him filling in all the information needed to pull the evidence they want to look at. Within a few minutes Sarge returned with a box filled with the clothes found hanging in the closet of victim two saying; "Word is out, you boys got your hands full on this one. You can review it all over on that table right now. Nothing leaves. You know the drill." growling his instructions.

Johnny tells Billy, "Write what I tell you. Hey, Sarge. Do you have a yard stick back there I can use? Thanks. O.K., Billy...this dress measures forty five inches from shoulder to hem. Taking into consideration the head measurement and lower leg exposed measurement, this person was about five foot five inches. Victim two, Ruth Silvan was only five foot, two inches. So her dress probably would have measured forty two inches. Look at these shoes. They're a Size seven. Ruth's autopsy said she was a size three and a half. This son-of-a-bitch is a cross dresser."

"You've got to be fucking kidding me. A man murderer who dresses up in women's clothes? What do you think, he had sex with them before or after he murders them? Billy asks.

CHAPTER 44

Angie and Freddy are eagerly waiting in the front of Gate six, Yankee Stadium for Johnny to arrive.

"Dad, over here," Angie waving her hand as she sees Johnny approaching. Johnny gives Angie a kiss greeting her.

"Hi honey. This must be Freddy," shaking Freddy's hand vigorously.

"Yes Mr. Vero. Freddy Redken. I'm glad we're able to meet."

"Dad, its ladies day. I get in free. Why do you have 3 tickets? Angie asks.

"I've got box seats for us, right next to the Yankee dugout along the first base line. I didn't want any hassle." Johnny responds.

"Wow, Mr. Vero, thank you," Freddy says with enthusiasm. "This is going to be a good game. They're playing the Dodgers."

Just as they were reaching their seats, the announcer says;

"Good afternoon ladies and gentlemen. This is your announcer, Charlie Goodman. Today's game is brought to you by Gillette for a smoother professional shave. Gillette has given a brand new meaning to the word, comfort with quick, clean refreshing shaves with more of them per blade. Each blade is alike offering equal and smooth shaves each time. The curtain is about to go up on our Lady's Day game this afternoon as the New York Yankees take on the Brooklyn Dodgers. It's a beautiful Sunday in New York. The umpires are discussing the ground rules with the managers of both teams. We have a great crowd here today folks. Looks like at least twenty nine thousand. Alright, the umps are finished. Here comes the marching band from the Bronx High School of Science taking their place on the infield. Please stand for the National Anthem. Gentleman, please remove your hats."

The Star-Spangled Banner

Charlie Goodman continues; "Thank you Bronx High School of Science. That was a wonderful performance. As the Umps speak with the team managers on the mound, let me tell you a little history about our stadium here:

April 18, 1923: Yankee Stadium officially opens for the Yankees' home opener. Babe Ruth hits the ballpark's first home run as the Yankees defeat the Boston Red Sox, 4–3.

 September 30, 1927: Yankees player Babe Ruth hits his 60th home run of the season, setting a new single season record. Here we go folks, throwing out the first ball is old timer Tom Overland and it's a good pitch, Tom. There all on the field as the umpire yells 'play ball.' Let's go over the batting order folks......"

Johnny leans in to tell Freddy, "You know Angie used to play the fife in her marching high school band. She looked so good out front in her blue and white uniform with all the tassels and epaulets. I loved the high hat that had the feathers and chin strap."

"I'd love to see a picture Mr. Vero," answers Freddy smiling as he eyes Angie.

"Yeah, yeah. Let's get back to the game here," Angie declares. "You know, 'Joltin' Joe DiMaggio has cemented his place in baseball with his fifty six game hitting streak. I say it's pretty good ball playing."

CHAPTER 45

"Miss Penett, Detective Vero is here to see you," Louise relayed into the intercom with a sigh.

"Send him in Louise and take a cold shower when you get home."

"Molly, you're not going to believe what I found as Billy and I went back to the property room and re-looked at the clothes in evidence."

"How, pray tell do you expect me to know what you found detective, unless you spit it out and I can add it to our black board."

"I measured the clothes and shoes found in evidence. What we found would fit a less than average man and not fit our victim two, Ruth Silvan. She was five foot two inches and weighed in at one hundred five pounds. She would have measured from shoulder to hem forty two inches. The dress measured from shoulder to hem forty five inches. Victim two shoe size is three and a half. The shoes in evidence are size seven. This sick bastard is a cross dresser. What we don't know is if he had sex with them before or after he murdered them. My guess is as good as yours," Johnny summarizes.

"Oh my God, necrophilia! What a sick bastard, having sex with a dead person. Ugh. This is becoming really macabre. I'm sorry Johnny. That really freaks me out. I want to go home and take a shower."

"I know, I know," Johnny says trying to help Molly with what she just heard. "This killer is cold and that's being far more than detached from his evil deeds."

"I don't know why God allows such horrific things to happen, detective."

"I guess that's one of the reasons we're here to help get these creeps off this earth and balance things out. It's sort of job security for us, you know Molly?"

"Awhile back you thought that our victims were not lesbians. So, how did the killer get these victims to rent a room and get in there with them and commit these heinous crimes if he was dressed as a woman," Molly inquires with such distain in her voice?

"Our suspect is not perceived as a threat to the victims. I have to put this all together and see why the suspect is not a threat along with a motive. You know, Molly, what is perceived as most probable is usually least probable. I'm heading back to the prescient. I'll keep you updated."

"Please," reply's Molly. "The Commissioner..."

"Yes, wants me and Billy to jump off a roof soon," smiling on his way out the door.

CHAPTER 46

Johnny arose earlier than usual this Saturday morning due to his tossing all night between the Old Crow Bourbon and the lovely lady that was in his bathroom running the shower. Not fully awake, rubbing his eyes with one hand and his balls with the other, gets out of bed to do first things first....take a leak.

"Good morning Johnny," a voice appears over the sound of the running water.

"Good morning, Grace. I'm sorry I can't drive you. I'll put cab fare near your purse. I've got to get to the prescient this morning."

"It's O.K. I have to meet my sister to shop for my father's birthday," her words echo from the shower. "I like how you use those handcuffs detective. Next time we need to handcuff ourselves to each other."

"Sounds like another date," flushing the toilet. "Do you have time for coffee?" Johnny asks, really hoping she doesn't.

"I'll grab a cup with her. I've got to hurry."

Picking up his police radio Johnny requesting a connection... 'Tschhhhhhhhhhhhhhhh... '"Detective Vero, I.D. 4225, to South Central Station, over."

"Go ahead detective; this is South Central, over."

"Connect me to detective Bradshaw, over."

"10-4. Hold on detective."

"Go ahead, detective Bradshaw are you there, over?"

"I'm here Johnny. Go ahead."

"Can you meet me at the prescient this morning? I thought of a few things we can use, over."

"Sure, right after breakfast, over," replies Billy.

"10-4. See you there, over and out."

"Thanks for the cab fare Johnny."

"You were really wonderful, Grace. I had a good time."

"Me too, Johnny. I hope to see you soon," closing the door behind her.

CHAPTER 47

"Billy we need to get updated information so Molly can get it to the Commissioner and the Mayor."

"What do you have on your mind? Billy asks. I'll add whatever you think and relate it to Molly so she can add it to the black board."

"Great. A few points;"

1) This guy is really comfortable with himself.

2) He cross dresses in public.

3) He must be non-descript and have very fine features to really look like a woman. He probably has a light beard or very little and can hide it easily.

4) Usually a first murder is sloppy and then murderers fix their mistakes.

5) He is opposite. Either he's setting us up by leaving his clothes he uses to dress like a women in the closet or, he got sloppy instead of getting better at it.

"Maybe he had to leave sooner than expected," Billy mentions.

6) That means he had another change of clothes in some sort of suitcase," Johnny reply's.

7) He must have had his regular clothes, as a man, not to be recognized when leaving.

8) Both bodies were in same position sitting upright, naked, legs open facing the door. This is for shock value.

9) He's about 5'5". He can't weigh more than one hundred thirty pounds, maybe a little less.

"I have to get my squad to jump in and help out. I'll meet with everyone first thing Monday morning. Thanks Billy. Enjoy the rest of the week-end."

He faintly hears the echo of Billy's voice that is by now down the stairs, thru the shuffling of all the papers and files on his desk."

"Ditto."

CHAPTER 48

Johnny walks into South Central Precinct Monday morning. Just yesterday, Sunday, was so peaceful. He and Angie spent the day at Central Park going to the zoo and rowing on the lake. The day ended with window shopping along Fifth Avenue before Angie returned to school. Folded under his arm is the morning New York Telegraph newspaper.

"Good morning Johnny," Billy's greeting. "I see you have the morning Telegraph. Did you read the front page?"

"How the fuck could you miss it! It's in big black bold letters. This is a story that is going to bite us in the ass."

"Yea, Chief O'Brian and Mayor Bernhard are in the Captains office chaffing at the bit, ready to do just that."

"Tell me when they stop staring at us through the blinds," Johnny asks Billy.

"Ah, here comes D.A. Penett," Billy mentions looking up.

"Vero, get in here," shouts Chief O'Brian. "You too, Bradshaw!"

"Good morning Molly. May I escort you to the guillotine"?

"I'm ready," Molly responds.

Johnny quickly stands and gives a slight bow as he stretches his arm out to help direct her path into hell and whispers, "After you, My Lady."

CHAPTER 49

Experience tells Johnny not to speak first at times and this is one of them.

"We all know what is in the morning Telegraph," Mayor Bernhard begins.

"I'll break it down to where we stand and what Mayor Bernhard and the Commissioner wants," Chief O'Brian chimes in saying. "We can't help what the newspapers print. That's why this columnist, Vincent Razzo got acid thrown in his face, and hands yesterday. It burned through his shirt and got a good portion of his chest and now is almost blind and probably will be scarred for life."

"I'm not saying he deserved this horrible crime to happen to him," Molly interjects. "He always wrote about the Italian mob and how he blamed them for everything, even running the city. He had no facts saying that the mob has committing the two Budapest Hotel murders using the dancers from the Flamingo Room. In last week's column, he wrote that the hotel and the Flamingo Room would be losing so much business, the mob would take them over to help launder money."

"O.K. We all realize that he is outspoken and that's why he was a target," Johnny speaks.

"I now have to have assign police protection to him twenty four hours a day," claims O'Brian. "Johnny, the Commissioner..."

"Hold up Chief. I can recommend 5 good detectives and Billy is s not going to be one of them. He will stay with me on these homicides. These murders are priority number one for all of us. The hospital states that Razzo is going to take months to recover and has a lot of surgeries in front of him until he is out of the hospital. You can use uniform men to be outside his room. When he's out, then we can assign a plain clothes detail. He's going to have a lot of time on his hands. He will either do a lot of reflecting or he's going to be so god damn mad, he's going to go after the crime boss himself."

"That wouldn't be such a bad idea. Maybe he'll lead us to this sick Bastard who did this to him and then like bowling pins we can knock 'em all down," Mayor Bernhard comments.

"I agree with detective Vero," says Molly sternly.

"I'll go along with that," snaps Bernhard. "Set it up Chief. I'll take care of the Commissioner"

CHAPTER 50

Mayor Philip Bernhard is being pressured by the newspapers to hold a press conference. He arranged to hold this on the court house steps at Federal Plaza for his backdrop. His reasoning is to show the entire city police force and legal system is backing him. He had police Chief O'Brian hand pick tough looking police officers to stand behind him knowing there would be a lot of photographs taken. He has notes he jotted down for things to say given to him by District Attorney Penett who in turn received the notes from detective Vero.

The reporters were all shouting questions to the Mayor...

Do you have a suspect?

Why aren't you releasing any information to the public?

What do the Flamingo Room and the Budapest Hotel have in common?

Is Vincent Razzo correct that the mob is behind these murders?

Is it true both women were dancers at the Flamingo Room?

Each question was like a shark sensing its prey, rubbing up against it before it was about to be devoured. As the reporters became more intense, the police platoon of twenty five men would take one step closer to the Mayor.

"I'll answer each of your questions. I expect you to be accurate in your notes. I will not be misquoted."

CHAPTER 51

Back at South Central Precinct, Johnny lifts his head from his notes staring at Billy saying; "You were right."

"About?" Billy asks.

"The killer. He might have had to leave in a hurry. He left the clothes he would wear as a woman in the closet. We have to go back to the Budapest and ask the housekeeper, Halina Elzbeta a few more questions. Let's go."

CHAPTER 52

Johnny and Billy enter Chester Riley's office at the Budapest Hotel. Within a few minutes housekeeper Halina Elzbeta enters the office asking in her Polish accent, "Yah. You call for me?"

"Yes Halina replies Mr. Riley. The detectives have some additional questions for you."

"Das O.K. Go ahead," Halina says nodding her head and fidgeting her fingers holding her hands together as they rest on her chest.

"Mrs. Elzbeta," detective Vero begins. "You said you immediately walked out of the crime scene and put your cleaning cart in front of the door."

"Yah, I told you dat already."

"I know. I have that in my notes. Did you at any time earlier start to go into that room and then stop to go somewhere else?"

"Yah, I tawt you know dat?"

"No," Billy answers. Why did you stop and not enter the room?"

"I start to put my key in door and see my cart was empty of fresh bedding sheets. I had to quick go to supply room. I run to basement and leave my cart in hallway next to door."

"Bingo, Billy. You were right. Did you hear anything coming from the room?"

"No! I no vant to know any udder business of people," Halina says.

"So, you came back from the basement and then entered the room and saw the body," Johnny asks?

"Yah, das is right."

"Thank you Mrs. Elzbeta," Johnny says, continuing to say, "As you said the Devil is not just in Europe but the Devil sure is in the details."

"I'm not," shrugging her shoulders and shaking her head, gesturing her hands, not understanding Vero's comment.

"It's just a saying Mrs. Elzbeta. You've been a great help. If there is anything else, we will be in touch to see you."

"I can go back to my cart now?"

"Detectives?" asks Mr. Riley.

"Sure."

"Go ahead Halina," Mr. Riley directs.

CHAPTER 53

Johnny starts to clear the fog from the mirror after stepping from the shower.

"Where are you going, Johnny, asks Marlene. You haven't finished washing my...?

Staring in the mirror, lathering his beard with the shaving brush, asks his self... *What*

are we missing? The smallest detail. We need something.

"Oh, detective?

"Marlene, I'm sorry. I thought I scrubbed you from head to toe."

"You missed a spot'.

"I guess I'll have to search you all over to find it the next time I put you in my arrest."

"O.K. I'm good with that. Can you drop me at the train station; I can't be late for   work"?

"Sure thing."

Wiping the leftover shave cream off his face with the towel he just removed from his waist, without missing a step, grabs his police radio from the kitchen table...

Tschhhhhhhhhhhhhhhhh..."This is detective Vero, I.D. 4225, to South Central, over?"

"Go ahead detective; this is South Central, over."

"Patch me through to detective Bradshaw, over."

"10-4 detective. Stand by."

"Go ahead detective Bradshaw, over?"

"I'm here Johnny, go ahead."

"We need to meet. I'll call Molly and go to her office. It's too crazy at the prescient,   over"

"10-4 Johnny. Be there shortly, over and out."

"Detective Vero, I.D. 4225, to South Central, over."

"Go ahead detective; this is South Central, over."

"Patch me through to D.A. Penett, over."

"Stand by, detective."

CHAPTER 54

"Miss Penett, Detectives Bradshaw and (sigh) Vero are here," are the words Molly hears through the intercom.

"Send them in Louise."

"Jesus Christ, Louise, I said send them in, not walk them in."

"I know. I just wanted to ask if you wanted coffee or...."

"No Louise, thank you. We'll be in the conference room."

"I don't know Johnny. Louise has eyes for you," comments Molly.

"Well, I wouldn't mind if she had eyes for me," replies Billy.

"What do we have detectives?" asks Molly with annoyance in her voice.

"I've come up with an idea to give a point system to the similarities of what we have," Johnny says.

"That's an interesting idea Johnny. Let's begin, show me," replies Molly walking to the blackboard with chalk in hand. "I apologize. Louise just pushes a bit too hard. Let's hear it, I'm ready."

Molly starts to write the heading, interjecting, with the turn of her head; "Don't worry Johnny, I won't make the chalk squeal", smiling.

Similar components with murder victims Hotel Budapest point system 1-5:

"O.K." starts Johnny. "You have better hand writing Molly, you write and I'll call out to you what I've put together."

> Sexually assaulted - 5
> Hair color: Victim (1) Auburn and Victim (2) Brunette
> So, I give this a score of - 3
> Childhood Run-a-Ways - 5
> Mother's unmarried - 5
> Victims used different last name
> from mother - 5
> No fathers around - 5
> Approximate same age - 5
> Taxi dancers at the Flamingo Room - 5
> Murders at Budapest Hotel - 5
> Bodies posed (same position) - 5
> Evidence (dance tickets) found on bodies - 5
> Victims clothing - 2
> (1)   Found on floor
> (2)   Not found
> Finger prints (Only partials not enough to process)...5

"Even if the finger print technician, what's his name, found any prints, there isn't a good way to tell for sure if they are male or female," Molly says.

"Kowalski, Kevin Kowalski. No shit, I never knew that" Exclaims Billy!

"Any more items detective?" Molly asks.

"Yes, two more," Johnny answers.

"Room Keys:
    Victim (1) none found - 5
    Victim (2) none found - 5
Victims did not put up a fight - 5

Look at the patterns. Let's look at the fact that no room keys found tells me these victims are his possessions and he wants the room keys as a reminder of his murders. What he does with the keys is a good a guess as any. Maybe he hangs them up or keeps them in a drawer as a reminder. It's the same thing with their clothes. Maybe he tries to wear them even though they would be small or maybe he smells them."

"I see the reasoning here with the point system Johnny," Molly says. "It gives us a purpose to see how he targets his prey. It's like he's hunting for them."

Johnny bragging says; "I was taught to be a cryptographer in the navy. Some things come in handy."

"Ah! Yes, Greek meaning hidden or secret." Molly says staring at the black board. "So, this killer thinks he has a hidden secret targeting young woman that meets his private needs.

"Johnny uses the same system for the women he wants to go out with," reports Billy with a wide grin.

"Well, detective, we'll just use this scoring for here and now."

"You're right Molly. I'm sorry. I was just kidding around," Billy says. "We need to look at all the number fives and see how we can view all the dancers that fit into that number. There must at least sixty out of the seventy five dancers at the Flamingo Room that fall into that number five category."

"Don't forget his other secret of being a cross dresser which he thinks we haven't figured out," Johnny concludes.

"Well not anymore," Molly answers. "We now know his secret and it's not hiding."

"I'll be here. This point system is really brilliant. It gives us direction Johnny. Good work," giving praise to him. "I guess we can also thank the navy. Maybe one day I can see your hidden secret point system," Molly says turning, smiling and giving Johnny a wink.

"Thanks, Molly. Let's go Billy. We have a lot to do."

CHAPTER 55

The Crosstown Diner neon sign is constantly aglow both day and night. It never flickers as some neon signs do because of the neon gas that escapes from the long luminous tubes. This is always a clean eatery with fresh food, coffee and deserts that is open twenty four hours catering to a lot of policeman and detectives in addition to the civilian public. The Crosstown Diner is also where Johnny's sometime companion, Audrey, slings the low price meat and vegetable blue plate specials to the customers.

"Hi Johnny, Shall I pour you Coffee?" Audrey asks with a smile that can welcome the hardest days of woes.

"Yes, Audrey, please and some eggs scrambled with sausage and toast," as he eases onto the stool at the counter.

"Coming right up," answering Audrey as she turns to the line cooks with a shout; "Give me an Adam and Eve and wreck 'em with a log. Let the raft drift with axle grease."

"Audrey, do you ever see any of the crowd from the female impersonator shows stop in here. You know before or after their performances?" Johnny asks.

"Sure plenty of them, Johnny. They usually like to take the booth in the back around the corner. You know, to keep to them-selves. A lot of folks don't understand them. They're very respectful. All the girls who serve them get some good tips on make-up, clothes, nail polish. You know, sounds funny, girly stuff. They have a lot of knowledge because they have to do a lot of searching to perfect how they look. I've seen them both in drag and in men's suits. They look pretty good either way. It's amazing. You must be working on something you can't tell me, so I won't ask as usual and if you tell me what to look for, I will."

As Audrey finished her sentence, putting down Johnny's breakfast with a fresh cup of coffee, a thought lit up like the Crosstown Diners neon sign. *That's another avenue to check out. The female impersonators have to search to perfect their look. Audrey called out my order to the cook in a special way. The impersonators have to go searching in special ways to fit their needs. There has to be specialty dress shops for women.*

"Are you alright, Johnny? You look like you're in another world," asks Audrey.

"Oh, yeah. I'm fine Audrey. I'm thinking about going out for dinner Saturday night. Can you make it?"

"Tell me the time and I'll have my dancing shoes on," Audrey replies knowing deep down that a relationship with Johnny is and always will be casual and nothing more.

"Glad to hear you're up to doing some dancing."

CHAPTER 56

Johnny knew that Audrey, being a platinum blond, would stand out at the Flamingo Room even though there were a few other blonds, platinum blonds and a few redheads. Audrey was happy to help Johnny knowing it was going to be part police business. It would also be a nice night with dinner, dancing and Johnny Vero.

"O.K., Johnny, let me be sure I have what you told me is correct. If someone approaches me with dance tickets, I'm supposed to take them. I take one ticket for each dance that should last approximately one to one and a half minutes per song. If they want to dance again, I only dance with the same man only twice in a row. Tell them they can dance with me later. I have to give others a chance to dance. You'll be dancing with me more than anyone else. There are other police whom I will not know, except Billy who may dance with me or not. I'm supposed to pay close attention to what the men talk to me about. If any get rambunctious, stop dancing and tell me or one of the housemen. I'm looking for any man with fine features that if dressed as woman would pass for a woman."

"You have it down pat. Let's go in," Johnny encourages Audrey as he opens the door.

Once paying the flat fee cover charge, they enter the beautiful hand crafted doors gilded in gold and silver that opened simultaneously by two housemen that gave each person the once over and sometimes 'pat' down the men to see if they are carrying a 'gat.' It is only to ensure that whoever entered passed their inspection not carrying a gun and to avoid a bad situation. Johnny just flashed his badge to the houseman who nodded his approval, opening the door.

The room was crowded with well-dressed couples dancing as the orchestra played. Johnny and Audrey were shown to a dinner table to a fast response of a waiter with menus, wine and beer.

"I'm quite impressed Johnny. I had no idea this was such a classy joint," Audrey whispers reading the menu before sipping her wine.

"I thought you'd like it. Let me order for you if it's O.K. Johnny asks?"

"Why yes. I'd like that Johnny."

"Cordon Blue for the lady and I'll have the porterhouse steak, rare."

"Yes sir. Your order will be done shortly," replies the waiter.

"C'mon Audrey, let have a go at it and spin before the floor show starts."

CHAPTER 57

Billy, climbing the stairs to the second floor reaching the detective's squad room, sees Johnny diligently at work hovering over files spread atop his desk. "Good Mornin', Johnny."

"Good Mornin', Billy. We had a good time Saturday night. Audrey likes to dance. There were few guys that tried to put the make on her but none that really would fit the fine features that if dressed as a woman would pass for a woman."

"Same here," Billy says. "The dancers I had pegged me right away as a cop and really couldn't tell me much except wanting me to call them, which I will do."

"Yeah, I know. Good luck. We need to get a list of Woman's specialty dress shops and female impersonator shows that are in town and hit the pavement. The shows may have a matinee so we'll have to see if the same performers are appearing in both matinee and evening shows. This is going to be a daunting task with no leads. Let's grab breakfast at the Crosstown Diner than we'll hit the streets."

"Audrey?" Questions, Billy.

"No. She's off today. Besides, we both know it's, you know... I also want to talk to victim one, Victoria Morrow's roommate, Susan Fleming again."

CHAPTER 58

Detectives Vero and Bradshaw's desks faced each other with Billy having the clearer view of whose head reached the top of the stairs to the second floor detective's spaghetti (squad) room before Johnny was able to.

"Johnny, Chief O'Brian front and center," Billy informs him.

Huffing and puffing from the two flights of stairs holding his chief's hat in hand with a fast paced cadence, O'Brian bellows without stopping, "Vero, Bradshaw, in the Captain's office."

"He better loose that belly and go on a diet," Billy whispers getting up. "He sounds like he's gasping for breath. I hope he doesn't keel over."

"Good morning," Replies Captain Sullivan.

"Let's cut to the chase," begins Chief O'Brian. I received a report that the original statement from Richard Lewis, if you recall who represents Irving Cohen and the Flamingo Room as attorney, stated that business has dropped off. That is bullshit! It actually has increased and so has the Budapest Hotel's business. All the publicity has brought out the lunatics to go see where the girls are coming from and where they're being murdered."

"So, we can rule out Vincent Razzo's theory that the mob is doing these murders to ruin both the Budapest Hotel and the Flamingo Room's reputation just to muscle their way in, buy these businesses to launder their money," Johnny speaks with confidence.

"We were just about to leave and cover some territory for specialty shops and female impersonator shows, Chief," reports Billy. "We feel strongly that our suspect is a female impersonator. The clothes we found in victim two's closet were not her size and could fit a small thin boned man."

"Good work, detective. Be sure to check that bath house that these men, girls or whoever they pretend to be frequent," directs Chief O'Brian.

"Great idea Chief," replies Billy giving the thought *that it was O'Brian's idea for the bath house well knowing it was on their list already.*

"Alright then, hit the pavement," Captain Sullivan says sternly pointing his finger to the stairs.

"I'll give an updated report to the commissioner with some hard nose bullshit," says O'Brian. "Now go."

CHAPTER 59

"Well, Johnny, where do you want us to start our search. We never got to Susan Fleming," Asks Billy?

Johnny answers; "Susan will have to wait. I think we need to save the bath house for last because I feel we, yes, I mean both of us are going to have to take part in getting in the tubs for a bath and maybe a message, and, maybe more than once. We may have to go in together the first time and separately after that."

"Oh, boy," exclaims Billy! "I wish it would be, alright ladies, Billy's here!"

"Let's start with the three specialty shops today," is Johnny's directive. "We have three to visit. All three are around the Budapest Hotel between Forty Fourth and Forty Eighth Streets. Any others are too far away. I feel our killer would keep it close to home."

Billy pulls out his list and reads from it; "Dorothee's, which has a crazy spelling, Andre's and Chantal's.

CHAPTER 60

The tingling of the bell rang when the door opened to Dorothee's specialty shop, signaling that a customer had entered.

A handsome older man dressed in a double breasted grey pinstriped suit appeared through an opened doorway.

Greeting Johnny and Billy; "Good morning gentlemen, I'm Dorothee, how may I help you?" The sound of sewing machines seemed to hum in unison to the beat of a Broadway show tune emanating from where he appeared.

Sizing the man up and down, both Johnny and Billy without looking at each other knew *his build was too large for the clothes they found hanging in victim number two's closet.*

Johnny starts with his usual introduction. "I'm Detective Vero and my partner, Detective Bradshaw. We're investigating a crime and we'd like to ask you some questions with regard to your specialty shop, if you don't mind"

"Not at all detectives. Ask away. You can also look around, I've nothing to hide. If I or my staff can help in any way, we would gladly help. Is this about the Budapest Hotel murders?

"So, you've heard," asks Billy?

"Hasn't everyone, detective?" answers Dorothee. "You know, we don't just put on shows. We are educated. We do read the papers, books, and listen to what people are saying. My heritage is ancient Greek. No pun intended detectives. My real name is Theodoros Stamos. Come, let me show you my girls hard at work sewing together some of our orders."

"Ah!" Johnny exclaims as they walk to the back area of the shop. "Now I understand why the name, Dorothee's. You devised it from your first name, Theodoros, by switching some of the letters around."

"Very good detective. You are quick," replies Dorothee.

"Wow!" Exclaims Billy seeing all the seamstresses are all men. "I wish my mother would have taught me how to sew," commenting, not to let Dorothee feel uncomfortable.

"Anytime you'd like to learn, detective, I'll give you private lessons," Dorothee says smiling, holding his hand sort of coupled between his chin and cheek. "Most of our work is specialty orders for shows and some for personal use. We do occasionally get orders from the prostitutes. You know the classy ones that work the high end hotel bars." Clapping his hands, Dorothee gets the attention of the seamstresses. Their machines all stop at once. Every seamstress looked up, in robotic form, toward the front of the room waiting for further instructions as if this was rehearsed many times.

"Ladies, these two detectives would like to say a few words to you. Go ahead detective," continues Dorothee.

"Thank you. We won't keep you. You all have heard by now, about the murders at the Budapest Hotel. We're looking for anyone who may fit the description of an exceptional beautiful slight woman, but really is a cross dresser. Excuse me. I mean a female impersonator. Do any of you think you have information now?"

Everyone just looked with a blank frozen stare, the same as a deer looking into the headlights of a speeding oncoming car.

"We will leave our information with Dorothee in case you may remember something about someone you know or heard of. Thank you again," Johnny says portraying authority.

Dorothee asks, "Anything else detective?"

"Not at this time."

Dorothee claps his hands twice and the machines start in harmony just as an orchestra led by its conductor begins an arpeggio.

"You know detective, who you're looking for, with that description, can fit most of the girls in the shows around town. I'll explain it better to my girls. I think I know what you're looking for. But why don't you give me more details and leave me your contact information," requests Dorothee.

CHAPTER 61

"O.K., let's go over to Forty Seventh Street to Andre's," Billy says checking his list. "You were kind of vague back there, Johnny."

"We can't give away the store. I want information to come from anyone that may fit into what we've established with our facts, not made up shit that will just throw us off our hard work. Maybe one of them will show up at our door with information who did not want to say in front of everyone else. I don't want to be chasing two rabbits. You won't catch either one of them. You know Billy, Dorothee mentioned something very interesting."

"Mmm, tell me. You want to take sewing lessons?"

"I know how to sew. I taught Angie. Another thing I learned in the navy. We may have to visit some of the hookers Dorothee mentioned. The high priced ones."

"Hey, I'm game for that. We can exchange that for going to the all men's bath house. Maybe we can get the department to pay for us," Billy adds as they both laugh.

CHAPTER 62

Andre's shop was quite elegant as Andre himself. Once opening the door that sounded a buzzer, a young lady helping a customer turned and said; "Someone will be right with you gentlemen." In her hand was some sort of device she used making a clicking noise. With-out hesitation, she clicked twice. A man in his forty's appeared. He has a slight build with fine features standing approximately five foot six inches weighing about one hundred thirty five pounds wearing horn rimmed glasses that were so light you hardly noticed them. He's dressed in a custom made, perfectly starched white shirt, French cuffs, tie, and vest. He was not wearing his suit jacket. Hanging from his neck was a tailors' seamstress cloth sewing ruler. Along the vests lapels were needles at his ready to place on clothing he would be measuring. Men and women would stand on a platform in front of a mirror wearing what was to be measured, pinned, and marked with tailor chalk. What went through Johnny's mind in a flash... *he could fit our cross dresser description.*

"Good day, gentlemen. I'm Andre," introducing himself in his British accent. "How may I assist you since we don't handle men's clothing? Something for a woman friend or wife," asking with a twitching of his lips indicating cynicism according to how Johnny studies peoples reaction.

"Andre, I'm Detective Vero and this is Detective Bradshaw."

"Why, yes. I've was expecting you blokes. You must be balls up with this investigation and knackered by the whole thing. Dorothee informed me you would probably be visiting my shop for a chin wag. Come, follow me," turning, using his fingers to gesture to follow him to the back room. Both Johnny and Billy glanced at each other as Billy whispers; "What the fuck is he talking about?"

"Excuse me, detectives, over hearing Billy's remark. I use my home words that just come out naturally. I'm from London. Blokes are gentlemen. What I meant was; you must be exhausted with this messy situation and need to ask questions. Please detectives, go ahead while I continue with this piece I'm working on. It must be done for a performance in one of the shows for tomorrow night."

Andre handled the piece he is working on as if it were a new born baby, gentle and kindly. Noticeably, there were only two sewing machines. All the seamstresses, both men and women, about a dozen in all were all sewing by hand. Only one was using a machine which was so quiet you hardly knew it was running.

"I see your eyes darting around detective. My shop is quite different from Dorothee's. We do most of our pieces by hand as you can see. We also get the more elaborate costumes that need repair or that were not made correctly the first time by the other specialty shops," saying with a chuckle.

"Tell us Andre," Billy begins; "You must have many customers from around town. I'm sure many are repeat customers. Have you seen anyone recently that you are unfamiliar with, maybe a new face in town, male or female?"

"You're correct, detective. There are many, many repeat solid customers both male impersonators and female entertainers. Many times the costume designers themselves will bring in work to be done because many times, we don't need the performer here to repair. It's only when we have to measure, would they have to come in. I rarely go to the theaters to do work on them. As you investigate this bloody tosh, you will find that our world is filled with twigs, berries and fannies."

"No one said these crimes were bloody, Andre," Billy lashes out.

"Again, detective, forgive me. Bloody is a British term for damn, tosh is nonsense, twigs and berries are male genitalia and of course fannies are vaginas. When I say, our world, you know what I'm talking about. It's filled with both genitalia. To answer your question, detective, I have not seen anyone that is unfamiliar with me or my shop. Feel free to ask my staff, both twigs, berries and fannies," giving a broad smile as he gave a swooping gesture to all those at their stations diligently at work.

CHAPTER 63

"Here we are, last of the specialty shops, Chantal's," Billy points out.

Chantel's is an upper class women's specialty shop in comparison from the other two, despite what Andre said. It caters to show girls, female impersonators, high society dames, and the hotel hookers. The entry is located on the ground floor of a building with magnificent gargoyle designs. Extending from the street curb to the front door is a black awning displaying the name, Chantal's, in gold lettering. The two front windows display magnificent pieces showing a variety of gowns, evening dresses, hats, gloves and custom shoes.

Johnny and Billy walked the long entry to the glass doors. A door man immediately, appeared in full regalia. He looked majestic with hat, gloves, and epaulets equal to a decorated soldier in a fourth of July parade.

"Good day, gentleman," tipping the brim of his hat with one hand and opening the door with the other. "Welcome to Chantal's. Our Concierge will be happy to direct your every need."

"Greetings, gentlemen, I'm Colette, which means victory of the people. How may I help you become victorious visiting Chantal's? We have three floors to accommodate your needs."

"Well, we are looking to speak with Chantal, whom I assume is the owner," answers Johnny.

"Who shall I say is requesting Monsieur Chantal's appearance?"

"I'm detective Vero and this is detective Bradshaw."

"*Monsieur*," Billy mumbles quietly to himself.

"Come; follow me to our V.I.P. room."

Escorted to the V.I.P room, they are seeing well dressed women being measured, each one standing on a raised platform, admiring themselves in the mirrors. Some, only wearing a bra and panties, did not give a thought to the two men passing.

Opening a glass door with curtains expertly placed, not to expose those who are sanctioned to this privilege, is a plush seating arrangement. This V.I.P room outdid some of the better lobbies of the surrounding hotels.

"Our hostess will accommodate you while you wait for Monsieur Chantal."

"May I get you some refreshment, coffee, tea, wine" Asks the hostess?

"No thanks, we'll just have a seat here."

"Thank you gentlemen. If you need further assistance, I'll be at my desk where you first walked in and I met you," replies Colette.

CHAPTER 64

"You know Johnny," Billy begins saying as he starts to pace. "It's been fifteen fucking minutes. Let's go find this son-of-a-bitch, Chantal, Monsieur Chantal," being sarcastic. At that moment, Colette appears.

"Monsieur Chantal will see you gentlemen now. Please follow me," directing them to the elevator. Once in, they were greeted by the elevator operator, dressed in a double breasted black and gold uniform much like the doorman, minus the hat and gloves.

Colette directs the operator saying, "Henry, directly to Monsieur Chantal."

"Certainly Colette," As Henry gestures for the detectives to enter the elevator car.

Once reaching the fourth floor, Henry opens the highly polished brass scissor doors pushing down on the control handle with the salutation, "See you on the rebound gentlemen."

Johnny and Billy step out, Colette is there to greet them; "This way detectives," turning leading the way through large mahogany doors. Both Johnny and Billy look at each other raising their hands and shrugging their shoulders. Billy, being his usual self, tilts his head to get a better look at Colette's backside as she leads the way.

"Monsieur Chantal, ces hommes sont des détectives Vero, ET Bradshaw de vous voir. Y at-il quelque chose d'autre pour l'instant?[1] "

"No thank you, Colette. Detectives... mmm. How may I be of help? Are you both?"

"Absolutely not Mr. Chantal, Billy exclaims!

"It's pronounced, Shahn-TAL, as a women's name. It is of old French origin as a surname which was derived from a place name meaning, 'stony.' It was originally given in honour of St. Jeanne-Francoise de Chantal, the founder of the Visitation Order in the 17th century. Shahn-TAL detectives, Monsieur Shahn-TAL."

Johnny begins; "Monsieur Shahn-TAL, as you may well know by now, we are investigating the murders that took place at the Budapest Hotel. We realize that your clientele is immense and it would take us days to search your files which would cause you a terrible interruption in business, so maybe you can lead us to what we are looking for?"

"I am at your disposal detectives. I or any of my staff will be willing to offer any information they may have to help you with your investigation."

Billy directs himself saying; "We are searching for a man of a slight stature that is a cross dresser and when dressed as a women really could pass as a woman. We see that many of your clientele comes from more than the female

---

[1] Monsieur Chantal, these men are detectives Vero and Bradshaw to see you. Is there anything else for now?

impersonator Broadway shows which could narrow our search by eliminating the prostitutes and high society dames."

"You're right detective. That would narrow my clientele down quite a bit. However, as you say from your description, it could fit more than forty or fifty performers, even myself. I don't get them all in here you know, although I would love to add more to our repertoire of clients. Many go to Dorothee and Andre. Please detectives look and ask around. As you see, I have four floors which one is sales, two are production, and one is my personal office, conference room as well as a small lounging area with sofa and kitchen for late night stays."

"We appreciate your co-operation, Monsieur Shahn-TAL," Johnny putting the emphasis on Chantal's name as asked. "We will look and ask around without interrupting your staff or clientele."

"Thank you detectives. Our doors are always open to you for your investigation as well as your purchases for pleasure. Let me call Colette to help you to where you would like to go. Ah, Colette, you're here already! Please take the detectives anywhere they would like to go and ask whomever they want to speak with."

Johnny and Billy look at each other with the same thought; *How did Colette know to be right there at that moment as well as beating them to the fourth floor when they stepped from the elevator?*

CHAPTER 65

"Orma, (Angie could not pronounce Grandma Norma as a baby as it always sounded like Orma which stayed with her). I'm so happy I was able to visit and spend time with you. I love your home here in Florida. I'll call a cab to take me to the airport," Angie saying giving her grandmother, Norma, an embrace of love and endearment.

"I'll have nothing of the sort dear. I'll drive you myself. It will give us some more time together and a chance for me to get out and do some shopping after I drop you. Do you have the tie you bought your father from the men's shop? It certainly is quite fancy. He always hated wearing a tie, you know. "

"I know, Orma. Now he wears one most of the time, even to the baseball games."

"Is he seeing someone special, wearing a tie? You know, dear, a special lady?"

"No. Not yet Orma. I would know. Dad and I are really close and share what's happening in each of our lives. We talk a lot when I'm home sitting on the balcony looking out at the river."

"That's good Angie. Usually your father is like the Secret Service Bureau, keeping everything a secret to himself. Your grandfather was the same way, bless his soul and rest in peace," making the sign of the cross.

"I'm ready Orma. I love you so much," Angie tells Norma.

"I love you too dear. Maybe you can talk your father into visiting with you. I'd love to see you both together. Although, we wouldn't be able to have girl talk," Norma adds as they both giggle.

CHAPTER 66

"Another day, another dollar," Billy quotes.

"Yeah Billy, but this day is going to give us more than a dollar. It's going to give us 'pennies from heaven.' Lots of pennies. Lots of leads," Johnny says happily.

Billy continues laughing, "Are you going to sing that song or are you hoping our leads will come from heaven?"

"O.K., Billy, what's our next list looking like," Johnny asks?

"Female impersonator shows with original all male review. There are three of them Johnny to be exact; 'In and Out', 'Jewel Box Review' and 'French Cabaret'. All are within a block from each other."

"Yes, and only a few blocks from the specialty dress shops," Johnny replies as he reviews his notes. "Let's get to these theaters before the shows begin and after the last performance if we have to depending on the cast members. I really don't want to sit through them."

"We need a break somewhere Johnny. All that time at Chantal's and a big fat zero of any information we can put to use. Everyone working there, we interviewed, really didn't hold anything back and weren't lying. One who didn't hold back was Nancy, the redhead. She gave me her number. She is part of Chantal's bevies of beauties, you know like the Sultan's Harem."

"You better make sure your redhead doesn't interfere with this investigation and fuck anything up, besides fucking you, until the killer is under raps, Johnny quickly snaps."

CHAPTER 67

"O.K. Billy here we are at the first theater for the show, 'In and Out'."

Locating the box office, Billy asks for the manager. They are directed to his office, one flight up, next to the dressing room. It is a huge room with constant activity of performers coming and going. It was difficult to determine if they were viewing men or women. Many are changing costumes, fusing with wigs, and make up in front of mirrors or were just lounging waiting for the next act. The entertainers were talking to themselves, to each other, talking about movie stars, the show, and gossiping. Johnny and Billy took in all that was going on; they see that there is a routine of preparing and that routine within its self, looked quite boring.

"You know Billy," Johnny begins; "These entertainers are not only mistresses of illusion, they are masters of illusion. It takes expertise to perfect their look and to believe they are that person in disguise. Look around. These entertainers are being taken to another place in their minds. We have to try to put ourselves in their mind set to see how our killer thinks."

Billy replies; "Well, Johnny, guess what? Their ain't no way I'm going to dress as a women and wear a wig and make up and all that shit just to see how they think."

"I know Billy. I'm just saying; I don't want anyone to feel confronted by an unsympathetic cop who would ask insensitive questions or show a condescending attitude. And you're right. You would look horrible dressed as a woman. Look how precise they all are being with their make-up and wigs," as Johnny continues as if someone just thru a light switch on in his brain..."That's what those strands of threads are that were found on the beds. Do you remember? "

"I remember the threads. What do you think they are? Billy asks being interrupted in mid question.

"I'm the manager, how can I help you gentlemen? You really should not be back stage. If you're curious, you'll have to pay to see the show."

"I'm detective Vero and this is my partner, detective Bradshaw...."

CHAPTER 68

"Angie, this tie is beautiful, pure silk. I think I'll wear it today. I'm glad you went to spend time with Orma. She loves you so much. She was always there for you when you were growing up. Went to all your school plays, recitals and to watch you march with your fife and drum school band."

Angie washing the sink filled with dishes answers raising her voice over the running water; "She's very happy Dad. She wishes you and I could visit together. She realizes how important your job is. She said it's just as important to get these evil doers off the streets to prevent what happened to grandpa and other victims. She said you're special not only to her but to the world for what you're doing. You know, Dad, I know you're special to me. You've always been there and I know you will always be there. I love you."

"Thanks Angie. I love you too."

"Where are you going wearing the new tie," Angie asks with a lilt in her voice turning the water off, drying her hands?

"To work. I have to meet with District Attorney Penett and continue on with an investigation. I didn't forget that I asked you that I may give you some information to present to your class and professor."

"Oh! Molly, huh?" Smiling to herself. "Tell her I say hello. I always liked Molly. She's such a nice woman. No Dad, I didn't forget. Whenever you want to give me the information I'll gladly present it. You know, hypothetical. "

"I certainly will. Will you be home for supper?

I may be late," Johnny asks heading toward the door.

"If you're going to be late, don't worry, I'll have supper with Freddy."

"Oh yeah, Freddy," mumbling to himself.

"O.K. Bye. See you soon honey."

"Bye Dad. Don't forget to tell Molly I asked for her."

CHAPTER 69

"Good morning Johnny. What's on the agenda for today?" Billy asks as Johnny places his suit jacket on the coat rack exposing his shoulder holster and gun before sitting at his desk.

"I see the captain is out already or isn't he in. Maybe, he's in the crapper with all the shit he eats," Johnny mentions rhetorically.

"Does it make any real difference Johnny?

"Gather up the squad and let's meet in the spaghetti room," Johnny directs Billy. I need to see what the hell is happening with the other files their working on and any other leads they got for our investigation. We need to finish visiting the other two male review shows and I have to meet with Molly."

"Ah! That's why the new tie," Billy exclaims.

"Fuck off!"

CHAPTER 70

Finishing interviewing the second show and gathering any information, from the 'Jewel Box Review' with all male performers, Johnny and Billy head to the last theater showing; 'French Cabaret'.

Visiting all the theaters, the detectives found that entry was easiest through the stage door. In each situation, the door is always unlocked. This makes it an easy access, so all the performers and theater workers could come and go without a hassle. Once inside, usually, there is a security guard to monitor and authorize entrance and departure of employees and visitors. Simply, this is to guard against theft and to maintain security of the premise. Although there is a chair and desk for them, they are nowhere to be found. This is consistent at every theater Johnny and Billy entered.

"Some security, heh Johnny," Billy sarcastically projects. "Look! There's a sign, *To Office* with an arrow."

"Sounds good Billy, let's follow the arrow."

Knocking on the open office door, a man jumped to his feet stammering; "You startled me! Who are you and what do you want? You shouldn't be back here."

The usual introductions were presented as Billy adds; "You should have better security at the stage door."

"We usually do. I'll be sure to speak with her about the lackadaisical attitude. I'm Monsieur Julian Moreau. How can I help you detectives," speaking through pursed lips.

Billy's mind is racing, thinking; *Oh, sure. Another fucking Monsieur.*

Monsieur Moreau is a slight man standing about five foot five inches to five foot six inches with very fine facial features speaking in a higher octave than you would expect from a man.

"By now you must be aware of the Budapest murders. That's what we are investigating," Johnny replies tilting his head to hear more clearly if that is a hint of a French Accent stemming from Moreau?

Fidgeting, Monsieur Moreau continues; "I don't understand. Why would those murders bring you here?

"We have to cover all angles and leads we get. How many entertainers are in the show, Billy asks?

"There are forty total including myself. This is a huge production. I still don't understand why you would be here questioning me or my girls," Julian harshly questions.

Johnny continues; "You say the show includes you. Are you also the theater manager?

"Yes and no. I'm in the show and I own both the theater and the rights to the show. I wrote it and direct it as well. I would much rather just be on stage and not deal with managing and owning it. So detective, yes to your question, I have to manage everything and everyone. As you see, I have to wear all the different hats, not just what I wear in my performance," relaxing with a smile. Please feel free to ask anyone of the girls what you want. We only have one performance each night which starts at 8p.m. You're both welcome to return and see the show, free of course."

Johnny respectfully considers giving the impression that if he could, he would. "Thank you Monsieur Moreau. We can't take any gifts and the tickets would be considered a gift. Our purpose is to ask if there is anyone of the performers that are new to you or unfamiliar, maybe, when you've been to the other shows or to the specialty shops."

"Our community is pretty tight knit. I or my girls would be gossiping about it non-stop. You know a new face. Excuse me detective. I see you staring at my family bible. Do you read scripture detective," as Johnny stops rubbing his thumb along the pages edge?

"Can you tell us your whereabouts on March thirty first"? Billy questions Moreau as he looks up from his desk.

"Why yes, I can. Here, right here. I'm always here detective. I practically live here."

"So, you were here all day and night, twenty four hours? Billy, seeking an answer.

"Just about detective. I come from my apartment directly here. I may have stopped for some coffee."

Billy concludes; "We'll be brief with asking our questions and see ourselves out. Thank you for your co-operation."

"You are welcome. Oh, I hope you find the killer. There are a lot of crazy people in society. Thanks to you, we can feel safe."

"Oh, one last question. Where do the performers get their wigs, Johnny asks?

Without hesitation Moreau answers; "At the periwig shop of course on forty ninth and Broadway. It's called *Vanity Hair Emporium* run by Gwendolyn Wright. She is the real thing detectives. What you see is one hundred percent la chatte.

After some time interviewing as many performers and theater workers as possible, Johnny and Billy find their way to the lobby instead of leaving their usual way through the stage door. The lobby is quite elaborate in its décor. At first entering, there is plush carpeting with magnificent mahogany stairway spiraling to loge seating. Hanging from the ceiling are huge crystal chandeliers that glistened brightly. Everything was properly placed including photos of everyone in the show as well as many movie starlets.

"Hey, Johnny, look at this lobby card. It's Moreau himself."

"Read what it says Billy under his picture."

"Julian Moreau is skilled at female impersonations being graceful with femininity. His rise to stardom began in regular appearances in vaudeville and several completed successful tours of the United States and Europe. He began his performances at an early age in France where he was born and raised performing at the famous Moulin Rouge Theater in Paris. Monsieur Moreau (meaning little dark) refuses to be a caricature of women which he feels would not be true. Rather, his dark

side reveals a true woman, not just imitating one. Although, Monsieur Moreau served in the French Foreign Legion with a professional fighting unit, he strives to present the illusion of actually being a woman which he considers his real side."

CHAPTER 71

Johnny and Billy are headed to D.A. Penett's office by early afternoon as Molly is expecting them.

"Hi detectives, Miss Penett is expecting you. I'll tell her you're here," Louise spouting her usual greeting.

"Send them in Louise," Molly replies.

"Molly, we're getting nowhere," Johnny blurts out entering her office.

"Well, good afternoon detectives," replying in an undertone.

"I'm sorry Molly. It's just we can't catch a break."

"Well, how's this for a break? The detail detectives you assigned to follow-up with victims one's room-mate, Susan Fleming just called me. She asked your detective when everything was over could she have the gold cross Vicky wore."

Johnny gleefully responds; "The son-of-a-bitch took her cross right off her neck."

"We never saw or found a gold cross," Billy mentions.

"Exactly," Molly says. "A souvenir to add to all of what he considers a souvenir."

"Molly when Billy and I were interviewing I remember there were strands of thread found on the bed. I didn't read anything in the reports. Can we find out about them"?

"Sure," Molly answers. "What are you thinking"?

"They're part of his wig. If we can find out anything about them, it could be a lead. This is good news about the gold cross, in that; it will be among the killers' personal things when we find him. Billy and I are going back to the Flamingo Room. I have another idea about the dance tickets. Is there anything else Molly? "

"Not at the moment. Glad you sent your men to re-interview."

"Yeah, me too. I also have them checking on any arrests for lewd behavior. Let's go Billy. We have a lot more to uncover. The list just keeps growing. "

"Oh! Johnny."

"Yes, Molly?"

"I like your tie."

Smiling widely responds; "Thank you, me too. It's a gift from Angie."

"Tell her, she has good taste in men's ties."

Billy gives Johnny a nudge with his elbow on the way out the door, thinking to himself...*see I knew it. He wore it for Molly.*

Without missing a beat, Louise sighs as they pass her desk.

CHAPTER 72

Two days have passed before arriving at the Flamingo Room. Johnny and Billy are greeted by Irving Cohen; "We meet again detectives."

Before Cohen could say another word, Johnny comments; "Don't worry Mr. Cohen you don't need your attorney. We just have a question about the dance tickets and how they're numbered."

"Sure, but please, call me Poco. Follow me to the office. I'll introduce you to our book-keeper, Doris. I'm glad she's back. Her mother's sister died recently and she had to take her mother to California to the funeral. This place goes to hell when she's not here. She is a wonderful person, very diligent and caring. She lives a solitude life caring for her sick mother and her constant boyfriend who is a leech, if you ask me, whom she also takes care of. Here we are. Doris, these detectives are investigating the two murders of our girls and have some questions about how the tickets work. I'll leave you to ask your questions. If you need me, I'll be up front."

Doris lacked any distinctive or interesting features or characteristics aptly fitting Poco's description. She seemed absorbed in her book-keeping job, otherwise uninspiring, run of the mill woman...short and stocky, adding to her dismal existence.

Billy thought; *she has a boyfriend? I guess there is someone out there for everyone, remembering how the hunchback of Notre-Dame, Quasimodo, kidnapped Esmeralda because of his step-father's obsession with her and then he fell in love with her.*

"O.K., Mr. Cohen. I'm Doris detectives. What questions do you have?"

Johnny begins; "I'm curious as to how the numbering system on the tickets work since we found dance tickets at the crime scene which led us to the Flamingo Room."

"Oh! Sure detective. Let me show you," pulling out a huge roll of tickets. "Each night rolls of one hundred tickets beginning with different starting numbers are used. Each customer must purchase a minimum sting of tickets consisting of ten tickets. The girls cash in their tickets each night. Some have as many as fifty tickets plus tips. They do O.K. It's all cash."

"Tell me Doris," Johnny begins, "How can you know if the tickets are real and someone doesn't get their own printed?"

"You certainly know to ask good questions detective. The tickets are both color coded and have stars on the back. Let me show you," Doris answers rolling out a string of tickets from the roll containing one-hundred tickets. "Each month contains stars, so there would be one star for each month. The tickets will have one to twelve stars on the back. We alternate the month with colors as well. Only the staff knows the color of the month. The un-used tickets are only good for the month the star and color represents. If customers don't use them with-in the month that the star and color represents, they're out the dance ticket and can't use it. Does that answer your question detective?"

"Yes Doris, loud and clear. You've been a great help," Johnny responds.

Billy was looking all around the office while Johnny was questioning Doris when he says; "Johnny, look at these pictures here in the frames. Will you look at this one," pointing to a picture showing many of the taxi dancers arm in arm with sailors.

"Oh yes Doris exclaims! That was an exciting week. The Navy fleet came into town for a week to spread their cheer, if you catch my drift. We were packed every night and mind you without one fist fight. Those sailors were real gentlemen."

"Johnny, look close," Billy says pointing to a figure in the picture. "Look real close Johnny."

"It's so sad what happened to those young girls," Doris interrupts. That is Ruth Silvan between those two sailors. That was about six months before, you know, she was murdered. Excuse me, I'm going to cry."

"It's O.K. Doris," as Johnny offers condolences to this elderly woman, holding her in his arms momentarily.

"Johnny, victim two has what seems to look like a cross around her neck."

"Holy shit Billy! I'm sorry Doris. You're right, another souvenir. We need to have Molly add this to our point system with a number five. Doris can I use your phone. I need to call the district attorney's office"?

"Go right ahead detective. I could never understand why people do such horrible things to one another. None of us has a halo. We all get out of bed each day and struggle with who we'd like to be and most of us are who we want to be without considering our dreams of course. Every now and then we fail and when we do fail, we don't bring great harm because of it. Sometimes, we may look back and say why I did this or did that. But not murder," as she starts to cry again.

"Hi Louise, its Detective Vero. Let me speak with Molly please."

"What do you have Johnny? Molly asks.

"I'm looking at a photo of victim two, Ruth Silvan, hanging in the Flaming Room's office and she's wearing a gold cross. For sure it's another souvenir. Add these to our number five board will you Molly?"

"Sure thing Johnny, considerate it done. Oh, by the way, all the arrests you asked about for lewd conduct this past year defiantly do not fit the person we're looking for. In addition, both victims, Victoria and Ruth, had no defensive wounds and all their finger nails were clean and no trace of a struggle."

CHAPTER 73

The Savoy Bath House on Lafayette Street had a reputation as the classiest, safest, and cleanest of all the bath houses in Manhattan. The Savoy is a Classical Revival style building designed to be imposing in appearance. It comprised its architectural style recalling ancient Roman public baths with classical pilasters, columns, arches and cornices catering exclusively to men. The Savoy is not a public bath house so it did not have to include a separate section for women. However, it did include steam heat, an amenity that was lacking in the coal fire furnace heated public baths.

Johnny and Billy are greeted as they entered the lobby by a young man in his late twenties sitting behind a beautifully hand carved desk. They both looked quizzically as to why he was sitting there bare chest until he stood to greet them, being completely naked. He stood as a magnificent Roman gladiator with an anatomically perfect physique, blessed by the Gods with enough genitalia for two men. Billy whispers; "My God, I'm jealous."

"Welcome gentlemen to the Savoy Bath House. My name is Maurice Warren. You are new to The Savoy. Here are the rules and rates posted for your convenience. Once you've decided, I can take you on a tour of the house. Will you bathing together or you may prefer separate baths?" We also have a community bath with ten or twelve bathing together."

Billy looking somewhat uneasy blurts out; "Why don't we do a private bath, with just the two of us."

"That's not why we're here. Remember, we want to mingle to get to know other people," Johnny adds.

"Many men are a little uneasy at first until you unwind a little. We do offer cocktails. Why don't you register here while I get you some towels and robes," Maurice suggests walking to a closet with fresh linens.

"O.K., I see you've registered, William Short and Jonathan Wadsworth," turning the registrar book. "Now comes, the painful part."

Billy bolts almost to a fighting position as Maurice continues; "I have to take cash payment upfront before I show you to the locker room."

"By cocktails, you do mean scotch and whiskey? Billy asks.

"Yes, William," Maurice replies. "Here is a scotch, on the house. You're quite a jitter bug. Drink up. You'll feel better."

Billy takes the shot glass and downs it in one gulp.

"There. I see you're relaxed already William. Do you need help with your clothing?" Maurice suggests in a question.

"No, no thank you. Where do we change?"

"Follow me gentlemen. Once you change, I'll show you our facility. I'll be waiting for you at my desk."

CHAPTER 74

Entering doors filled with condensation from steam, Maurice points out; "This is the community bath I mentioned to you and the last part of the tour."

Every man that was in the community bath followed Maurice with their eyes as he walked passed them projecting himself like a show horse prancing to the judges.

"The idea is to relax and make new friends. Have a good time gentlemen. If there is anything I can guide you with, I'll be happy to help."

"Thanks Maurice," Johnny politely answers as he drops his robe on a lounge chair. Stepping gently into the pool, he now noticed that every eye is now upon his nakedness.

"Come on in William. It's magnificent," Johnny suggests, laughing aloud.

Billy thought to himself glancing around the pool *imagining every man as an alligator waiting for its prey to enter their territory.*

CHAPTER 75

Breakfast at the Crosstown Diner is as regular to Johnny as his daily shave and shower. The only difference is, Audrey, most days, is catering to the diner customers and not catering to Johnny in the bedroom or shower.

Billy arrives seeing where Johnny is seated not missing Audrey's platinum blonde hair pouring Johnny's coffee. "Here comes Billy, fill his cup too, will ya Audrey?'

"Sure thing, want to order now?"

"Just toast this morning," Johnny answers.

"Same for me," says Billy as he slides into the booth. "You know, Johnny, after that day visiting the Savoy Bath House, I had to..." hesitating as he looked around as if someone might be listening.

"What? I'm not a psychic. If I was, we wouldn't have to do all this gumshoe work?"

"Then we'd be out of a job without all the investigations we have to deal with, no Johnny, Billy asks rhetorically? "I spent the week end with Nancy, the red head from Chan-tal's. Remember her, I bet you do? I had to be with a woman after spending hours at The Savoy Bath House being in the pool with all those men naked, particularly after the message therapist. We took shower after shower together. She must have invented these different positions that I never thought existed. They got me so deep inside her I never wanted her to leave. She even taught me to have multiple orgasms within a few minutes apart. I'm in love with Nancy. You know that Sinatra song; Nancy with the laughing face? We laughed, drank and you know one thing she does....."

"Here's your toast, more coffee?" Audrey asks.

"No thanks."

Johnny leans in toward Billy to whisper as Audrey attends to the next booth. "I understand, Billy. I did the same with Audrey. We used the handcuffs again. You should try it with Nancy. Remember this; you doing her, better not interfere with this investigation. Now that you're into her (smiling), try to get some information out of her. You know, on Chantal. What the hell!" Both laughing.

CHAPTER 76

The Vanity Hair Emporium is located exactly where Monsieur Moreau said, Forty Ninth and Broadway. Proprietor, Gwendolyn Wright, was quite available to greet Johnny and Billy.

"Just as you say detectives, we do get many female impersonators here since we do offer quality hair pieces, more than any other periwig shop. And yes, many can fit the description you're asking about, that's why so many can pass as women."

"How do you fit the wigs?" Billy asks.

"We, I or one of my assistants, Tabitha or Raquel that you see over there, producing a special order piece, can tell approximate size just by looking," Billy measuring them up and down with his eyes.

"The entertainers hide most of their hair under a fitted net type holder, something like a tight shower cap. They pin the hair piece to their hair and the net which gives a real good fit. Our wigs are not inexpensive detectives. They can run from twenty seven to sixty dollars and as high as seventy five. Real custom wigs are priced according to all the variables that go into hand making them," continues Gwendolyn.

"Wow that is not cheap. What are they made of?"

"A mixture of fake and real hair. When there is more real hair, the more expensive. The fake hair is hard to tell if you're not an expert. Most of the entertainers purchase the wigs ranging from twenty seven to thirty seven dollars."

"Who purchases the more expensive wigs with more real hair?" Johnny asks.

"Besides some of the high paid prostitutes and my wealthy clients, a few show people. Some come to me from Canada as well."

"O.K. Who purchases a better wig that may be local? Let's say from one of the shows."

"I have a few. Let me get my customer card file."

Billy standing at the counter thumbing through the file, writing names comments to Johnny; "Well, well. Look what or who we have here Johnny."

On their exit, Billy comments; "Moreau was right Johnny, Gwendolyn is all woman."

"He failed to mention Gwendolyn's assistants. Va-va-voom!"

CHAPTER 77

Tschhhhhhhhhhhhhhhhh...the familiar sound stemming from the police car radio.

"This is detective Vero, go ahead over."

"This is South Central detective. I'm putting through D.A. Penett, over."

"Go ahead Molly, over."

"Number three at the Budapest Hotel detective. I'm on my way, over. Drop what you're doing and get there now," exclaims Molly!

With the police siren glaring and the red extension light stuck on the car roof, Billy carefully maneuvers through the streets racing toward the Budapest Hotel. Johnny is on the police car radio with Captain Sullivan getting some detail as to what took place in what room number and to pacify the brass about headway being made with the leads.

"I hope so Vero," is the captain's response. "I don't want this to hinder you from becoming Lieutenant in the near future. Now we're looking at sick serial killer and he is on the loose. Chief O'Brian is out of town to a special conference with other police chief's from around the country along with Mayor Bernhard, lucky for us. The shit is going to hit the fan when they get back. D.A. Penett will meet you there. Get back here as soon as possible. I want a report on those leads you're telling about. Do you understand, over?"

"Yes, captain, over and out," not giving Sullivan any opportunity to say more.

"Johnny, it looks like we will have to be putting a lot of overtime in on this. What is this killer thinking of each time he sees them die?"

"Billy, people view themselves better than others view them. He feels superior in some strange fucking way. Maybe he's punishing someone or him, each time he kills them. Step on it Billy. This God damn this son-of-a-bitch is getting to me now."

CHAPTER 78

Entering the lobby, Johnny and Billy are greeted by the Budapest house detective, Chester Riley; "Detectives. I can't say I'm glad to see you, again. You know what I mean, under these circumstances. Follow me," as they did into a waiting elevator.

Johnny immediately asks the elevator operator, "Did you see or hear anything that might be out of the ordinary. You know, something you know doesn't feel right in your gut"?

"No sir, business and riders as usual. Here we are. Watch your step getting out," as he said hundreds of times to hundreds if not thousands of hotel guests. Johnny realized that even they are just another passenger in his elevator making small talk if any to all those who step inside his car.

"Well, if you do, go see Mr. Riley immediately."

"Yes sir detective," is his reply so nonchalant.

Chester mentions as he leads them down the hallway; "He forgets a lot, you know being a war vet. What he does remember are the numbers of all the rooms, their locations and floors they're on. He can add twenty or thirty numbers with the snap of your finger. Right here detectives, room 70-6."

The police standing at the entrance greet them saying; "D.A. Penett is in the room. Good luck detectives."

"Molly," Johnny states entering the room.

"How many God damn tweezers do we have to buy Johnny?" is her reply.

"Shit, Molly. I really don't have one."

"I've got you covered," is Molly's response. "Don't worry; it's not the one you bought me. Now you have to buy Louise a new one," handing it to Johnny with a smile knowing *Louise is going to wet her pants when he brings her a new one.*

Johnny starts with directions coupling questions all into one. "Same situation and same positioning. Mr. Riley please go to get the person that found her. Before you go, why is this room number 70-6? Why is there a dash between seventy and six?"

"We have seventy rooms of which six are called Presidential Suites. This is the sixth suite. The other five are all on different floors with different room numbers, a dash, then either 1,2,3,4 or 5 to distinguish which Presidential Suite it is. Again, this is suite 6. I'll be right back detective."

"Don't forget the registration card. I'll look at it here. Billy why do you think a suite, a presidential suite and not just a room," Johnny asks rhetorically?

"Billy, get a cellophane bag ready." Slowly, pulling a dance ticket from this victim's vagina, Johnny holds it up to the light looking to see how many stars and what color it has.

"How many stars Johnny," asks Billy?

Molly retorts; "What the hell are you talking about stars? This is not a beauty pageant."

"No Molly, nothing like that. We found out that the dance tickets are coded with stars to distinguish what month they are issued against a certain coloring system they use," Billy quickly explains.

"This is a current ticket with the right amount of stars for the month," Johnny answers putting into the evidence bag.

Finger print specialist, Kevin Kowalski arrives with the photographer, who goes by the nickname, 'flash,' stating; "This is so sad, seeing such young beautiful women found this way. I'm going to dust every inch of this place."

Molly looking at the victim with such antipathy, sympathy, grievance, and sadness all rolled into the expression her eyes radiate, begins to recite;

'What though the radiance
Which was once so bright?
Be now for ever taken from my sight,
Though nothing can bring back the hour
Of splendor in the grass,
Of glory in the flower....

Johnny continues picking up on the verse...

'We will grieve not, rather find
Strength in what remains behind;
In the primal sympathy
Which having been must ever be?
In the soothing thoughts that spring
Out of human suffering.'

Each person in the room turns to look at Johnny in disbelief as Molly finishes the poem...

'In the faith that looks through death,
In years that bring the philosophic mind.'

Turning to Johnny, Molly says; "Well what do you know, a flatfoot that can quote Wordsworth? I'm impressed Johnny."

"Twice Molly. You liked his tie the other day too," Billy reminds her as his grin widens. "You know, he also plays the cello and listens to classical music," noticing Molly's head as it lowers along with her jaw in disbelief.

"Remember how I want the photographs, don't you flash," Johnny asks deflecting the stares and any comments in the making?

"I do detective."

"I also want a couple of close-ups this time of the nylon on her neck. Got it"?

"I do."

"Can you tell if she had a gold cross on," Johnny continues. "Look everywhere from top to bottom to see if it might have been dropped."

Chester Riley re-enters the room. "Detective, this is Herb Glickman. He's the maintenance engineer that found the body."

"O.K. Mr. Glickman why did you discover the body, Johnny questions?

"I got a report there was a loud banging coming from this room. I have to respond to all the reports and requests," Glickman answers.

"Where are the reports, do you have them with you?"

"I have them here detective and the registration card," Riley mentions as he hands them to Johnny.

"I'll take the registration card," Billy says stretching out his hand.

"Here's the coroner," the policeman at the door says sticking his head in.

"Good. He'll be able to tell us approximate time of death," Molly points out.

Johnny directs the maintenance engineer; "O.K. Mr. Glickman, tell me everything about this here."

"It's all in the statement that is with the original report of the room noise Mr. Riley asked me to write. I'm feeling sick seeing her dead. I think I'm going to throw-up."

"I want to hear it from you Mr. Glickman, from the moment you got this request or report of the room noise. How the information gets to you and then what? Take him to your office Chester. We'll be down soon. Get him some water and don't go anywhere."

"Gotcha, detective. C'mon Herb. Take deep breaths as you walk," Riley instructs him.

"Let's go see Mr. Glickman, Billy. Keep the registration card and hold this report as evidence. Molly would you please have all the policemen in the hallway turn the mattress after the body in removed and Kevin is done dusting. I want to see if there is any evidence that can be used."

"Sure thing Johnny. I'll be here until the body is removed."

Billy whispers to Johnny once in the hallway; "You know Johnny; she is the cat's meow."

"You know Billy, you're a real wisenheimer."

CHAPTER 79

Once finishing with Mr. Glickman with any fill in information, Johnny instructs Chester to bring the desk clerks two at a time and then the bell hops one at a time which Chester does as instructed introducing the desk clerks to the detectives; "Pamela and Arthur."

Johnny started with specific questions such as:

- What time do you start?
- When do you go to eat?
- How many breaks do you take?
- Do you go outside to smoke?
- How many times do you go to the bathroom?
- How many check-ins and check-outs do you do?
- Do you arrive early and stay late before and after your shifts?
- Does anyone checking in not match how they sign the registration card?
- Have you noticed anything or anyone out of the ordinary in or around the hotel?
- Look at these registration cards. They all have a note stating registrar requested certain room number. Can you describe these people who signed in?

Each of the clerks answered the detectives' questions directly and honestly. Johnny knew that having two together would be more apt to nudge the others memory to say the truth.

Pamela remarks saying; "Yes, I remember seeing a man dressed very smartly in a double breasted suit and hat come in every day from 11a.m. to approximately 3p.m. and sits in the lobby holding a book he takes from his brief case and the daily newspaper the hotel provides. He drinks coffee in the morning and orders a sandwich with a bellhop at lunch."

"I don't recall," mentions Arthur.

"Yes, you do. After I pointed him out to you on or about the second day he came in, you said how nice he dresses."

"You know Pam, now I remember. You're right. He's been coming in every day for a long time now, probably a month. Does just what Pam said and leaves. We usually don't get anyone who does that," Arthur agreeing.

Chester chimes in; "They have told me about this man. I've been keeping an eye on him detective."

"O.K., tell me what color suits he wears or his ties. Does his hat match the color of his suit? When he wears a hat, does he leave it on or takes it off? Does he get up to go the bathroom? Does he order the same sandwich all the time? How tall is he? What about his build, short, stocky?" Johnny asks Chester drilling him as he pushes the bit deeper with each question.

"Well detective, this is a big hotel and needs my attention everywhere and I don't have any help," Chester answers Johnny.

"So, in reality, you really aren't keeping an eye on him. What about the individuals who signed in requesting these room numbers. Anything pop into your mind Arthur?"

"Let's see. I signed in Miss Morrow. Jeannette signed in Miss Silvan and Pam, you signed in Miss Cummings. You see here detective, we put our initials in this box as to who registered the guests."

Johnny pursed his lips with frustration and disproval thinking; *How did we miss this important fact that could help identify the person who checked in.*

"O.K. Arthur, where's Jeannette," Asks Billy?

"Oh, she's gone detective."

"So, where do we find her? Do you have her address"?

"No, I mean she's gone... Dead!"

Billy could not contain his *sigh*! "How about you, Pam"?

CHAPTER 80

"Jesus Fucking Christ Sullivan! I go out of town for a police conference and another fucking murder at the Budapest Hotel. Three murders and we are no closer to getting a suspect than when we got called for the first one," bellows Chief O'Brian, that was heard throughout police headquarters. "Did you see the Goddamn front page of every newspaper in town," restating it word for word?

"CITY IN A PANIC; SERIAL KILLER STILL AT LARGE...
MAY CAUSE MAYOR NON RE-ELECTION.

"I thought we are on the same side here and we would have had someone in custody by now. Where are Vero and his fucked up partner? This is the only station house under my command without a lieutenant. We both know we want Detective Sergeant Vero to fill that position and that will be coming down the pike. But for now do I have to bring one in here to help you?"

"Calm down Pat. You're all wet here. What do you think we're doing, jerking off? Vero and Bradshaw have been working double time on this even giving up some vacation time. Do you see all those boxes? They're filled with letters from anyone who wants to marry the killer to those who want to torture him. Some claim to know who it is and want a reward. We can't without man power, follow-up every one of those by chasing ghosts. We are on the same side and we want this sick bastard put away and off the streets too. I'll send you a copy of all the goddamn reports from interviews and autopsies. Pat, I know you pull rank on me but we're also friends. I know you're getting heat from the Mayor and the Commissioner and I will meet with them if you want me too. But don't come in to my station like a fucking Nazi storm trooper. Look out in the spaghetti room. It emptied out. I can't have that in my house. Let's stay friends, Pat. One day when we retire and we're having a drink, we'll be congratulating each other about how this was solved."

"You're right John. I don't need the reports. I have enough papers on my desk to feed a goat for a year. And why the hell do you call the squad room the spaghetti room?"

"Because there's so much going on out there, so many cases at one time, like stands of spaghetti, you have to put a lot on your fork at once hoping none of it falls off. So, you use a spoon to help support what's on your fork as you twirl the strands to get enough into your mouth so you want more. That spoon is our detectives, keeping it all together."

"What's this police force coming too? Tell Vero and Bradshaw I asked for them," roaring with laughter on the way down the stairs leading to his chauffeured police car.

CHAPTER 81

"More coffee Johnny, Billy," Audrey asks with the hot coffee pot in her hand ready to pour?

"Fill 'er up Audrey," Billy answers. "Pour more for Sir Galahad here too. We have a lot of shit to cover and will be awhile. We need peace and quiet from the spaghetti room to look at some evidence."

"Ten- four. If you need anything else, I'll be here," Audrey says smiling using 'cop' lingo.

"Billy read this last report on victim three. We need to get updated before going to question the hookers at the Metro Hotel. It's a class 'A' joint with..."

"With class 'A' broads, Johnny. You know, Audrey's no flat tire herself. I think..."

"I think you should be quiet and start reading that report," Johnny interrupts.

"O.K.... Ethel Cummings/ twenty four years old/ brunette/ originally from Indiana to N.Y. for Broadway/ in a few 'off Broadway' plays/ No living relatives, never married or has children/ lived alone on Bleaker St, fifth floor walk-up/ neighbors said kept to herself/ strangled with nylon/ recent sexual activity/ ticket from vagina up to date with the correct stars/ all belongings left behind/ gold cross jewelry found tangled in nylon stocking on her neck/ her clothes on floor/ No room key found/ one finger print found difficult to read. Fingerprint lab says it looks like whoever it belongs to was gripping the head board and it must have been rubbing on the wood."

"Ah, again, we have a lot of similarities to add to our score card with number five's. Remember Billy when Glickman said there was a report of banging? It was the headboard when they were having sex. I now think as he's fucking them, he is tightening the nylon around their neck to watch them die and not fuck them after they're dead. It must have been her print grasping at something for help and the gold cross got snagged in the nylon and the killer got spooked from the knock on the door and left as soon as he could not having time to get the cross. Glickman's report says the desk gave him a work order to see about the banging because they got a call from the room next to 70-6 reporting the banging. The guest went to knock on room 70-6 door but no one answered then he called the desk."

"So, Johnny, the killer is getting more daring or genuinely crazier in his spree to murder, not caring? That doesn't fit his M.O. He's been pretty meticulous and consistent with method of operating with many of the number five similarities on our chart."

"With all that we have it's like we have nothing except that he is consistent with certain things. He doesn't take their clothes particularly their undies to hold or smell. He takes the room key and the gold crosses for souvenirs and reminders to and for what, re-live what he's done? Those items must be representative of something, don't you think Billy? We now know that victim two, Ruth Silvan's clothes were found in a trash barrel in the basement of the hotel by one of the uniformed detail men. We still don't know how he was dressed leaving that room since his lady clothes were hanging in the closet. My brain is going haywire."

"Right now, Johnny, the killer is in control. As soon as we figure his angle for a motive, we'll be in control. I wish we would get some anonymous tip that would pan out. Look at the registration card Johnny. It's marked that the room number was requested by victim three, Ethel Cummings. The other two, Victoria Morrow and Ruth Silvan both did the same. The hotel manager said it is quite common for people to ask for a certain room. It is special to them or they have been in that room at another time and want to come back for whatever reasons."

"Let's get out of here. I have to stop to buy Louise a tweezers. Shit! Do I have to?"

"Yes you do Johnny. I think you should gift wrap it," Billy says laughing.

CHAPTER 82

Both detectives began to slide out from the booth they occupied to pay their tab.

"Do you see what I see, at the cash register," Johnny asking Billy...*thinking it was a woman he wanted him to look at.*?

"Holy shit, I do, seeing the cashiers' expression being ice cold." I'll pretend to be in a hurry with all these files and come along side of him!" Billy exclaims.

"I'll get him from behind."

Just as planned, Billy comes alongside the man standing in front of the cashier fumbling all the files he was carrying. "Excuse me sir. These files are heavy. I just want to set them here and I'll pay my bill when you finish."

Acting nervously, the man turned to Billy from his distraction and took his eyes off the cashier. Instantly, Johnny draws his revolver from his holster and points it at the man's head stating firmly; "Police. Put your hands on the counter where I can see them."

Shaking, the man complies with Johnny's command as Billy handcuffs him immediately. Patting him down, Billy pulls out the gun from the thief's suit jacket side pocket. "You're under arrest. Let's go," escorting him to their car.

"Oh my God! How did you know I was being robbed by that man," asks the cashier visibly upset and crying, thanking Johnny in-between sobs?

"You learn how to read people. Their body language, their demeanor and a lot of experience," replies Johnny, not admitting he saw the gun pointing to the cashier.

"Johnny, are you all right," Audrey asks excitedly approaching Johnny with a hot coffee pot in hand?

"Yeah, I'm O.K. Listen; this young lady needs help to calm down. I have to help Billy," slapping down his check with cash not waiting for his change picking up the files Billy left.

The uniformed police car with its red lights flashing was pulling into the parking lot from Billy's call to dispatch after locking the thief in his car. The two uniformed officers were out of their patrol car as it seemed, before it came to a complete stop.

"Officers, take this man into custody. Book him for armed robbery at this diner. Here is the weapon he had," Johnny giving directions, as Billy hands over the gun that was wrapped in a handkerchief he used to protect any fingerprints. "You both can share the collar."

"Thank you detective. We can really use it," answers the officer escorting the robber to their patrol car.

"Do you know who I am," asks Johnny?

"Detective, everybody knows who you are. Thanks for this bust. My partner and I owe you one."

"Yes you do. Return the cuffs he is wearing to my desk by the time I get back."

"Yes sir."

"I'm glad you gave them the collar. That's all we needed, to deal with that, on top of all this," Billy mentions, pointing to the stack of files.

CHAPTER 83

The Metro Hotel is palatial to New York, catering to upscale worldly travelers. The lobby floors are marble that shine to show your face as if you were looking into a mirror. There are huge marble columns appeareded to stretch to the sky. Couches and chairs were plush velvet that offered you such comfort you never wanting to get up after sitting. There is a concierge service that caters to the guests to include such tasks as restaurant reservations, night life, taxi service, tickets to special events, travel arrangements and the like.

As usual, the hotel was bustling with activity. Off to the south side of the lobby appears an entrance to 'The Nostalgia Hideaway' catering to gamblers to be considered 'high rollers.' Many of whom would gamble huge amounts of money with one toss of the dice. Although gambling, and who detectives Vero and Bradshaw are going to talk to is illegal, it still exists through secret doors and hideaways as its name depicts, separate from the bar and lounge. This is where exactly Johnny and Billy were headed. In eye's view, Johnny sees the person he came to speak with, the Madame of 'The Nostalgia Hideaway.'

"Well, lookie, lookie, who wants my cookie? Homicide detectives Johnny Vero and look who's along for the ride, Billy 'the kid' Bradshaw?"

"Hello Monaca. It certainly has been awhile. You're looking fantastic, as usual," greeting her with a kiss to each side of her checks.

"You both are looking good yourselves. Are we here for business or pleasure?" Monaca asks.

"We're investigating the homicides at the Budapest Hotel," Billy mentions. "You remembered my days of playing ball under 'Billy the Kid' Bradshaw. I'm impressed Monaca."

"We all have something behind our names. I'm originally from Monaco, so I took on the name, Monaca for my business. It's kind of exotic."

"I would love to talk to you about it, but we've got to go straight to what we came here for Monaca," Johnny points out.

"I'd love to get whatever it is straight between us detective, anytime," giving Johnny a wink. "You were saying about the murders at the Budapest Hotel. In a way, I wish they were here. The curiosity seekers would be filling the rooms every night. But then again my girls would be uneasy and that's not good for business."

Johnny begins; "We looking for a cross-dresser who could in your opinion pass as a beautiful woman or a good looking guy."

"Believe it or not, we get some of them from the shows. My girls often say that they are either bi-sexual or straight but defiantly not homosexual the way they know how to please a woman. We don't get many here, but those that do come, pardon my pun, could fit the description you describe, Johnny."

Billy questions Monaca; "Is there any one of these individuals that are repeat customers, maybe asking for the same girl?"

"I think better with a drink. Walk me over to the bar. What will you boys have, on the house?"

"We'll pass Monaca. You know, on the job," Billy says proudly. "Maybe on another visit."

Smiling, Monaca answers; "There are maybe two now that I think of it. Both of them are French or at least sound like they speak with a French accent. You know that most girls don't really look or care about their faces, except for you Johnny. Yours is a face me or my girls would never forget."

"These Frenchman you mention, can you tell me what they look like. Height, weight, hair, age what the girls say about them. Can we talk to the girls since we're here," Johnny asks?

"Let me call up to Lilly. She's a favorite among the French since she is a Parisian." She should be finishing with a customer.

Lilly entered the bar eloquently dressed in shear white chiffon giving an appearance of floating innocence. As she drew closer, she removed the soft white scarf from her neck wrapping it around both Johnny and Billy saying; "Ce charmant messieurs, deux ensemble?"

In response Monaca answers; "No Lilly, not two lovely gentlemen together. These gentlemen are detectives. They want to ask you some questions about your French clients. They are also friends of mine so you have nothing to hide or worry about. Coming from Monaco, my first language is also French detectives. I just don't let it be known."

Johnny begins; "Lilly thanks for coming down to speak with us. We won't take up much of your time. As Monaca said, we are only here to ask you about your customers that may be French and possibly a cross-dresser. He is probably very good looking with fine features for a man and not being very big, perhaps five foot, five inches tall with a slight to small build. Any such customers?"

"Are you boys buying me a drink at least," Lilly asks, as Johnny throws a five dollar bill on the bar?

Lilly signals the bartender with her sleek long feminine fingers that displayed freshly red nail polished finger tips.

"Since, you're both in 'my house', detectives. Let me ask you...There are three men here for business with us. One is running down the stairs, one is running up the stairs and one is in with one of the girls in her room already. Can either of you tell me their ethnicity?"

"That seems impossible, Lilly," Billy quickly answers as if he were aiming a dart at the bull's eye that rarely hit it.

"Well," Lilly continues. "The one running down the stairs is 'Finish.' The one running up the stairs is 'Russian.' The gentleman in the room with the lady is 'Himalayan.'"

Laughter erupted between them all.

"You got us Lilly," interjects Johnny. "Your point is well taken. It is hard to distinguish where a person is from without really knowing and if they don't have an accent."

"I have two clients; one is French and speaks the language. The other pretends to be French speaking only English with a fake accent. He's cute and likes to role play. I bet you detectives are good at role playing, no?"

"What kind of description can you give us," asks Billy?

Lilly raises the shot glass of whiskey to her mouth like a well-oiled machine throwing her head backward emptying all the liquid in one fell swoop of a gulp. She signals the bar-tender as he refills her shot glass.

"The one client who role plays is short and portly. However, the real Frenchman may fit your description detective. He is about five foot five or so. He has a slight build and could pass for a woman dressed in drag with his fine features. But I'll tell you detective; he knows how to please a woman and is larger than most men by two or three inches and I don't mean his height, if you get my drift. He's just the opposite for a man of his small stature. My clients don't say much about themselves but he did say he is from one of the shows or specialty shops. I forget which. He speaks perfect French when he is here."

"Tell me Lilly," asks Johnny, "how often does he schedule time with you?

"I never know. It's whenever. No particular schedule. He just shows up and will wait for me if he has to."

"What about the color of his eyes," Bill asks?

"You know detective, I never really looked that close," as she closes her eyes and asks; "What color are my eyes"?

Billy stares at her closed eyes, giving notice that she is a beautiful woman stating;

"You got me again, Lilly. I really wasn't looking at the color of your eyes. Touché."

Monaca chimes in and says; "If the Frenchman shows up and we can detain him, I can call you detective. However, I won't jeopardize my clients or my business. I'm sure you understand."

CHAPTER 84

"That's your job detectives. There must be a dozen reasons why a hotel guest asks for a certain room just as the clerk said. If I can come up with anything from the point system board or reports, I'll gladly throw what I have into the mix. I'm the prosecuting district attorney and will go the limit with this sick person. In my opinion, he should not live another day in this world. He certainly does have a lot of issues. It's up to you to uncover what they are and that is going to lead us to him. We can put our brains together and list reasons why specific rooms were requested," Molly points out twirling her pen between her fingers.

"Romantic, special occasion, used the room in the past being nostalgic." Billy points out.

"Yes, but why and what special occasion would someone choose that number? Why that room to be romantic in or what event to re-live?" Molly asks. "Let's list them."

Reasons to choose a certain room number:
*Used on honeymoon
*Nostalgia for first time having sex (not married)
*Birthday matches room number
*View
*Near exit
*Age matches room number
*A Lucky number
*Significant date matches room number
*Woman conceived in that room

"That's a lot of reasons to choose a room with a specific number. How the hell are we going to narrow this down to the reason our killer is choosing these numbers. Molly what would make you choose a certain room number and you Johnny?" Billy questions.

"For me, I would choose either honeymoon or baby conceived," Molly answers.

"I would probably choose to be near an exit," Johnny exclaims!

"And I would pick the room for a lucky number. You see, right here with three of us, we have four different reasons we would pick a certain number for a room. We have to put this into the mix and hope for the best since there is no rhyme or reason any person would pick a number for the room they want," Billy adds.

"Except for the only reason he is choosing those room numbers. We need more background on our killer and victims to put this together. Go back and re-visit the evidence detectives. For victim one, Victoria Morrow, it has been confirmed that her funeral and grave site have been paid in cash by an unknown person as we knew signing with an X. That's a dead end. By the way, Johnny, do have a new tweezers for Louise?"

"Thanks for reminding me, Molly its right here in the box," reaching into his suit coat side pocket. "I did not gift wrap it like I did yours, I want you to know,"

"Hand it to her on the way out. I want to hear her sigh," Molly laughing as she stands to dismiss the detectives from her office.

CHAPTER 85

Detectives Vero and Bradshaw enter the lobby to the Budapest Hotel at 10:45 a.m. to await the arrival of the well-dressed man scheduled to arrive at eleven a.m. They each take a seat opposite from each other facing the chair usually occupied by the mystery man. Johnny made sure that Chester Riley was also there as the house detective. Awaiting the signal from Pamela who will recognize him when he arrives, gives Johnny the hand gesture and nod of her head to indicate that he just walked in the lobby. His head turned and his eyes scoured the lobby before sitting, always in the same chair that could capture the entrance doors as well as the corridor leading to the elevators. After removing his hat, he takes a book from his brief case placing it on his lap as the bellhop approaches to take his order for coffee handing him the morning paper.

Waiting a few minutes to analyze his movements and demeanor, all three moved toward him forming a semi-circle. Both detectives flash their badges each grabbing one of his arms as Chester comments; "I'm the house detective, Chester Riley, bring him to my office."

Johnny commands; "Frisk him, Billy"

"Here's his gun."

"What's going on? I have a license for that," he blurts out. "Bring my book and briefcase."

Sit down and we'll ask the questions. Show us some identification."

"Reach real slow," Billy adds.

Chester reaches for it reading; "He's a private eye and has a license for the gat."

"O.K. now you can start flappin' those lips, Mr. Walter Thomas," Johnny says while reading the identification. "Who are you working for and why are you here every day from eleven a.m. too 2p.m.?"

"I work for The Geneva Insurance Group with its headquarters in La Chaux-de-Fondsl, Switzerland. I work out of their New York office."

"It's all here, detective, in his brief case along with his book, a bible, I assume he reads," claims Chester.

Billy says; "keep talking."

"We're here to search out an art thief who has stolen approximately one million dollars of insured art from different hotels around the globe that we had to pay out. If you don't know detectives, there is art hanging in the entry hallway and lobby of the Budapest Hotel worth close to that by artists such as, Claude Lorrain and Franz von Stuck. Isn't that right, Mr. Riley? The Geneva Insurance Group just wants to protect its interest."

Chester comments; "I'm not aware of this."

"Who the fuck owns this hotel," Billy asks rhetorically?

Chester answers; "My pay check says Bulgaria Corporation with this hotel's address."

"We don't want it widely known detectives. Sometimes, it's better to keep things quiet and let the guests just view the art as just that, oil paintings. Imagine if it were known? How much more staff would have to be on hand to continually protect it? The few oils are right in view of where I would sit and read my bible and newspaper."

Johnny asks; "How would you know if the paintings were switched during other times you're not here, Mr. Thomas?"

"Easy. We have around the clock surveillance here with three to four hour shifts. Our company rents a room by the year in case we have to freshen up or make calls either before or after our shift. This hotel is so busy, we just blend in. I'm the only one that has been detected as a daily occurrence in the lobby. This was a test to see how the hotel personnel would react and how long to find me and the paintings out. The Geneva Insurance Group wants to know everything about what and where they are insuring. From now on, these paintings will have to be all put in the lobby, under armed protection in a roped area if the Budapest wants us to continue to insure their paintings."

Thinking for a moment, Johnny asks; "Mr. Thomas, do you have any idea who the art thief might be or a description? Maybe a name or any lead? Do you realize that there have been three murders here at this hotel?"

"Yes, we know. That's an important reason why we have surveillance here. Yes, we are working on a few leads from other art thieves in prison who want to talk and make a deal for themselves. "

"O.K. Walter, you're free to go about your job. Billy, let him have his gun. I would like you to keep us informed of any leads you may get. Here's the number that you can reach me. I think you have the right idea to move that art work so it can be with an armed guard. Good luck. Don't forget your briefcase and book."

On the way out, Johnny asks Billy; "Are you thinking what I'm thinking?"

"It crossed my mind too, Johnny."

CHAPTER 86

"I understand Captain, that Chief O'Brian was on the warpath right in your office," Johnny says greeting Captain Sullivan.

"We're old friends Johnny. He was blowing off steam he was getting from the Mayor and the Commissioner. You know Johnny; this would be such a coup for you that will provide you with enough ammo, along with you passing the test of course, to reach the rank of lieutenant even though in many ways you are taking that responsibility now as Sergeant. That will prove to be in your favor with my recommendation."

"Yes, sir, thank you. The exam is still some months away. We have some theories we're working on. We encountered a private eye at the Budapest who works for the insurance company that insures the oil paintings that hang there worth a lot of money. Many of the paintings they insure have been stolen from other hotels around the world totaling millions. They are staking out the hotel. Billy and I have a theory that the murders could be a deterrent to steal the art right under everyone's nose while there's so much chaos going on," Johnny responds.

Billy adds; "The evidence is still kind of sketchy. Although there are a lot of similarities, there are a lot of differences with each murder. Captain, we're working hard and long and need to hit the evidence trail again. Can we get going here, if that's o.k. with you"?

"Get going. I need updates as you progress," the Captain says raising his voice with each word so both Johnny and Billy could hear him as they both jolted from their chairs as fast as they could to leave already in the hallway.

CHAPTER 87

Back at their desks after more days of hitting the streets, mulling over file after file of collected evidence and interviews, Billy continues to flip through the pages mumbling to him-self.

"C'mon, Billy, these murders, once we solve them is going to put you to Detective Sergeant. Before we go back to The Flamingo Room, read me what you have."

"You're right. The files at the wig shop show that Monsieur Moreau, Shahn-Tal and Andre all purchase high quality wigs. Both Moreau and Shahn-Tal have some sort of French background."

"And could fit the description of what we're looking for Billy. Keep going."

"The dance tickets found in victims one and two were up to date just like victim number three with the stars and color for the months they were found. We don't know if the killer knew the victims didn't use their mother's name. We have the similarities of our number chart. We don't know who paid for Victoria Morrow's grave. All three victims were taxi dancers from The Flamingo Room. We have two missing gold crosses and room keys. Victim number three, Ethel Cummings' gold cross found tangled in nylon. There is no evidence of a struggle with any of the victims."

"What about the photos of the knot on the nylons around their necks, asks Johnny? Pass them to me will ya Billy...Well will you look at that. They're identical knots down to the length on each side of the remaining nylon."

"O.K., so what if they are?" Billy states.

"Well, it means he has made this knot dozens if not thousands of times because he would not have time to re-tie it to meet his expectations. He ties it quickly to the point of it being perfect every time. Who the hell does that and why? Let's go back to Doris' office at The Flamingo Room and re-look at the pictures on the wall."

"I see what you're saying. It takes me after all these years, to retie my tie to get the length I want. You know Johnny, it seems the city is burning all around us and we're not even throwing a small bucket of water into the flames that surround you and me with this case."

I know what you mean, Billy. Not enough to make a path to see our way out."

"Johnny, it's late and it's Friday. Let's take the week-end and kick back. I have plans starting tonight with Nancy the red head..."

"Oh, yeah, from Chantal's. O.K. Monday morning bright and early. Remember... get something out of her besides putting your dick in her."

CHAPTER 88

Billy knew that some things are not only wrong, but are downright wrong, double wrong, because he's a cop. His instinct could not put his finger on that wrong feeling he gets about Nancy. It didn't stop him. It actually gave him a rush of adrenalin that was arousing to him. It's that adrenalin that makes him love being a detective at times, chasing down the bad guy, literally pouncing on him like the king of the jungle takes down its prey until it conquers to devour it.

Nancy looked exceptionally tantalizing in her sleek black dress trimmed in shear lace with a side panel that showed her leg with each step, giving sight to her mid- thigh, all of which accented her striking red hair. Every man's head turned as they were being escorted to their table. Billy slipped the maître d' a few bucks to impress Nancy of the better seating in the area set aside for romantic interludes.

"Billy, I'm glad to be with you here and now," Nancy says smiling as she slides a little closer in their semi-circle booth making it easy, thanks to the plush leather.

The waiter approaches with menu's asking for their drink order.

"Pinot Noir for the lady and I'll have a double scotch on the rocks. I hope you don't mind me ordering for you Nancy."

"Why no Billy, I like a man who is in charge."

The night progressed with dancing, dinner and drinking. Everything became seemingly less hurried. Soft music played and the alcohol took its effect knowing it had a job to do as it carried out its assignment without fail. Nancy took Billy's hand, placing it in the opening of her dress for him to feel her soft skin, not caring that the rush of the jungle animal became aroused within him.

"Go ahead Billy," whispering in his ear continuing with a sigh. She could not believe what she was saying, pushing toward him instead of away. Billy's finger starts to trace the outline of her thigh thru the opening as his hand slides upward, feeling her thrust forward.

Billy releases a chuckle as his voice deepens; "I can hear your heart."

Like her heart, Nancy's mind was racing, not believing the words released from her lips; "I'm getting wet." Looking Billy in the eye, covering his lips with hers, finding it hard not to say; "I didn't wear nylons or underwear."

Not waiting for the check, Billy takes out two twenties and a five dollar bill from his money clip placing them on the table. He knew far too well it would not only pay for their entire check, but would also give the waiter a gratuity he would not see for weeks. Billy took Nancy by the hand as they slide from the booth together. Hurrying out to the street, he hailed a taxi. Climbing into the back seat, they continued where they left off, giving the address to the driver in-between deep breaths, and sighs. Not missing a beat, both continued, touching the un-forbidden places of each other's body that finally found their way to each other's embrace.

CHAPTER 89

Johnny didn't have to remind Billy how they left off saying Monday morning would be bright and early. It almost appeared Billy didn't even touch one step coming from the front doors that lead to the apartment house he lived at. It was as if he was flying in the clouds just missing some of the neighborhood kids on their way to school. "Hey Detective Bradshaw, let's hear the siren," a few of them chanted as Billy was getting in the police car that just pulled up with Johnny behind the wheel. Reaching over to the switch that puts the siren at the ready, Billy flips it pressing the horn making a deafening shrill equal to one hundred klaxons blaring all at once.

"Now get to school before I take you kids to jail!" Billy shouts as they start running.

"Well Billy, you're in a good mood for a Monday morning."

"Yes, I am Johnny. Like I told you Friday, I spent the week-end at my place with Nancy. It was one big love making time that we had. I got her a cab earlier so she could go home to change and get ready for work. She is magnificent, Johnny. Smart, can hold a good conversation and likes to cook and she is all woman, and likes to be handcuffed and man can she........."

"O.K. Billy, I get it. We've got to get you back on the ground again. We're going to The Flamingo Room to visit with Doris. Remember those pictures on the wall; we need to look more closely to see who is standing all around our victim, Ruth Silvan."

CHAPTER 90

"Oh, Good morning, detectives, did you miss something the last time you were here," asks Doris?

Johnny begins by saying; "We're sorry to disturb you Doris, we need to look at the pictures that are hanging in your office, if you don't mind. Are there more in any other offices?"

"You're not disturbing me at all detectives. Monday is always busy since a lot of our business is over the week-end you know. There may be some in Mr. Cohen's office, but more of the type with him and the politicians and not the dancers or patrons. He's not here now, too early. But I'm sure he wouldn't mind if I let you in his office."

"Thanks Doris, maybe after we take a look here." Billy answers. "Doris, do you have a magnifying glass?"

Billy scours the pictures. Slowly he places the magnifier over each face, looking at each man and sailor hovering around the dancers and particularly, Ruth Silvan.

"Johnny, look! Use the magnifier and focus in on this guy behind Ruth Silvan next to the sailor. What do you see?"

"It's hard to tell. Part of his face is behind our victim and part behind the sailor. Doris, do you recognize this guy? I'll point to him."

"I really don't detective. I rarely go to the floor. I'm usually gone by the time it starts to get busy. I'm sorry."

"O.K., Doris. Thank you. Please ask Mr. Cohen or dancers if they recognize him."

"I will. I know where to reach you."

Reaching the squad car the radio transmission signal is sounding off...tschhhhhhhhhhhhhhhh. "This is Detective Vero, 4225. Go ahead."

"This is South Central detective. Hold for D.A. Penett. Go ahead Miss Penett I have Detective Vero."

"What, No" Exclaims Johnny! "Let's go Billy. Number four at the Budapest."

"Jesus Christ, Johnny!"

CHAPTER 91

The Budapest's lobby was busier than usual as many people and newspaper reporters were standing at one particular spot with flash bulbs sending bursts of light into the air. Johnny and Billy moved as quickly as possible toward the crowd thinking that the murder was right in the middle of the lobby. Chester Riley intercepting, signaling to follow him without drawing attention and not to alarm the hotel guests.

"Not there, follow me. That's the new oil painting display that premiered today with armed guards and the private investigator, Walter Thomas. You remember him? He's having his picture taken with the paintings. It will help him keep his job. We'll go up the service elevator, this way. You're not going to believe this, detectives."

Stepping from the elevator car, Johnny and Billy see many of the uniformed policemen bemused at the door where there was a lot of commotion. Stepping from the room being held by her arm by a police officer is D.A. Penett.

"Get her a chair," can be heard as Johnny, Billy and Chester get closer.

"Molly, are you alright," asks Johnny?

"It's a mess in there detective. I thought I'd never see anything like this in my life. I think I'm going to be sick. Please someone; get me an evidence bag… quick."

"Molly, sit down. Here's a chair. Stay with her Chester. Officer, get her a glass of water and that bag to throw up into. Let's go Billy."

"OH MY GOD!" Billy shouts out.

"Officer, seal off this entire fucking floor and get two other uniforms to help you knock on every door and start asking who heard what."

Stepping out into the hallway, Johnny asks; "Molly, are you going to be O.K.?"

"I will Johnny. I need a minute to go back in there."

"Take slow deep breaths. That helps."

Their eyes could not conceive what they were viewing. Blood soaked through the sheets covering the mattress, bed covers, pillows and the walls as if an artist's brush stroked the blood of unsung martyrs that once stood tall across the land leaving a crimson swathe of battle from pillar to post. Sitting on the night table was the head belonging to the body lying on the bed. Fresh streams of dark liquid imitating running rivers of chocolate syrup that once flowed from its origin to its basin were drying quickly. The body was sitting upright in the bed naked with its legs spread apart. Blood was dripping from the neck portion of the head onto the night table continuing to the carpeted floor. The head faced toward its body with eyes staring in bewilderment to where it belonged.

"There's a uniformed officer with Miss Penett. She'll be O.K." claims Chester. "I have the registration card here detective."

"Beverly Hart, Room number 30-6. I guess this is another one of those presidential suites, right Chester?"

"Yes detective one of six, remember?"

"I have a flashlight and tweezers Johnny. Do you want me to…?"

"Sure Billy. Bag it and tag it. We know what it is. However, check to see if the stars and color card is for a current month before it gets too stained. I guess we all better be carrying a tweezers from now on until we catch this animal. O.K, who can tell me, who found number four, Beverly Hart?"

"We have a special crew that handles the room service for all of the six presidential suites," replies Chester.

"O.K., Chester. Who are they and where are they?" Johnny asks sternly.

"There are three teams with two on each team. The team that serviced this room is Harriot and Kathleen. They are in shock and are being cared for by the hotel physician."

Billy almost in disbelief blurts out; "This fucking hotel has its own doctor too?"

"Yes detective. We have to be prepared for any situation. We have a lot of dignitaries and special guests. We've also hired more in-house security. They're being processed, fingerprinted and their background checked. You know military records and all that. They should be all starting around the same time, about another week," Chester answers.

"It's about fucking time," Billy mumbles to himself.

"Well go to wherever they are and be sure they don't leave until we speak to them. I don't care if they faint or puke. Have the doctor revive them. They don't leave until I get there and come right back."

Molly re-entering the room looking as white as the sheets before they became blood soaked.

"I've called for more uniformed officers. We need to question a lot of people today and search the entire building and crevice."

Johnny seeing Molly a little weak in the knees grabs her arm; "Are you going to be sick again? Do you want the hotel doctor?"

"No. I'm alright now. Thank you. Look around. Her clothes are on the floor and no blood on them. Her personal things are on the chair all arranged neatly too without blood on them. So, our victim, Beverly Hart, removed everything or our killer removed all her clothing and put everything in a neat order before having sex and then cutting her head off. He is one cold sick son-of-a-bitch. The hotel has its own doctor, Molly asks almost in a stupor?"

"Look at this!" Johnny carefully lifts the blood soaked nylon with the untouched letter opener that is standard with the suite's desk ensemble. "Let's bag this and include the letter opener."

Billy holds open an evidence bag, commenting; "It's really starting to smell bad."

Chester snaps to attention, after returning, as he heard his name being called by Detective Vero.

"I have an important assignment for you. Find out what kind of publicity the hotel and the insurance company put out about the new arrangement for the oil paintings being displayed under armed guard."

"I'm on it detective," as Chester leaves the crime scene.

CHAPTER 92

Johnny and Billy join Molly in her office having coffee, at the section for just that, to sit and talk.

"I've got plain clothes officers posing as desk clerks at the Budapest and around the clock detail in the lobby, as elevator operators and strolling the halls thanks to Mayor Bernhard approving my pleas for the extra men and overtime;" Molly reports. "The autopsy for Beverly Hart has come back with many similarities as the others, age, hair, height, weight which I've added to our numbering chart."

"I've assigned some undercover detectives to sit at The Nostalgia Hideaway. We feel that our killer might be a frequent visitor with one of Madame Monaca's girls, adds Johnny."

Billy points out; "Beverly Hart's background is again of a 'Hollywood' hopeful with dreams and aspirations of stardom and the silver screen according to other taxi dancers and her brother."

"She has a brother you were able to interview," asks Molly?

"I'll get to that in a minute, Molly. She lived alone in a single room occupancy boarding house on Sullivan Street. She lived a quiet life according to neighbors with no visitors. She paid her rent on time and many times a few days before it was due. We found a picture of her with her mother and brother according to her brother, Sylvester who we were able to speak to. We found him living in Yonkers on Warburton Avenue. He told us there was no father around although they always used their father's name, Hart. Beverly is wearing a cross in the picture which was not at the crime scene. Sylvester mentioned that Beverly had friends at the dance hall, as he called it, but she never mentioned any murders. He said she just hung with the dancers that wanted what she wanted, Hollywood and stardom. She said there were a few of them that would go to the Broadway shows and go out for a drink afterwards together."

"I guess you already know that the hotel room key was not found. He must consider it keep sake," Molly concludes, thinking to herself... *It's kind of bizarre that this is another relative of victims in Yonkers."*

"We would classify the gold crosses and room keys more like souvenirs and trophies," Billy says.

Being interrupted by the intercom, Louise's' voice is heard...."Miss Penett, there is a Mr. Walter Thomas here to see you."

All three look at each other bewildered as Molly responds; "Send him in Louise."

"I know I don't have an appointment, Miss Penett, but I had to stop by to give you my thoughts on the Budapest Hotel murders before I move on to another assignment. This time I'll be going to Austria where there is a huge art gallery under suspicion. Oh, hello detectives. I did not expect you here, but I'm glad that you are. First, let me tell you the answer you asked Chester Riley about any publicity regarding the armed guard for the oil paintings. We only had one article in the Daily Post in the theater and art section."

"So, not too many people would really see or read it unless they are into the arts, is my take," Molly putting in her opinion.

"Correct, Miss Penett."

"If we are thinking that our killer is part of the theater and art life and read about the publicity, using it as a distraction to do the killing, we will have to go back to the female impersonation shows and see who reads the Daily Post. What do you think?" Billy concludes.

"Yes, Billy, we will," Johnny answers quickly.

Mr. Thomas continues; "That is not my reason for being here. Rather to tell what I think."

CHAPTER 93

"Please, Mr. Thomas, tell us your reason for your visit," Molly asks?

"O.K. Miss Penett. Chester and I were talking about the private sector of detective work and we got to the room numbers where the murders were committed. If you recall, I usually have a book open to portray that I'm reading. It's my bible. It keeps me calm. I don't read it on duty, mind you. However, certain numbers in the bible contain certain meanings."

"What are you talking about? Numbers are numbers", Billy states.

"Go on Mr. Thomas," Johnny is quick to cut Billy's thought short.

"Well, the room numbers are as follows; Room numbers eighteen, forty, seventy (dash) six, thirty (dash) six. Let me break them down for you. It can get very complex with many interpretations"

"Just a minute, let me get the black board."

"O.K. Miss Penett...

"Room eighteen: The significance of this number comes from its symbolic meaning for bondage, both oppression and spiritual. The children of Israel were in bondage to several nations for eighteen years. Number one denotes singleness and eight denotes new beginnings. Eight survived the flood; circumcision took place on the eighth day symbolizing a circumcision of the heart. Jesus showed himself alive eight times after his resurrection from the dead."

"Hold up a minute. Let me write it," Molly asks.

'He works alone'.

'He takes his victims into bondage and abuses them.'

'He kills them because he is giving them a new beginning, somewhere, somehow.'

"O.K., continue Mr. Thomas."

"Room forty: This number symbolizes a period of testing. The Jews wondered the desert for forty years. Jesus was tested during his forty days of fasting by the Devil. The flood... it rained for forty days and forty nights. Being that the number four is used in forty, we see on the fourth day of creation, God separated the night from day, light from dark. Now the number zero, visually, resembles a circle. We're dealing here with meanings of cycles, time, like what comes around, goes around. As a numerical value, the zero can be interpreted as a void, a representation of non-existence, like death. When we begin to contemplate zero, we soon find ourselves on an endless adventure. Go ahead, Miss Penett, make your notes."

'So, testing. He is testing himself, us, how many he can kill before he is caught?'

'Separation of night and day, light and dark. Maybe good and evil?'

'He is creating a void of non-existence by death and he is going to lead us on an endless adventure.'

"Continue, please, Mr. Thomas."

"Can you think of anything else, Mr. Thomas like room number 70 (dash) 6 where victim number three was found. Is there any significance with the dash between the numbers, Johnny asks with intense concentration?"

"That is an excellent question, detective. You are well versed in your puzzle solving. If you have done any bible reading, you may recall that Moses after breaking the Tablets because of his anger with his people because of their idolatry had to face God. His anger and frustration had become replaced with love and compassion. When he returned to the Lord, in the book of Exodus, said; 'Oh, this people have sinned a great sin, and have made themselves gods of gold. Yet now, if thou wilt forgive their sin-; and if not, blot me out of thy book.' That dash is found nowhere else in the bible. Contained in this little punctuation mark are all the emotions of a man who had given every fiber of his being to these people. He loved them, cared for them and patiently led them when others would have given up. But Moses consumed by love and overcome with emotion, pauses as indicated by the dash and then pleads for God to take his own life rather than the lives of the people. The number seventy denotes possible judgment. There were seventy elders by Moses and Israel spent seventy years in Babylonian captivity. The number six denotes the number of man and the cities that were given as cities of refuge where the manslayer was permitted to flee."

"Wait, wait, wait, continues Molly. You're telling us..."

"I'm not telling you anything, Miss Penett. I'm simply giving you a theory based on what numbers in the scriptures represent that may tie into your killer. It's up to you or you detectives whether you want to use this theory or not."

"Yes, Mr. Thomas, I want any theory or idea that can lead us to the sick bastard! Let me get my thoughts here as I continue writing. So, the killer is passing judgment on his victims but yet shows love and compassion toward them even though they have committed sins against God by killing them and wants his self to be free?"

"Yes, Miss Penett. He knows he can't plead to God for them, so he is helping both God and his victims in his mind, thinking he will flee to wherever the city of refuge is in his mind. Only he knows where that may be."

"This is a really sick fuck," Billy states!

"O.K., Mr. Thomas. Victim number four found in room thirty (dash) six asks Johnny?"

"The number thirty denotes mourning and sorrow. Both Aaron and Moses' death were mourned thirty days and again the number six."

"Yes, six, man's number, cities of refuge. I get it," states Johnny. "So, he is mourning his victims."

"It seems the devil has found his self a fiddle," Molly states.

"And he has a prodigy that is willing to play arpeggio on his fiddle," Johnny concludes, making it sound like an underlying theme from Homer's Odyssey.

"One more thing I'd like to share with you before I go detectives, Miss Penett..."

CHAPTER 94

As Johnny, Billy and Molly sit staring at the board without Mr. Thomas present, Johnny asks; "Well, do you want me to add what Thomas' last thought is, or, are you going to Molly?"

"O.K.", as Molly turns to the blackboard. "I'm going to asterisk this along with all the other theories Mr. Thomas offered. He thinks the killer is going for seven victims because according to Thomas, the number seven means divine perfection of completeness using the example of Mary Magdalene when seven demons went out from her symbolizing total deliverance."

"You think the killer will stop his killing at seven, thinking he has completed his divine task," asks Johnny?

"How and who the fuck thinks of these things," Billy stammers?

"You know what I know, Billy. Whatever motivates this sick prick is going to keep us all up at night. This is the reason we chose this job. Fight crime and remove the demons that roam our streets."

"I like that!" Billy chimes in. "We are crime fighters. You can be *Johnny Thunder*. Molly can be *Sheena of the Jungle* and I'll be *The Shadow*."

It's alright Billy. If I'm going to be anyone who fights crime, I'll be *The Blonde Phantom*," Molly interjects.

"But Molly, you're not a blonde."

"Correct, Billy. That's why she's called that, *Blonde Phantom*, because she's not really blonde, *Phantom, fake* and really…"

"O.K., yes, I get it. You're really a brunette."

"Fun is over," Molly quips. "Let's get back to the drawing board"

CHAPTER 95

"Well, hello Johnny Vero. It's been awhile since I've seen you," is the greeting walking into the neighborhood butcher shop that also sold some groceries and dairy products for customers convenience and to avoid them going to the large A&P grocery chain store.

"Yeah, Tony it's been awhile. Angie wants me to pick up a roast she's going to cook on Sunday. She'll be home from college for a few days and wants to do some home cooking."

"Not many kids go to college these days Johnny. She's lucky. She was here this morning and said you would be by to pick it up. She was with a nice young man. I think she wants to impress him. Whadda you think. Are they serious," Tony asks?

"I hope not. She is too young and has time left to finish her education and concentrate on what she wants to do with her life," Johnny answers as he watches Tony prepare the roast that Angie ordered. "That's some hunk of beef Tony. That's way too big."

"I know. I'm going to cut it for a rump roast. It will be a lot smaller. That's what Angie asked for. It makes a great pot roast with some potatoes and gravy."

Johnny diligently watches Tony slice the knife so smoothly through the meat on his butcher block. He could not help to have a flashback of the slaughter in room 30-6 and how the victims head was sliced from its body.

Tony throws the roast on the scale, commenting; "Perfect, three pounds. It will shrink just enough to feed four to six people, Johnny, depending on who's eating," slamming the meat back on his butcher block to tie and wrap it so it looks official.

Johnny is watching Tony slip the string under the roast holding one end in his left hand and the other end in his right hand, so the two ends will eventually meet. He wraps his fingers around and through the string creating a loop. He then slides the loop gently to meet the rest of the beef using one side of the string tugging it as he pushes the other side of the string causing both sides to form a knot, squeezing into the beef. One last pull of the string and it all comes together forming a slip knot that squeezes the beef to perfect form.

"Tony, show me how you do that knot again, slowly and please pack some extra string for me to go will you?"

"Sure Johnny. Want a job, laughing?"

CHAPTER 96

Once Johnny got settled in and put all the groceries and the hunk of beef away from Tony's, started thinking; what *can I use to practice tying this knot Tony showed me?* A flashback hit him as if he got hit in the head when you see sparks or stars. *That's it! I can roll a towel up like I used to when I would go swimming at Tibbett's Public Pool, living in Yonkers as a kid. I wonder what happened to all my friends that used to hitch hike together to get there. Eh, can't go to that memory now. I'll practice tying it around this towel... Brilliant!*

CHAPTER 97

Johnny and Freddy's nostrils were filled with aroma's that put your mind somewhere else as they sat out on the balcony drinking their beers saying very little to each other. Johnny's thoughts were; *I've got to get back to practicing that knot on the towel.* Freddy seemed to be in a world all his own.

Opening the glass door to the balcony, Angie asks; "How are you two doing? You have time to finish your beer before we sit to eat". Both acknowledged, gesturing, by raising their bottles.

Johnny could not help to think; *what is this fancy dinner all about? I hope it's not an announcement.....marriage. Oh God, not a baby!*

The time arrived and Angie sang out as it might be performed in a rhythmic show tune..."O.K., let's go. Go wash up and come sit.

Passing the table, Johnny quickly glanced seeing the table was set to look like a magazine ad. Linen, polished silverware, fresh flowers, wine glasses with place settings for four, not three. Now he thought; *what's going on, place settings for four. We are only three here, who else is invited without me knowing? I hope it's not...*

Ah! Perfect timing Angie thought to herself as the doorbell rang.

"Dad, please get the door."

CHAPTER 98

Johnny could not believe his eyes as he used them to measure this elegant woman wearing tailored grey wool pants that sat on her natural waistline having her legs looking as long as one of the Rockette dancers from Radio City Music Hall. Her red stripped blouse opened at the top showing a simple pink rose pendant necklace. Johnny stood mesmerized, momentarily. In the doorway holding a box of pastries, stood... Molly.

"Molly?" Almost in a question, Johnny blurted out.

"Johnny," was Molly's response, staring at each other awkwardly.

Angie hurried to the door interrupting the silence, "Molly, I'm so glad you're here. Come in, come in," greeting each other with a kiss. "Dad put the pastries in the refrig. Just in time. Dinner is ready."

"Thank you, Angie. Can I run to use the powder-room?'

"Sure, to your left."

Angie turned to face her dad, smiling. The look in her eyes spoke volumes to Johnny.

CHAPTER 99

Angie's dinner looked scrumptious. The roast was perfectly cooked showing the most beautiful pink inside making your pallet moist knowing it was going to melt in your mouth. The potatoes and carrots were roasted in the same pan which Angie continuously basted with the Au jus she prepared with red wine and spices to be used later as a side dipping sauce. She picked up this culinary delight from the head chef at the Parisian Hotel who was her mother's friend, when visiting her mother in France over a summer vacation, before entering high school, many, many years ago.

Johnny, still easing into the fact that the guest sitting next to him is Molly and

is keeping the conversation to the dinner chatter light, not talking police business or talking 'shop', as it were. Trying hard to concentrate on the conversations being heard, he had only one thing on his mind... *Wanting to practice tying the knot as he watched Angie cut off the sting so she could slice the pot roast, which was a reminder to him.* The room filled with smells warming your soul down to your marrow.

"Angie, this is so nice of you to invite me. I have not had a meal like this since....since

my mother was well enough to cook."

"I'm so glad you accepted. Is your Mom ill," Angie asks?

"No, she passed away when I was about twelve. My aunt, being my mom's sister and my father raised me. I'm sorry. I didn't mean to go there."

"I guess we have things in common Molly. My mom went to live in Europe when I was about the same age. My Dad has raised me both as a mom and dad."

"He's done a great job," Freddy interjects.

"Freddy, what are your plans for finishing college," Molly asks, easily taking her out of the spotlight as a seasoned trial attorney knows how to manipulate those in the court room?

"I've decided to go on to become a dentist and I'll be attending the University of Illinois at the Chicago College of Dentistry after this semester here at St. Johns."

"But first he's going to Spain, for the 'Running of the Bulls'," Angie inserts.

Johnny sighed, thinking; *Wow! I'm so fucking happy. Maybe a bull will gore him to death. No, no, I can't go there for Angie's sake. I'm always thinking like a cop trying to get to details. This, I never figured,* as he mustered up something to say. "Freddy that's great news. You're going to make a wonderful dentist. Congratulations! Running of the Bulls. You're going to do what many dream of Freddy."

As diner finished, Molly offered to help clean up. Angie asked her set the table for coffee as she placed the pastries on the table, removing them from their box.

"Angie told me these were your favorites, Johnny, from Ferrara's bakery. Did you know that Caruso thought their coffee was marvelous, but especially loved their cookies and cakes which they are famous for. This was a place where an opera lover, such as myself, would like to go after a night of Verdi or Puccini, "explained Molly. Caruso is from Naples, Italy, the same town my grandparents came from with my father.

"Yeah, well wait 'til you taste Angie's coffee," Johnny said proudly, puckering his lips and kissing his fingers throwing them into the air as an expression of perfection.

"If you're Grandparents and fathers are from Italy, how come your name doesn't end in a vowel," asks Freddy?

"Good one, Freddy. My Grandfather's name was shortened when they landed on Ellis Island because the ships manifest had their name as Penett. Originally, it was Penetto. So, you had a choice. Accept your new name that matched the manifest or go back to Italy and start all over. Many adopted the new spelling of their original name. They did that much of the time. Some names were changed to the name of the town they came from. Everything was moved very quickly. According to my father, you put your luggage in one area then moved to another area for a medical exam and questions that lasted about three minutes. You were asked if you were ever arrested or in prison. They looked at your eyes, ears, and throat. Don't dare sneeze or cough. You'd be sent back to Italy."

"That is really interesting. I never knew that. In a way, it's kind of sad not to have your real name," Freddy sort of questions, not really knowing how to respond.

"We are the same person, even if our name changed. It's what's in your inner being. What's in your heart, soul and mind set," answers Molly.

Desert finished, Angie says; "Let's move into the living room. I have a surprise for you Molly. Something similar, you might say to opera. Guess what Dad's going to do," Angie questions rhetorically walking into the living room, bringing Johnny's cello from the corner out to the center, moving the coffee table?

"Angie, I spoke to you about putting me on the spot. I haven't played in a while, at least three months.

"Johnny, I heard about your playing the cello. This is exciting", Molly says as she pats Johnny on the knee sort of reassuring him it will be O.K. "Consider this a practice session. What will you play for us"?

"Well, I haven't played The Six Suites for Unaccompanied Cello by Johann Sebastian Bach in quite a while."

"A private recital. I'm so happy to be here," Molly enthusiastically comments.

CHAPTER 100

As the evening drew to a close, Johnny walked Molly to the elevator while Freddy and Angie finish cleaning up. Turning to face him after he pushed the call button, Molly gives Johnny a hug saying; "You have a great family in Angie. She is so proud of you. You've done a wonderful job raising her. You are a good man and a great detective, Johnny Vero. I'm so glad Angie thought to ask me for dinner. I'll see you soon. We need to solve these murders. I think we have to seriously consider Walter Thomas' theory. I'm glad we didn't talk about them here." Moving her head in the opening of the door as it moved to close so Johnny could see her, Molly continued talking; "I'll have Louise call you to come to my office."

Angie and Freddy came out in the hallway leaving for a late night movie.

"Want to join us, Mr. Vero. We're going to see 'Mr. Lucky' with Cary Grant and Lorraine Day"?

"No, you kids go, have fun, and remember not too much fun. Thanks Angie. That was a nice surprise. I really enjoyed that;" as he thought...*Oh, shit, the string and towel! I have to practice that knot more.*

CHAPTER 101

Johnny turns the police squad car onto the quiet winding tree lined block, right in Manhattan, rarely seen, known as Morton Street. Pulling up to the house that sat in the middle of the street and attached on both sides as the architecture mandated, stood a magnificent brick three story home with six stairs leading to the front door framed on each side with pillars, resembling the entrance to a Roman garden. Johnny wondered *how Nancy could afford to live here, where not many families could,* ever mention what he *thought* to Billy.

"Pull right here, Johnny. I'll only be a minute. I want to surprise Nancy with this necklace I bought her. What do you think," Billy asks, as he opens the blue velvet box?

"Billy, it's beautiful. I think she'll love it. Try not to dawdle. We have an appointment with Molly at her office, remember?"

Ding Dong, Billy hears releasing the doorbell button. His heart racing anticipating Nancy's reaction as he feels his suit jacket that holds the blue velvet box, reassuring himself of his visit.

The door slowly opens to a man wearing pajamas and bathrobe sitting in a wheelchair with both legs missing from the knee's down. Within an instant appears Nancy, placing her hand on the man's shoulder....."Oh, detective. This is my husband, Staff Sergeant Roger Enwright. Darling, this is Detective Bradshaw. I told you about the murders at the Budapest Hotel. Detective Bradshaw is investigating them and all the specialty shops that cater to the show people," her eyes becoming red starting to tear up.

Billy just stared momentarily, frozen without emotion, feeling paralyzed, much as the man sitting in the wheelchair.

"I'm sorry detective, would you like to come in," asks Roger. "Forgive me for not standing," smiling at Billy. "I lost both legs when I stepped on a land mine as my unit pushed forward to stop the Japanese from taking the Aleutian Islands so they could not use it strategically for other attacks. We lost that battle to the Japs and I lost my legs there. I'm just home for a spell from the re-hab hospital. I have a few more months there... (*Sighing*) maybe a year," patting Nancy's hand that is on his shoulder. "Did you serve detective?"

"Err, no, no thank you. I won't come in. Yes, I was Navy Shore Patrol. I'm so sorry to disturb you. We stopped by your place of business, (*knowing in his mind he had to think fast for an excuse to stop here*) Mrs. Enwright, but you weren't there and we did not have your telephone number and got your address from the office. We would like to ask you more questions about some of the 'show folk' that frequent Chantal's. It can wait. Here is my card," fumbling through his pockets feeling the velvet box reminding him why he stood there. "Either you can come to the station or we can come to Chantal's again, at your convenience.

Sergeant, I salute you," as Billy takes a step back, snapping to attention, bringing his hand to his brow, as he watched Nancy's tears stream down her face.

In respect, Roger returns Billy's salute saying, "Thank you detective. I hope you find this terrible person. I've seen a lot of gruesome sights fighting. From what I hear, this could be as frightening as the battlefield."

"Good luck to you Sergeant," stammers Billy, turning to leave.

CHAPTER 102

A meat clever could not cut through the silence nor did the blank stare on Billy's face after explaining to Johnny what just take place.
Just emptiness...

CHAPTER 103

Billy, in a conscience state of un-conscientiousness, goes through the motions as he did dozens of times before, entering the courthouse building housing Molly's office...showing his badge to the policeman at the front desk...pushing the elevator button...stepping in the elevator car...pressing the floor button for his destination...stepping out to the receptionist area, greeted by Louise.

"Good morning detectives. Miss Penett is expecting you," buzzing Molly on the intercom. Not waiting for Molly's response, both Johnny and Billy continued walking, opening Molly's door. Louise gazed in wonderment turning her head to follow their direction, without a word to them.

CHAPTER 104

"Good mornin,' detectives. Billy, you look pale. Are you sick? Looks like you're going to throw-up. Do you need to use my bathroom," Asks Molly?

CHAPTER 105

Billy thwart off Johnny's (almost) command to take a few vacation days to get his mind clear and settle back into his work of solving murders. Instead, he felt he had to stay busy or else he would have just gone on a drinking binge.

"Billy, I'm sure Nancy has an explanation for getting involved with you. Maybe the two of you can work through it. Her action is really a reaction to something that caused her to accept whatever the relationship is between you two. Maybe she wants a divorce and feels guilty or just a simple, you know, like me and Audrey and..."

Billy interrupting; "And Grace and Marlene and whoever else you have in that black phone book of yours. The difference Johnny, is, I want to have a long term relationship with Nancy, not a slam-bam, thank you ma'am, see you next week. I know it works for you and the list of women you see now and then. But someday, you'll meet someone and so will all the others in your little black book. They'll all meet someone, and all of you will want to settle down with whoever that person is. You remember when you felt that way about Simone before you got married?"

"You're right, Billy. I guess me, Audrey, Grace and Marlene and all the women in my 'little black book,' are on the same wave length when it comes to satisfying our sexual needs. You know I'm here for you. I support whatever your decision is as to how and what you're going to do."

CHAPTER 106

Johnny and Billy approach the top step leading to the spaghetti room catching Captain Sullivan's eye through the glass of his office. Using his index finger signaling for them to come right in to his office, changing to both his middle and index finger pointing, indicating that both of them get in his office right away. Already waiting with Sullivan is Molly and the Commissioner who has become distraught by not having these murders solved, begins by saying; "Excuse me, Miss Penett. What the fuck is going on with this goddamn investigation detectives. I don't see any progress or arrests?"

"It's O.K. Commissioner, I've heard worse. I have to support all the efforts this prescient and detectives are doing to solve these murders. Every time we put a piece of the jig together, another piece comes to the fore front that has to be put into the puzzle. It's quite involved. This city or I don't know anyplace that has experienced a serial killer in a long time. Who knows? Maybe as long ago as Jack the Ripper," Molly sternly answers in defense of all who are working on these horrific crimes. "Remember too, we got side tracked from Vincent Razzo having acid thrown on him that had to be investigated."

"Maybe so, Miss Penett, but this is my city and"...

"This is our city too," Commissioner, interrupting. "I want to get re-elected as District Attorney and these two detectives want to get promotions in their career. We love this city and this sick motherfucker is going to get caught by us right here. We have very good theories that are turning into strong possibilities. How's that Commissioner? Put that in your pipe and smoke it!"

"I like your brashness, Miss Penett. I will accept what you just said, even though I don't like it. I'll even campaign for you when it's time," rising, picking up his hat and walking out.

Johnny, Billy and Captain Sullivan stood with stares of shock as Molly grabbed her briefcase and purse to leave, paused and turned, stating; "Get your fucking asses to my office now!"

Sullivan himself, in disbelief of what he just witnessed, waved his hand to both detectives in a shooing motion not knowing what else to say or do as he stood awestruck. Almost in a whisper said, "Go, go."

CHAPTER 107

Quickly arriving at Molly's office as she directed with exuberance, Billy could not hold back by saying; "Holy shit Molly! That was not the Molly we're familiar with. I guess you became crime fighter, *The Blonde Phantom*, for an instant. Thank you."

"It was getting quite tense in there. You did 'kinda' shock us, I must say;" Johnny chiming in to Billy's surprise.

"Yeah, well, he was pissing me off. My father taught me well. I told you once Johnny, my family is from Napes, the region of Campania, where the Guapparia got its start. You probably are more familiar with the term, Mafioso, from Sicily. Let's get started here. We've got to get something solid here fast. Let's focus on the positive leads and I want to put Walter Thomas' theory into the mix."

CHAPTER 108

"I like Walter Thomas' theory a lot," Molly begins. "I myself and my assistants have spent a lot of time on what he said and how the numbers written in those bible verses have the meaning he said they did. I think this investigation has got a powerful direction that was handed to us by someone well versed in the Bible. It just makes so much sense when we analyze it. How do you both feel about it?"

"In theory it sounds great, Molly. And it probably is the best thing to go on right now. However, it seems like another dog chasing its tail. How do we find a cross-dresser who knows about the Bible so intensely, believes what is in the Bible and what God says and is as sick as he is, " Billy points out asking?

"And picked up using a slip knot just like my butcher did on the roast Angie made. After viewing the photos, he used this hundreds, if not thousands of times, because it is the same in every photo. Equal in length, and knot, to perfection, Johnny points out.

"Excuse me... Miss Penett," hearing Louise over the intercom. "South Central is trying to reach Detective Vero."

"Thank you Louise," Johnny answers.

"Use this phone detective," Molly directs.

"We have to go, Billy. Sorry Molly," Moving toward the door. "

We'll pick up on this, don't worry. I believe Walter Thomas is on to something. Our contact at the Nostalgia Cafe' thinks the person we are hoping would show up may be there now."

CHAPTER 109

Johnny and Billy sped through the city streets with siren blasting and a red light flashing from the magnetic mount beacon light atop the roof.

"Do you believe this fucking traffic? All for Frank Sinatra appearing at the Paramount Theatre," Billy yelling and pointing at the traffic trying maneuver thru and around it as the cars pulled to one side.

"The Paramount is on Forty Third and Broadway. Shoot over to Third, Billy. We'll make better time. Can you imagine how it feels to have all these people coming to see you? Every seat in the house filled all 3,664 of them. What they sacrificed and paid to come and see you," Johnny asks rhetorically? I remember, my Dad took me and my mother there the first week it opened in November, 1926. It snowed early that year. The show was 'God Gave Me 20 Cents."

"I think I got short changed, I got a dime," laughingly Billy taunts.

Waiting anxiously in the bar is Monica having a drink. They see her wave, signaling to join her at her table.

"Oh, detectives, I'm sorry. I tried to keep him here but he didn't want a drink which I offered on the house. I thought it might entice him to stay. You just missed him by one, maybe two minutes. I watched him exit through the kitchen doors. I wondered why he (fading and slowing her sentence) *didn't.. use.. the.. front.. lobby*," as she turned her head to keep time to Billy's running after this mystery man hoping he was still in the kitchen area or back ally.

Flinging the door wide open, feverishly looking, not to be seen. The mystery man just seemed to evaporate. He started kicking the stacks of garbage ready for pick-*up hoping this man would suddenly appear squealing for mercy...Don't shoot, don't shoot!* Instead, he thought *not only is he a cross-dresser, he's an illusionist that can disappear with passing thru a doorway.*

Johnny and Monica, now joined by Lilly, were sitting enjoying a round of 'Old Crow'. Pulling up a chair, Billy joins in on their conversation hearing Lilly give a description of the man they think they are looking for as the waiter pours Billy a whiskey.

"You know, I'm going to have to ask you both to come to the station to give our sketch artist a description," encourages Johnny.

"We will detective. I promise. Both Lilly and I will...

"You know, Johnny," Billy says interrupting Monica; looking at his watch, "We could be off duty. We deserve a little R&R."

"I think you're right this time, Billy. Monica what do you have to offer that's on our menu?"

"I'll get the ladies lined-up for you guys. Come, no pun intended, follow me. I owe you for this. This menu is on the house. Lilly, you have another customer asking for you."

CHAPTER 110

Both lying naked, Johnny had a tough time absorbing how this temptress now straddling him, pulled his hair, getting him closer to her as she reached for a blindfold. Tying it tightly making sure he couldn't see, he felt her breath close to his ear.

"You're mine, she whispered," feeling her nipples teasingly pass back and forth over his lips. Aware of the metallic clicking sound, *ZZZTTT...ZZZTTT,* (he's heard so many times before), realized, *she used this technique to distract him to quickly handcuff him to the bed.*

He wasn't sure how he felt *losing control, losing his senses, feeling claustrophobic.* After all, anytime he used the cuffs, it was always the other way around.

CHAPTER 111

"Billy, pull out your notes from the file at the wig shop. What do you have there?"

"Johnny, the squad is waiting for the morning briefing," snorts Captain Sullivan from his office door.

"On my way, Captain. Bring those notes with you and give them a refreshing glance while I give the briefing," instructs Johnny, as they begin walking.

"All right, listen up you 'shits' and quiet down," bellows Johnny to the room filled with police officers and fellow detectives. "I need more uniforms on the Vincent Razzo hospital detail. He's got a long way to go and still needs twenty four hour guarding. Your sector supervisor has the schedules. Hoffstra and Bullock...nice police work on the liquor store murder-robbery and apprehending the perpetrator. I don't know how you two fat-heads pulled it off, (*everyone chuckles a bit before giving halfhearted applause*) but who knows, you may earn your gold detective badges one day after all. I thank everyone for the diligent efforts and gumshoe work gathering all the information we need for our Budapest Hotel murders. We have some good leads we working on, getting us closer to this sick bastard. Three more items to cover and you'll be on your way:

1) Be sure to buy your Irish Sweepstakes tickets from Captain Sullivan. You know how he is about his beloved Ireland.

2) The stake-out rotation detail for the gambling operation located at 'Phil's' candy store on Fifty Fourth Street is on the back board.

3) The under-cover operation for the dope dealing cock suckers coming down from Harlem. Johnson, you're up. Give us the details"

CHAPTER 112

"Billy, your notes indicate the files at the wig shop show that Monsieur Moreau, Chantal and Andre all purchase high quality wigs. Both Moreau and Shahn-Tal have some sort of French background. Andre is British, so he's eliminated."

"Yeah, Johnny. But if you recall, Moreau is the one that fits more than Shan-Tal," (Mimicking how they were corrected in the pronunciation of his name.) Moreau speaks French with an accent and lived in France and was in the French Foreign Legion. He's slight build, right height, is in the shows and dresses like a woman. C'mon, Johnny. Remember your math. One plus one is always two. Moreau is adding up to equal one plus one. Johnny, the light on your phone is flashing. You really should change the ringer so we can hear the Goddamn thing at least."

"Homicide, Detective Vero. How can I help you," not even glancing at Billy?

"It's Molly. I need you to come right over and pick up this arrest warrant. You are not going to believe this. Your fingerprint specialist, Kowalski, picked up this new technique he learned from the Los Angeles Police training and found a latent print at the Budapest, in victim three's room. See you in a few minutes. Step on it!" - Click.

CHAPTER 113

Opening the arrest warrant he's done so many times, Johnny reads:

United States District Court
Southern District of New York, City of New York

ARREST WARRANT

Johnny did not have to read the rest of the gobbledygook listed on the arrest warrant. He knew exactly who and where to go to make the arrest.

"Billy, look at this 'pinch' we 'gotta' make," handing him the warrant.

"Beat me daddy eight to the bar," Exclaims Billy! "How the hell did this person come into this investigation?"

"As I was telling Johnny over the phone. Fingerprint specialist, Kowalski picked up this new technique he learned at the L.A.P.D. training they offered. He found a latent thumb print in victim number three, Ethel Cummings, room. The print matched up to an earlier arrest for the same charge. Now, we're finally getting somewhere. What are you two waiting for? Go, go, go.

CHAPTER 114

It makes sense now, Johnny. The hotel clerk, Pamela, gave a great description of this person signing for the room with victim three. The question is, how the fuck is it, we couldn't put Pam's description to the person on the warrant"?

Johnny stared at the warrant as Billy wrangled thru the traffic to get to their destination, cutting of the red light and siren a block before their arrival. Meeting them was a marked Black and White police car with two officers as back-up.

Rushing through the doors of the Flamingo Room, they were greeted by Irving Cohen;

"Detectives..."

"One of the uniformed officers put up his hand stopping Cohen from interfering as Johnny and Billy continued down stairs.

"Oh my God detectives, you scared me," Doris spurts out in a startled voice.

"Clara Blum, A/K/A, Doris Zollermann, you are under arrest for prostitution," Johnny declares.

"I have to handcuff you, Doris. Or should I call you Clara", Billy states.

"What's going to happen to my mother and my Georgie," Doris asked rhetorically?

CHAPTER 115

Directly to central booking where Clara Blum was photographed for her mug shot and fingerprinted. Johnny and Billy waiting in the interview room for her to be processed to ask a barrage of questions.

CHAPTER 116

"I guess you're used to this," Billy starts. "Tell us Clara, why did you do this?"

"Do what, detective? I've really done nothing wrong. I just arrange for meetings between two consenting adults for a date, nothing more. I collect a small fee," declares Clara.

"We call it prostitution," claims Billy. "You've been arrested for this before along with gun possession, so you know the drill."

"We all know that is not at all what happens when you booked those rooms. You were setting up prostitutes. You were their 'pimp', states Johnny in an ominous tone. "We even found your partial print in the room of Ethel Cummings."

"Those other arrests were when I was eighteen. It was a long time ago. Look at my records, detective. I needed money, so I started to prostitute myself, by myself and then got hooked up with some guy and he started to 'pimp' me. I loved him and did what he wanted. I, we, made a lot of money. He was killed shooting 'craps' in a dice game up in Harlem run by 'Big Dee'. The gun was for protection. I had to care for my mother and I still have too. What do you want from me, detective," Clara trying to win the detectives over to her sympathy?

"We just want the truth and the details, Clara. You had to know after the first murder what you got involved in," Continues Billy.

"I knew these girls and they wanted to succeed and go to Hollywood and become movie stars. I was just helping them to achieve their dream."

"Oh, because you fucked up your dreams," snarls Billy.

"I really sobbed when I found out about Vickie. I sobbed with all of them. I loved them like they were my own girls," Wiping her tears with a lace hankie she removed from her dress sleeve.

"Is that why you paid for her burial at that cemetery in Hollywood," Billy asks taking a chance it was her.

"Yes, yes. I had to do that for Vickie. Oh my God, I'm so sorry. She was special. She was the daughter I never had and always wanted. She loved me and I loved her. We would spend a lot of time together, having lunch and going to a show off Broadway every now and then. She introduced me to Ruth, Ethel, and Beverly. They all had the Hollywood attraction to become movie stars and were willing to do whatever it took, just like so many of the stars. You know, perform sexual favors for advancement... 'the Casting Couch,' as it's called. They were just doing this to save enough money and have a little nest egg while they got started in Hollywood. You know, rent, food, clothes, and auditions. They all spoke about sharing an apartment as each of them moved out there."

"Why the fuck didn't you come forward after Vickie was murdered," asks Billy.

"Why, detective? Because I was scared and didn't want to get involved. Look where I am now. What would have happened if I came forward and the killer thought I knew something? He would track me down and what, kill me too? And, like I said; I need the money for my mother and my Georgie."

CHAPTER 117

Johnny and Billy turn toward the one way mirrored glass as they hear a rapid succession of tapping by Molly, indicating to leave the room.

"Good work so far detectives. What we need is her involvement in all this. If she only did as she states, find out how she got paid and for what. At that, we will only have her on pandering charges which brings a misdemeanor charge along with a fine and maybe a six month sentence. Since her earlier charges were so long ago, the judge will not even allow it to be brought up. Also, she will prove that her mother needs her support, so the judge will give her probation verses jail time. Let her sit before you go back in. Go get coffee, while I see what bail to ask for. She meets in front of the judge in the morning. The Flamingo Room attorney, Richard Lewis already called my office asking about bail. They want Clara back to work too. We're assured that Clara acted alone, in that, The Flamingo Room and Mr. Cohen was not involved at all."

CHAPTER 118

"Here you go Clara. I got you fresh coffee and a sandwich. You can make a telephone call to your mother or Georgie and let them know you probably won't be home until tomorrow after you appear before the judge," states Johnny.

"Thank you detective. I would like to call as soon as I can."

"O.K. Clara, you can do that, but first tell us how you were able to arrange your customers and the girls to meet and how you got paid. All of it, Clara," asks Johnny?

"First, detective, they were not my customers. It really is a very simple operation. I use a telephone answering service that the men called to arrange meeting the girls. The girls would give their customers the number while dancing. They were all quite good at detecting who wanted to meet with them and not just dance. Once the men had the number to call, who knows if they were repeat customers or not. I would then call the service from a pay phone to get the messages, call them back with instructions of paying and time and day to be at the hotel. They would have to pay first."

"How did that work. Paying you?"

"Once again, detective, it is very simple, Western Union. I gave instructions to wire the money to the Western Union office located on Forty Eighth Street and Lexington. I would collect the cash; call the customer through the answering service leaving the set up instructions for them of the day and time for the room at the Budapest Hotel. They would call for their messages. I never spoke to any of them. I had no idea who they were, what they sounded or looked like. I would check in at the hotel myself since the girls did not want to be seen or known, meet them in the room and pay them and I would leave. If the customer showed up or not, we got paid. So, you see detective, I just set up a meeting for two consenting adults to meet for a date. As I said, there is nothing more. Can I call Georgie now?"

CHAPTER 119

"All rise. Hear ye, hear ye. The United States District Court, Southern District of New York, City of New York, is now is session. The Honorable Judge Roberts presiding. Please be seated and come to order."

As soon as the courtroom clerk read the docket and swears in Clara for her testimony, Molly asks; "Your Honor, I am requesting bail to be set at $25,000 dollars as to the depth of Miss Blum's crime with the possibility of her knowledge and involvement of four murders of the women she helped to meet men for prostitution."

"Your honor, Clara Blum admits to only arranging for two adults to meet for a date and nothing more. This would cause a hardship..." states her attorney being interrupted by the judge before he could finish his sentence.

"I'm well aware of your hardship appeal, Mr. Lewis. I've read it. Now step back. Miss Penett, do you have any proof of Miss Blum's involvement in these four homicides and not just as Mr. Lewis states?"

"Not at this time Your Honor, however..."

Interrupting Molly, Judge Roberts continues, "I am going to release Miss Blum in the custody of Mr. Lewis. Since Mr. Lewis is also the attorney for Miss Blum's place of employment, I see no flight in her future for this misdemeanor offense. Apparently, she also needs to get back to work to help support her invalid mother which Mr. Lewis attests too. Miss Penett, if you come up with any proof of Miss Blum's involvement in the horrific crime you speak about, you can re-file. Miss Blum, are you aware of these charges"?

"I am your Honor."

"I'm going to impose a fine of $2,500 dollars Miss Blum," states Judge Roberts.

"Your Honor, I can't..." starts Clara

"Your Honor, the Flamingo Room will pay the fine on our way out." states Mr. Lewis.

"Your Honor, can we ask that Miss Blum's passport be surrendered," Molly requests.

"Mr. Lewis, do you have any objection?"

"No, Your Honor."

"So, ordered."

Judge Roberts raps his gavel. The court clerk jumps to her feet to read the next case number on the docket, Molly sighing as she arranges her papers into her folders.

CHAPTER 120

"This mystery man, cross dresser, who disappears by walking thru a doorway is now going to be called 'Opaque Man'," states Billy.

"Not any more. Look at the artist's sketch from the two ladies you sent over from the Nostalgia Cafe'. Who are they anyway, Johnny," asks Molly?

Billy and Johnny dart their eyes toward one another, blivet, thrown off guard as to how to answer Molly.

"Well, Molly," stumbles Billy, "They, um, are, you know, ah, from the Metro Hotel. They work at the bar in there,"

"I know who and what they are. I just wanted to see if you would up front with your civilian contacts that supply you with information. They are just contacts, right detectives?"

Not answering Molly, Johnny holds the sketch in front of him and Billy.

"Holy shit, Johnny. Do you think it is who I think it is?" Exclaims Billy!

"It's now coming together, isn't it detectives," Molly asks rhetorically?

"We are going to have to start a twenty four hour stake-out. Thanks, Molly. Let's go Billy."

CHAPTER 121

"Yes, Captain, we have some suspects lined up from the artists' sketch. We're just about to set up twenty four hour surveillance, "explains Johnny.

"Good work detectives," Captain Sullivan says interrupting the morning briefing. "You see gentlemen; this is how good detective work gets accomplished by using your brains and good old fashioned gum-shoe. Of course, your civilian snitches can help as well as was done in this case. Carry on, detective. Be safe out there men," as Sullivan leaves the room.

"Okay. Here is the stake out schedule going on the back board. Read it and weep. We have two suspects. Make you arrangements with your personal shit that you have to so you can meet your schedule on the list. It starts tonight," giving instructions hearing the mumbling beginning. "You know the drill, now go," raising his voice over the noise of everyone getting up talking at once to walk to the back board..."*For those who have not purchased an Irish Sweepstakes ticket from the Captain, better do so this week, if you know what's good for you.*"

CHAPTER 122

"Miss Penett, Detective Vero in on the phone, line one," hearing Louise's voice over the intercom.

"Hello detective. What..."

"I need two search warrants, Molly. We have to eliminate one of the two suspects we feel that look like the sketch. One of the suspects is giving our stake out teams a run for the money. It seems he might be on to us. We need one for their business and one for their apartments. How soon can we get them?"

"I'll have them for you this afternoon. I'm meeting with one of the judges this morning and he is pretty amenable towards search warrants. Give me all the information, names, and addresses."

CHAPTER 123

Detective Bradshaw with search warrant in hand, along with eight police officers and two female officers to detain any women if necessary; enter Chantal's Specialty Shop causing a lot of commotion and disruption. Giving directions, Billy gets the officers distributed among the four floors. The female officers collect all the women, both employees and customers to the main area on the first floor to determine who is who before releasing any women customers while the search is being conducted. The few male employees were being detained on the second floor.

Monsieur Chantal hearing the entire racket comes quickly down the stairs from the hallway outside his office door almost falling, misjudging the bottom step.

"What the hell is going on here," Chantal asks trying to sound like he is control?

Handing him the search warrant, pressing it into Chantal's chest, Billy advises him; "Step aside and let us do our job and we will be out of here as quickly as possible. We have a search warrant for here and at your apartment where Detective Vero is with another police detail."

"My friend is there. He can let them in. I must call him. What are you looking for?"

"Just stay put right here. Read the warrant, it's all outlined for you. You're not calling anyone. Now sit down and be quiet."

CHAPTER 124

After sometime of searching, nothing was found to implicate Monsieur Chantal, the police entourage pack up and leave. Walking out the front door, Billy hears a voice calling; "Billy, Billy, wait," as he feels Nancy's hand grabs the inside bend of his elbow, pulling him around to be face to face. Darting her eyes and turning her head around waiting for all the police to pass them, kisses Billy softly and whispers; "Please, give me a chance to explain. You owe me that, Billy, please, please. When can you come over? I need to tell you and explain things. This has not been easy for me. Try to understand. I need to ..."

Okay, Nancy. I will pick you up, where, here or at your house Friday after I get off, probably around 7:00 P.M."

"At my house, please," giving him another kiss, slowly letting go of his hand as she watches him walk away.

"Let's go detective," *snickers* one of the female officers.

CHAPTER 125

Johnny is going over the details at the morning briefing for the search to be held at Monsieur Moreau's theater and apartment:

"The Captain has agreed to get some of you approved for overtime tomorrow for our search warrant on a suspect for the Budapest Hotel murders. We have the theater to search which has the Broadway hit show, 'French Cabaret,'" (*There were a lot of different sounds coming from all the policemen in the room... grunts, moans, hisses, and sighs*)...as Johnny continues in a loud resounding bellow; ***"Simmer down and shut up!"*** The silence becomes eerie as he continues; "This is a big search. I will be at the theater with you and Detective Bradshaw will be at this person's apartment. We want this done simultaneously. This is a person who fits the artist's sketch from our Civilian Informant and description of who we might be looking for. He has given our stake out teams a real work-out keeping up with him, sometimes shaking them. He has murdered four innocent women. We are the voice of these women now and don't ever forget that. We are going to assemble here in the morning at 0800 hours. For those who forgot how to use your military time, it is 8A.M. That is 8A.M. ready to roll in the parking garage. Are there any questions? Bullock, put your hand down, (*everyone giving a loud laugh*). You're dismissed.

"Johnny, if you need me, call. I have to go see Nancy. She got to me at Chantal's when I was leaving after the search. I'll see you in the morning."

"Good luck, Billy."

CHAPTER 126

Seven o'clock on the dot, Billy rings the doorbell to Nancy's front door. Nancy, knowing it was Billy, ardently scurried to answer the door. Once the large mahogany door opened, Nancy grabbed Billy by his suit lapels pulling him toward her kissing him with such tender love and compassion. Billy could not think of anything else but the intense passionate love they have shared for one another, not giving thought to...

"I love you Billy Bradshaw," whispers Nancy, feeling Billy's body becoming more endearing. "Come in, we'll finish this inside," leading him to the living room to pour some Scotch whiskey for Billy and mixing a highball for herself.

"Billy, I want you to know this now. My marriage has been a sham."

"Nancy, you don't have to..."

Let me explain," handing him his Scotch, sipping her mixed highball, as they sat together on the couch. "My mother was an alcoholic. My father left my mother before I was born, never ever hearing or knowing who he is. I dropped out of high school to help my mother pay the bills. My mother always told me; *I would amount to nothing and I came from trash and would always be trash and that marrying Roger would be the only thing that would save me from being nothing.* So, after a few years, I married him. We didn't have a honeymoon and we lived like shit for a few years until he was drafted into the Army. It was sort of a blessing and a malediction. We got a steady income from the Army that helped. In turn, I would help my mother until she died from cirrhosis of the liver. I had a lot of different jobs for a spell while Roger was away. Then I landed this job at Chantal's and it's a good job. I don't have to do things I did to get extra cash. It pays well and is a respectful job."

"How can you afford to live here? This is some joint," Billy asks.

"Roger's parents are quite wealthy. They wanted him to prove that he can earn a living on his own before they brought him into the family business that manufactures women's apparel. That's how I got with Chantal. He buys from them. It's good for both Chantal and my in-laws and their business that I am there. I never loved Roger. I'm sorry he became disabled. Even if he didn't, I was going to file for a divorce. I'm in a quandary, Billy. Roger has a lot of rehabilitation to go through. He was sent to Walter Reed Medical Center where he will be treated and probably will be there for twelve to eighteen months for both physical rehabilitation and the mental depression he is now suffering from. He may come home during that time and maybe not. It's up to the doctors' evaluation concerning his mental improvement. I don't want to add to his depression by divorcing him right now. He has a position in the family business when he is discharged. His parents bought this house for us. You have to understand, Billy."

"I'm falling in love with you, Nancy," speaking softly as he puts his arms around her, kissing her with such meaning, making Nancy weak, releasing a *sigh.*

"I already know, Billy. I love you," taking him by the hand un-buttoning her blouse and dropping her skirt and slip as they continued walking toward the staircase leading to the second floor bedroom, stopping to kiss on every few stair steps, until Nancy was completely nude falling onto the bed.

CHAPTER 127

Everyone gathered early as planned in the police parking garage for some last minute instructions handing out a description and sketch of who they are looking for and for what they are looking for; *Monsieur Moreau is a slight man standing about five foot five inches to five foot six inches with very fine facial features speaking in a higher octave than you would expect from a man.* Johnny delegates, as to who was going where and with whom. On search warrants, he always liked to make a big show having all police personnel shouting orders to cause chaos with scare tactics so everyone in the premises becomes confused and not able to react quickly.

"Billy, you have your team. Wait for my call once you are and your teams are in his apartment building. Now go. My team; "I want you to see your diagrams for this theater. There are a few floors to cover. There may be as many as forty or more people that are in this show and may or may not be there. Bullock, I want your team to contain them in one place while the rest of us to a search. Hoffstra, you and your team at all entrances and exits. The rest of you, with me. Let's roll."

CHAPTER 128

Monday morning's briefing was a high point since Captain Sullivan was giving praise for a job well done with the search warrants.

"I want to thank everyone for your good work on the search warrants that was conducted this past Saturday. We were able to find extremely important evidence and information indicating this individual is our number one suspect. Unfortunately, he is not anywhere to be found and seems he has disappeared. Some of the people in his show indicated they overheard him making arrangements to leave the county." Seeing Police Chief O'Brian and the Police Commissioner walking into his office, comments; "I'll turn this briefing over to Detective Vero, now"

"Thank you, Captain. All right, you have a description and our suspect's name. Remember to tell your C.I.'s he is a cross dresser and may be dressed like a woman. We've been informed that his replacement for the character he portrays in the show is already filling in. We've contacted the bus stations and airports to be on the look-out, just in case he is still around. We know how that usually goes. Keep sharp and be safe, Go..."

CHAPTER 129

Molly was waiting for Johnny and Billy. Right on time, Louise announces their arrival, Molly thinking; *I could set my clock with Johnny Vero. He is a man of his word.*

"Hello, Molly", both Johnny and Billy offering their greeting.

"Great work, detectives. Billy's search found three gold crosses at Monsieur Moreau apartment. Your search, Johnny, finding Moreau's bible, was all marked with chapters and verses to the numbers agreeing to what Walter Thomas pointed to about the meanings of why certain room numbers were chosen. All evidence points that he's our man! No room keys. I and my office staff have been working all week-end and on the telephone to ICPC making arrangements."

"Arrangements with the International Criminal Police Commission," Billy questions"?

"Yes, it is located in France," answers Molly.

"Look at the board as to what Walter Thomas said about victim four, Beverly Hart in room 30-6 and what it represented."

"Number thirty denotes mourning and sorrow. Both Aaron and Moses' death mourned for thirty days and number six denotes the number of man. The cities that you give the Levites shall be six cities of refuge, where you shall permit the manslayer to flee. My weekly Wednesday Catechism class never covered this in depth shit. So, Molly, what you're saying is Monsieur Moreau, or you think he fled to a city of refuge. Where," asks Johnny?

"France, where he originated from. That is his city of refuge. He can't finish his seven murders. He knows we are on to him. All arrangements have been made for you and Billy to travel there and meet Inspector Laurent. He is in charge of the ICPC French office in Lyon, France and is looking forward to meeting American detectives and helping in any way. He speaks perfect English. I know your passports are up to date; we had to be sure of that. Here is a little hand book of easy French expressions along with your plane tickets for you both. Your flight leaves Friday from New York Municipal Airport. We can meet again Thursday and go over any new information that may come available."

Johnny thinking; *I've got to let Angie know. She can't think I'm going to see her mother who is living in France doing her art and now living with some French artist named Beariee or something like that.*

"Johnny, please know that Angie can call or come by and see me or I can call her if she has somewhere I can reach her to let her know when you'll be home. This may take a while. Mayor Bernhard and the Commissioner have approved all the expenses for as long it takes you both to find this bastard!" Reports, Molly.

"You know, Molly, I've started seeing this woman and it's starting to get serious and...."

"Sorry Billy," Molly interrupts. "I understand. You can tell her you may not see her for, I don't know, maybe a few weeks and won't be able to be in touch with her. You can tell her you are going undercover, but not where or for what or when you will return. Same for you Johnny, with Angie. We can't let anyone know what you are doing and where you are doing it. Remember the war time expression, 'Loose lips sink ships'? We don't want any unguarded talk. I'm sure either one will speak about it, but that's how it goes. You both look nervous. I thought you'd be happy about this," Molly expresses.

"It's just the flying. You know over the ocean and all. That's all. I just don't want to run into Simone and what's his name."

"France is a big country, Johnny and you're a big boy. Keep your mind on our business of getting this son-of-a-bitch. We'll meet again on Thursday."

CHAPTER 130

"Okay, Johnny. I'm looking at this itinerary. We have to make a stop for refueling in Casablanca, Morocco. From there, it's a little over a thousand miles to the Lyon airport in France. What do you think, we we'll meet Bogart and Ingrid[1] at Rick's cafe, both giving a capricious laugh.

---

[1] Humphrey Bogart and Ingrid Bergman are actors in a movie; 'Casablanca'. Bogart runs a bar called Rick's Cafe' in Morocco.

CHAPTER 131

Bonjour la France

Finally coming to a full stop on the tarmac after an arduous trip, the aircraft door was opened by the stewardess exactly the same moment the stairs rolled up to disembark. Exiting the plane, Billy, tapping Johnny's shoulder, as he points to a large black sedan pulling up, comments; "Looks like our ride is here. Ah! Fresh air. Do you remember what we rehearsed for our greeting?

"I do, Billy; Bonjour, Monsieur Laurent, comment allez-vous? Nous sommes des detectives, Vero er Bradshaw. Merci de nous rencontrer."

"I'll let you do the talking. How the hell did you memorize that"?

The doors open to the sedan. Four gentlemen step out, all dressed in the same garb; French police tunic uniforms with white baton and gloves tucked into their belt. All wearing the recognizable Kepi hat.

The man leading the group was a large man of stature. As he got closer he seemed to be in his fifty's with a ruddy complexion, as if he worked his entire life on a farm and not investigating crime. His facial features were sharp with chiseled edges that featured a thin mustache, looking quit handsome, perhaps belonging in the French movies or theater.

"Ah, you must be Monsieur Laurent," as Johnny spews out his rehearsed French greeting......

"Very good detective. Please, Inspector will be fine. No formalities here. However, I do admire your attempt at our language. Did you take it in school?"

"No, inspector. Johnny's a quick study. He memorized it on the plane. And as long as we are doing away with the formalities, please call us by our first names, Johnny and Billy."

"Here is the second car. My men will take get your luggage and bring it to your hotel. You must be tired and hungry. Let me take you for dinner and wine as my guests before the night draws upon you with torpidity."

"I could use a good dinner and nice wine to unwind, Inspector," comments Billy.

"Well, then, let's proceed with the proceedings," as he continues giving orders to his men;" Soyez sûr d'obtenir tous les bagages et porter à l'Hôtel de Ville."

CHAPTER 132

The bedside phone continues to ring jolting to Johnny. Morning arrives quickly due to the six hour time difference, it being midnight at home in the United States and 6 A.M. here and now in France. Lacking sleep from their journey, a rare steak and too much wine, was no help to either of them struggling to get to the phone. The ringing continues blaring like a fire alarm siren that could not be shut off.

"Hello, hello," stumbling to answer the phone.

"Bonjour, dètective. It is morning here. We need to start our day. It is getting late already. I will meet you in the lobby for croissant and cafe' au lait in forty-five minutes." - Click.

"Johnny, Johnny, Johnny!" Each cry from Billy getting louder and stronger. "Get up,! barging into Johnny's room via a door that connected their rooms. We only have forty-five minutes to shave, shower, and dress....for both of us! That was Inspector Laurent. He is in the lobby ordering our breakfast already. Johnny! Get up Goddamn it! I'm going to shave."

"Ahhhh, fuck!"

CHAPTER 133

"Ah, detectives, once again, Bonjour. I have taken the privilege of ordering you breakfast," watching the waiter place their plates.

"Il y aura quelque chose d'autre, Inspecteur" The waiter asks?

" Non, merci, nothing more. Juste le chèque, s'il vous plaît."

"I don't know how you Americans eat such a hearty breakfast. Eggs, bacon, toast, jam, coffee. I think it clogs you up before you start the day. I have this information from your office we are going to be using to track your killer. I made copies for you both. If you look at page two, we have information showing that the person you are pursuing is not Monsieur Moreau, but rather is, Monsieur Jean-Paul Vincent. We were able to use the finger prints your New York Bureau sent to us that was gotten from the raid you conducted on his home and business. We are told that he may have fled here to his home thinking he would be safe here as some sort of city of refuge?"

"Yes, it is a bible reference of sorts, where a manslayer can flee. We assume it is here since he was born and spent a lot of his life here," Johnny explains.

"We have been looking for Jean-Paul for some time now, searching the globe. He killed his father, or we believe he killed his father after his mother committed suicide. His father was quite a religious zealot always quoting the scriptures and punishing his son, Jean-Paul for the slight infractions the boy would do, rather than following what his father interpreted the scripture to mean and how he thought Jean-Paul should behave. His father wanted his wife and Jean-Paul following the scriptures according to his interpretation. He was very abusive to Jean-Paul. His mother hung herself with her nylons by twisted three of them together to make them strong enough to hold her. It seems this too is a bible reference to have three cords in a marriage. This was in the suicide note she left referencing a bible metaphor about three cords. One cord is the husband, the second cord is the wife and the third cord is God. If you put God into your marriage, it becomes very strong. The note she left made reference to that, explaining why she used three nylons and that she felt God was not in her marriage but rather the third cord was the devil. The husband and wife ran a butcher shop and would raise and slaughter hogs they would butcher and sell. It is believed Jean-Paul killed his father and fed him to the hogs blaming him for his mother's suicide, because of his abuse to them both mentally and physically. We can't prove it, just speculation until we catch him and he confesses."

"Can we see where they lived and where she hung herself," asks Johnny?

"Sure, détective. I have a car outside. If you both are finished with breakfast, we shall go."

CHAPTER 134

The automobile they rode in was quite un-comfortable, considering its small size compared to American autos. Some of the streets were still being repaired from the bombing that took place during the war which gave a lot of uneven swaying and continual bumping as Inspector Laurent maneuvered side to side avoiding the pot holes and large boulders that lined the streets as workmen diligently continued to work, avoiding the traffic.

"Je suis de`sole` de`tecives. Excusez la turbulence. I have no control over the Streets, only my driving, which is getting a bit of a work-out. I hope you don't get, how you say; milady en voiture? Ah, yes, car sick."

"It's fine, Inspector. It's much better than Billy's driving back state side. It's all falling in to place now, you know, what you said, Inspector. We have this theory that co-inside with what you were telling us about our suspect, Jean-Paul Vincent and his background. His father, being a religious zealot and how he mistreated his son, Jean-Paul and his mother and all. We would not be surprised if he did kill his father and fed him to the hogs. It all fits now. The knot he uses to strangle his victims matches the knot my butcher uses to tie a roast. The strangling representing his mother hanging herself. But why the decapitation, Johnny questions?"

"It must be a universal knot that butchers use that is fast and easy," comments Billy.

"Yes, however, it does not excuse him no matter how he was mistreated to kill his father and now you say he killed four innocent women in New York. Many have been mistreated in their lives and even orphaned and have not done these horrific infamous crimes. I'm sure you've heard of Charles Dickens, Edgar Allan Poe and your famous Babe Ruth. All orphans and look how well they turned out. There are many, many, more my friends. In his father's mind, his way was the only way. He felt he was doing whatever it was to his son and wife for God, and in God's name. How many wars have been fought in God's name? That is dangerous thinking," Laurent converses. "You were saying about your theory detective, something scriptural"?

CHAPTER 135

"Here we are," Inspector announces, pulling the automobile into this run down dilapidated home that displayed a huge sign that read:

'CONDEMED PAS DE PLICE TRESSPASING'

"Every so often, we come out and continue to sift through everything and look for any evidence. No luck over the years. We won't give up."

"Tell us, Inspector, we read that Jean-Paul Vincent was in the French Foreign Legion. Why couldn't he be found through those military records," asks Billy?

"He is a genius at deception as you have seen, détective, changing himself from a man to a woman. Once we matched the prints your New York office sent us from his apartment to his military records, we believe he found a way to disguise his fingerprints when he saw fit. Thankfully, he didn't at his home. Keep in mind again, détective, he is characterized by solipsism. His philosophy deals with madness as a complete, self-contained, world that only the self exists. That is a world that sane people are not able to enter."

"I believe we understand, Inspector. However, don't you think that this location, if it is a crime scene has been compromised, you know even by kids finding out that this place was once a horrific murder scene, coming here, drinking and telling scary stories, maybe with some girls to get them laid?"

"Oh oui, détective, yes, yes. I do enjoy your unvarnished way with words. We have over the years made a few arrests as you say for the young wanting to impress their girlfriends. In doing so, the novelty has worn off and we can tell if there has been any new activity here. We even had a stake out for many, many months after Madame Vincent's suicide and Monsieur Vincent's disappearance, thinking Jean-Paul would come back to... as you say... the scene of the crime. Unfortunately, he out-smarted us, fleeing, with his mastery of disguise."

"Do you mind if we get out and look around," Johnny asks?

"Of course, détectives, S'il vous plaît, be my guest."

CHAPTER 136

The three seasoned detectives carefully and slowly eyed whatever each room held in their minds eye, taking one step forward at each turn of their head.

"I see all the cabinets, draws, and furniture has been dusted for prints," states Billy, seeing all the remnants of the powder used to dust the areas.

"Oui, oui, yes. More than once, just in case, as you mentioned détective, Jean-Paul returned to the scene of the crime. Please, feel free to look, touch, or move things. New eyes are always welcome," suggests Inspector Laurent.

"My God! What is that stench," Billy asks in a muffled tone covering his face with a handkerchief he quickly removed from his back pocket?

"I'm sure you have smelled the stench of death, détective. Perhaps only human death. This is both human and hog's stench of death combined with pig shit and years of decay. When you exit the back door, you will see where and how the hogs lived. Adjacent is the building where they slaughtered and prepared the hogs for sale. The front of that building is the butcher shop where they sold the pork meat. The store front faces the next street. This is where we believe Jean-Paul fed his father to the pigs. We even took their excrement to the lab to test since there were no hogs left. The last step has rotted. Watch how and where you walk. I wouldn't want you to get your shoes covered with the evil that is in the ground. We removed most of the mud and dirt to the other side where we had tents and testing equipment set up along with our crime laboratory. Do you know that the first crime lab was set up right here in France in 1910. We also have a series of written records like, 'A treatise on Forensic Medicine and Public Health', by our French physician Foderé. We've learned a lot since then."

Johnny's mind started to race...*This is all so falling into place. The butcher's knot on the roast from Tony's, being the same knot that was used on all the victims except the last one, Beverly Hart. Jean-Paul knew where and how to cut thru the neck and bone. He learned well from his father. Ah, the student turns on his teacher!*

"I'm sorry, Inspector. My mind wandered. So, what did the pig shit show. I mean about having anything human in it," Johnny asks holding his hand to his face to act like a mask?

"The examiner said it was inconclusive. Which to me says; could be. So, I am going with my theory," answers the inspector.

"Inspector, have all the utilities been cut off," asks Johnny?

"Oui, les services publics have been shut once we finished. We have a few hours before dusk and have plenty of daylight left. Why do you ask," states Inspector Laurent, giving Johnny the answer he hoped for?

CHAPTER 137

Once Detective Vero entered the slaughter house, he almost fell over from the first breath he took after opening the door and stepping in. The stench was ten times worse than in the living quarters. Billy started coughing, bending over starting to dry heave making a wretched sound.

"Are you going to be alright, détective, asks Inspector Laurent?

"Yeah," musters Billy. "How come the neighbors' don't complain?"

"They do. As a matter of fact, the entire place is going to be torn down."

"When," Inquires Johnny as quick as a snapping turtle. "How soon?"

"Oh, in about one month. We have no reason to keep this site as a crime scene. It has been condemned."

"Let me ask you, Inspector. The utilities have been shut off as you said. Tell me about the water supply," Johnny inquires.

"France has made great advances in the last one hundred years, détective, in an effort to provide safe and reliable potable water. Unfortunately organisms surviving the water treatment process still cause illnesses in the population. What is your interest in the water supply?'

"I read something about 'Heavy Water' in the system here. What can you tell me, Inspector?"

"What the hell is heavy water," Billy asks, as he carefully calculates his every step? "Water is water, choking out his words."

"Ah! Détective, you certainly do your homework. Heavy water is much like ordinary water but has higher freezing and boiling points. It is used in certain nuclear reactors for cooling. It is water formed of oxygen and deuterium. One commonly repeated assertion is that the Germans lost their supply of Heavy Water in Norway and thus were never able to achieve nuclear fission. Before WW2 the Vemork Hydroelectric Plant in Norway was the world's largest producer of Heavy Water. In 1939, the Nazis had felt so pressured by the French Atomic bomb project and so fearful that they were well behind that they created a special top secret project under a German Army Ordnance (Heereswaffenamt) to develop an atomic bomb for Germany. It was known as Projekt R masqueraded as a fake rocket fuel project. Heisenberg was never aware of this project and was not trusted to join it. Hitler was panicked into invading Norway by France and England sending mercenaries and equipment to Finland via a railway line from Narvik in northern Norway in support of Finland against Russia. Hitler feared an alliance between France, England and Finland would cut off Germany's supplies of Iron Ore from northern Finland. France purchased the entire Norwegian Heavy water supply. This Heavy Water was first sent to Scotland. In a twist of irony, this entire water supply of Heavy Water was secretly flown to France, via Perth and ended up shipped to France where it was promptly captured by the Germans. This led to another sabotage attempt, sinking of the ferry with the cargo of Heavy Water. The drums floated free of the ferry never to be recovered. Well, never recovered by the proper authorities."

"So, Inspector, that indicates to me, that these never re-covered drums of Heavy Water fell into the hands of underground German sympathizers working right here in France, pouring them into your water system." Johnny interjects. "You are correct again, détective. Now I truly understand why your American office sent you here. Would you like to transfer to our police here in France, détective. Be part of the world famous International Criminal Police Commission?"

Billy lets out a burst of laughter saying..."Are you kidding Inspector. Johnny's ex-wife lives here in France. It took a lot just for him to agree to come here for this investigation, right Johnny, asking rhetorically?"

"Is that so, détective. Is your wife, excuse me, ex-wife French," Laurent inquires.

"Yes, complete with her given French name, Simone. Exquisite on all counts. Beauty, brains, talent, and most of all, making a beautiful daughter with me. She is an artist and took her art over myself and our daughter."

"Ah! Les Artistes are so soulful and have an internal fabrication engine powered by conscious and unconsciousness. Their mind seems more visceral than intellectual. They are driven by the inner spirit and very hard, if not, impossible to stifle. From what you describe, she must be a perfect work of art herself. Beaucoup trop mauvaise. Much too bad."

"It took a long, long time, inspector for my heart to recover. I had to focus on acceptance for my daughter to raise her properly. She has accepted her mother's choice even though it creeps up on both of us once in a while and invades our well-being."

"Tisk, tisk, tisk," expresses Laurent shaking his head side to side simultaneously.

"Inspector, let me ask you...since Heavy Water is much like ordinary water but has higher freezing and boiling points as you said and is used in certain nuclear reactors for cooling, couldn't it's effect act to preserve evidence in the water pipes that might have human tissue.? How soon can you get the water pipe removed and sent to your lab," Billy asks, misdirecting the subject of Simone.

"That never crossed our minds, détective. I will have the water pipes removed, not waiting for the demolition and sent de laboratoire. Our scientistes are very, how you say...brilliant."

"Good, Maybe you can get some solid evidence to help prove Jean-Paul is a diabolical, cruel, and a fiendish self being. He is heinous."

CHAPTER 138

It has been years since the war ended. Most of Europe was still rebuilding, including France that suffered staggering losses including massive property damage. Detective's Vero and Bradshaw knew they would have to wait days before the report came back from the French lab to determine if any human evidence was latent within the water pipes due to the water formed of oxygen and deuterium which they hoped would preserve any indication of human remains. Not wanting to step on Laurent's toes, and nothing more at the moment to figure out where Jean-Paul Vincent may be living or hiding, Johnny and Billy were going to take in some of the sights and some of the most famous landmarks in the world, starting with la Tour Eiffel (the Eiffel Tower) named after the French engineer, Gustave Eiffel. .

When arriving at the Tower, it still manages to amaze who ever stands before it.

"Holy shit, Johnny! I never knew how huge this structure is. Oh, my God!"

"I never knew it either, Billy. It's almost scary standing at the bottom. Look at the informational sheet. It is 1,063 feet tall, including the top antenna. It is 108 stories."

"Listen to this. The tower sways slightly and the sun affects the tower and heats it up, that the top moves 7 inches away from the from the sun. The sun also causes the tower to grow about 6 inches. How the hell is this possible. It has five billion lights. This is almost unbelievable."

"The French nicknamed it; "The Iron Lady." Are you ready to ride this Iron Lady, Johnny?"

"Let's do it, Billy."

CHAPTER 139

After an exhausting few days of taking in the sights of Paris, Johnny and Billy were happy to return to their Hôtel de Ville at each days end. This hôtel is an important structure which has been the site of the municipality of Paris dating back to 1357. It's magnificence is a combination of a palace designed by Italian architect Boccanegra in a style that combines Italian Renaissance and French Classicism. Hôtel de Ville is adorned with 108 statues, representing French cities and notable Parisians. The interior is quite exquisite – it features long ballroom *(Salle des Fêtes)*, beautiful staircase decorated with chandeliers, statues and coffered ceiling. Johnny and Billy quickly made their way to the hotel's bar and lounge, The Lè Chesterfield which is masterfully an influential visual design style known as Art Deco, which first appeared in France just before WWI. Art Deco was the last splendidly self-indulgent decorative style, described for luxury and leisure, for comfort and conviviality. It is an exciting style and should, like the archetypal drink of the period, the cocktail, be enjoyed while it is still laughing at you. Once Johnny and Billy entered, they were hit with an explosion of sophistication, abstract, lavish colors and beautiful women.

The light sound of jazz was playing. It was during WWII that jazz became embedded in the French psyche, becoming associated with freedom and the resistance. It became the sound of liberation. Johnny and Billy bellied up to the bar, scoping out their surroundings as rout as checking your watch when your stomach starting to growl to see if it was time to have something to eat. Here they were aided and abetted by the bartender, Marcel, who greeting them cordially; "Bonjour messieurs, how may I help the American dètectives. News travels very fast here?"

"How about a Scotch and water for me and Old Crow bourbon for him," replies Billy? "I love all the English speaking Parisians."

"Ah, qui. The war you know. Makes you learn quickly things you never thought you would have to learn. I don't know of this 'Old Crow,' you mention. If you don't mind, I see you looking at our lovely ladies sitting at the far end of the bar. Let me mix the cocktail known as 'Pepa,' named for Pepa Bonafe, a French silent film star. I concocted this rousing brandy and vodka cocktail with a secret ingredient that t will make your dick hard for hours," claims Marcel.

"You invented this cocktail," questions Billy?

"Please, trust me. Once those ladies observe me mixing these drinks for you....well, you'll see."

CHAPTER 140

Although the war had ended for a few years, the stigma and activity that stemmed from its spoils continues with prostitutes, that at one time, provided soldiers with an escape from the filth and slaughter of the trenches. Prostitution and war often go hand-in-hand. The French government played a part in the sex industry. Bordels Mobiles d Campagne or Bordel Militaire de Campagne (both abbreviated to BMC's) is a French term for the mobile brothels to supply the soldiers who were facing combat in areas where brothels were unusual. Nothing can unleash sex like war. After all, when a soldier knows that he might die tomorrow, the thing that might pop up in his head and his pants, is having sex tonight. Since the known history of ancient Roman wars to modern warfare, sex has decided wars and thus changed the world. Seductive spies and even officially sanctioned brothels were used as part of strategy for victory during wars.

The prostitutes that frequented The Lè Chesterfield bar and lounge located in the Hôtel de Ville, were not a carry over from the war. They are a new sophisticated woman, melded into all those eyes that fall on their erotic silhouettes and expressions of femininity, on their faces, that hold the natural beauty of these women. These eleemosynary goddesses give way to an articulation of male fantasy and desire. Years after the war ended, people were rediscovering the beauty of life, just getting dizzy from the dark cloud of enmity that continued to be lifted from them.

Detectives Vero and Bradshaw were no exception to their male fantasies or desires. To be with such a beautiful woman in her natural beauty, one could only dream about.

The interior of the hotel's pub in its Art Deco design was just as exquisite as the rest of the hotel, crying out in its majestic glory; *Welcome. Let me embrace you. Sit; be warm and fed in my arms.*' The shallow lighting and music created the perfect ambiance to allow the 'Pepa' cocktails to take effect as Marcel suggested. Shifting in his seat, Johnny sensed one of the ladies of the night gazing, lingering, almost to a point of burning him with her glare. Against all his experience and strong will, he looked back to her. Those eyes seemed to reach across the room as a war arrow drawn from its quiver, directly into him, to touch the inner soul. She didn't drop her gaze, as a demure woman might. Instead, *she appraised him, boldly measuring with her eyes.* Just a hint of her tongue darted along the seam of her mouth to whet her lips. Her eyes smoldered as if *she'd read his very erotic longing and the fantasy in his mind, never wavering until she was able to see the emptiness diminish within his countenance.*

He shifted again, trying to adjust for the heated blood rushing into his manhood, just as Marcel predicted. The corners of her mouth turned up giving Johnny a chance to digest the fluorescence that seemed in her eyes. Clearly, *she found his interest amusing. She found him tantalizing.* She stood, walking toward Johnny until she reached his personal space where she could pick up what his energy was about to tell her.

"Hi. I'm Charlotte."

CHAPTER 141

In spite of her good-girl persona, Charlotte, was very bad. She captures the dark fantasies within every man. Charlotte is a self-assured woman and appears submissive. However, she knows exactly what she wants and is not afraid to chase it.

Once she introduced herself to Johnny, continuing her glare, *she felt he would have wanted her to wait for him to initiate the greeting. Such a fanciful notion, she thought. Men and their ego's always coincide with their penis.*

"Hello, my name is Johnny. I'm a tourist visiting France for the first time with my friend here, Billy. Why don't you bring one of your friends over? We can have some cocktails and something to eat. I'll ask Marcel to get us a booth."

Charlotte extended her hand. ...."My pleasure Messieurs," turning to signal her companion to join them at the booth as Marcel summoned the waiter to bring them.

"Bonjour, Monsieur's. I am, Yvonne. "

"I'm Johnny."

"I'm Billy."

The four after being escorting to their booth, sat to slide in, almost without thinking, who would sit next to whom in the order they wanted. It was as if the waiter was tucking them into bed for the night. All he had to do was read them a bedtime story as he handed them each a menu.

"May I suggest the menu for the evening," whispers the waiter?

"Sure, quips," Billy. "Two of Marcel's famous 'Pepa' drinks for the gentlemen, and,

Ladies... wine for you both"?

"Oui, merci."

"May I suggest Blanquette de Veau with a red Bordeaux, starting with Soupe à L'oignon, finishing with a Éclair au chocolat for desert. I will bring your cocktails and wine for all momentarily," snapping his fingers to the staff.

Johnny, Charlotte, Billy, and Yvonne all started to speak at once as soon as the waiter removed himself to tend to his duties.

A quiet, yet a burst of laughter erupted amongst them, each *knowing it was going to be an epicurean evening with a lascivious ending, like the a Éclair au chocolat they would have for desert.*

CHAPTER 142

Johnny was thinking *that the average hooker would have acquired every trick in the book and knows every secret that would make a man pulsate through his entire body. They had to be the masters with the art of lovemaking, the best of fucking.* Charlotte proved true to her calling.

She gave a *soft sigh.*

Johnny *thought it was more of a moan.* His stomach clenched and looked down at her and thought, *she is beautiful, admitting to himself, more beautiful than Simone, his ex-wife who was exquisite. H*e continued to kiss her soft inviting lips, along her neck down to her waiting breasts with nipples that summoned Johnny's mouth. She convulsed around his hardness as she became almost violent in her frenzy to please herself and her client simultaneously in a way that was long lasting and unfaltering, making Johnny's body shudder as he released himself into her. He did not want to leave his intemperate thirst for this seductress Jezebel. Reluctantly, he withdrew, rolling over on his back.

"Merci, monsieur. You certainly are a great lover. Not many men can..."

"My ex-wife is French. They are fantastic in their sexual escapades."

"Monsieur, this escapades, you speak of?"

"Adventure, excitement, fun," Johnny replies snickering.

"Oh, Qui. I had fun," rubbing his chest, placing her head into his shoulder.

CHAPTER 143

Ring... ring...ring... ring...ring...ring...

The telephone would just not shut up, seemingly getting stronger...

ring... ring... ring... ring... ring... ring.

Stirring slightly, Charlotte in a hypnotic state of sleep, reaches for the phone removing it from its cradle, lays it down on the bed next to Johnny's ear.

"Bonjour, bonjour, dètective. Dètective, are you there, this is Inspector Laurent? Bonjour, we need to meet. Bonjour, dètective."

"Yes, yes, qui, qui," Johnny responds, raising his voice to resonate as he wipes the sleep from his eyes.

"Let us meet, say, 12 noon for a light lunch and then we must continue our business. This way you will still have time to enjoy your guest."

"Have you found..." - Click.

Johnny realizing his thought was cut off by Inspector Laurent, pulls Charlotte closer.

"Mmmm. Ah, Monsieur! Let me shower and freshen up before we continue qui"?

Watching Charlotte sashay butt naked, he could not help but wonder; *How did Laurent know I have a guest in my room?*

CHAPTER 144

Both detectives arrive to meet Inspector Laurent at 12 P.M. sharp in the lobby café. Being on time is a necessary evil for Johnny's wrist watch.

"Once again, dètectives, I've taken the time, to order your lunch. It is a fresh baguette, cheese, and one slice of ham. Simple, but delicious, and of course your morning cafè, or as you say; coufee, heh, heh, heh," eagerly pronouncing it the way he previously heard Billy order."

"Bonjour."

"Bonjour."

"I see, you waste no time getting to know our magnificent city and our women. You never seem to be Désorientée.

"Désorientée Inspecter," asks Johnny?

"Qui, you never became disorientated with our time difference or culture.

"Remember, I was married to a French woman."

"Qui, qui,"

Let us get down to business. The testing of the residue in the pipes at Jean-Paul Vincent's' parents' home did not show any form of human evidence. So, the scheduled demolition has been moved forward to an earlier date. My investigators have been working night and day to get us closer to finding this animal with no conscience. We think he may be right here, under our noses."

"What are we waiting for, let's go," Exclaims Billy!

"Qui, qui. We shall. You Americans need to enjoy the moment, like you did last night. We found an informant willing to give us adequate information to Jean-Paul."

"How did you...?"

Interrupting, Laurent continues... "When babies are hungry or uncomfortable, they only know how to tell their mothers by crying. The mother gets to know what each cry means. It is only as adults that we become more difficult, qui? We hide our feelings. We put up barriers. Too often, we really don't know what anyone feels or thinks. We use a disguise, not like the baby who lets it's mother know its needs. As our profession dictates, we must remove the barriers and disguises to persuade those willing to come forward to give us the information we need to get the dangerous people who commit crimes away from society. The war has taught us the machinations of the devil and how to extract the details we need, breaking down the barrier dètectives, and letting us know what we want to know just as a baby let's its mother know what it wants."

Instantly, their eyes darted toward each other, both knowingly, from their military background, exactly what Laurent was eluding too.

CHAPTER 145

This must be the worst automobile ever, thought Billy, getting into Laurent's car once again, stating; "I don't know about you, Johnny, but I'm glad I got laid last night since we might be killed in this thing you call an automobile, Inspector."

"Qui, monsieur, I am glad your aphrodisiacal evening (starting to snicker in mid-sentence almost not able to finish his thought, finally filling the air with gasps of laughter) will be remembered as a smooth ride and not one that endangered you."

"Inspector," Johnny begins.

"Qui."

"Billy and I both know what you alluded to with your informant. We both served in the military. My question is, how did you find this informant"?

"We have had to collaborate with the I.C.P.C.[1] on this one. This is where you belong, dètective, with the I.C.P.C. in France.

"Right now, I could not do that, with my daughter still attending college and my ex-wife lives here."

"Oh, yeah, Simone!" Billy almost shouts to drown out all the racket the automobile was making.

"Oh, qui, yes. Forgive me, you mentioned that. The police are emerging as an essential tool of collaboration to the I.C.P.C. since the end of the war. I've made many contacts as we exchange ideas and information. I've seen the hand of the devil myself over the years, dètectives. A woman wrapped in cloth and locked inside a piece of luggage. A prostitute, much like your case, strangled and mutilated. Another found with her hands and feet covered with some sort of stain to signify purification, after she was raped. One body or partial body found in their bed covered with blood and burned with acid. We could never tell if it were a man or woman. A man tied and bound, nude from the waist down. We could never identify him. There are many, many more, as I said, the hand of evil. I know what you're thinking, dètective, why don't I go to the I.C.P.C. After my retirement from the Prèfecture de police de Paris, I have been invited to join them, as I plan."

"And, your contact and the informant," asks Johnny?

"Ah, qui!" Exclaims Laurent. Agent, Antoine Blaisè. A good man, I must say. Knows his business and how to extract what he wants. We will be meeting him momentarily."

---

[1] International Criminal Police Commission

CHAPTER 146

"Here we are monsieur's, Saint-Cloud, the I.C.P.C headquarters. The first half of the ride is over, less than 10 kilometers from Paris. You can now relax. Come, let's meet Agent Blaisè. He is a wonderful man and is incredible at solving crimes."

CHAPTER 147

Before entering the building that was graying from its original pristine stone, anyone must have been ardent of its Gothic architecture. This distinctive style of French Gothic was expressed most powerfully. Its characteristics seemed to always lend themselves to appeal to the emotions, whether springing from faith or from civic pride much like the I.C.P.C itself. Once through security, the three were escorted to Agent Blaisè office on the sixth floor.

"Ah! Bonjour, bonjour, monsieur's. Welcome to The International Criminal Police Commission. I am Agent Antoine Blaisè. Inspector Laurent informed me all about you both", extending his hand in a proper meeting. "Now, just tell me, who is who."

"Bonjour, I'm Dètective Vero."

"And, I'm Dètective Bradshaw, bonjour. Your English, Agent Blaisè, is perfect."

"Ah, qui, merci. I attended Oxford University in England graduating with a degree in Civil Law. Well, let's us sit." Calling to his assistant... "cinquante et un et craquelins pour nos clients."

"Qui," continues Laurent..."You will enjoy this cocktail with your crackers. Pour a little water in and it turns cloudy, almost a yellow."

Agent Blaisè (laughing) interjects..."Inspector, I was going to surprise them with our little demonstration. It is fine. It's all in fun. Let me show you what we have already uncovered."

Agent Blaisè wheels a board over that had all sorts of markings as to the reported whereabouts of Jean-Paul Vincent that were numbered one to eight.

"Tell us why there are two circles around the number six," inquires Billy?

"Because that's where we feel Jean-Paul Vincent is according to our surveillance and informant's information," answers Blaisè.

"So, when can we get this sick bastard," asks Johnny?

"In a bit. We are anxious also, my fellow inspectors. We must be sure that we can't prove he killed is father and fed him to the pigs before we turn him over to you. We would have priority to indict him. We, like you, want first hand to celebrate this victory of capturing a serial killer. No crime is more frightening than serial murder. Not only are these crimes most brutal and sickening, but the serial killer usually targets a particular type of person, as you know...children, prostitutes, women, elderly women, young boys, male hustlers, hitchhikers, then selects his victims at random from this category, so none of us are safe, really, because we all belong to one or more particular group, qui"?

"We appreciate your thoroughness, Agent Blaisè. We would have to take into consideration all the details as well. This is a worldwide headline and we understand," states Johnny.

"Wait a minute," exclaims, Billy!

Johnny taps Billy's foot three times without anyone noticing, indicated to be quiet!

"Dètective," questions Blaisè?

Billy realizing he spoke as usual without thinking, understood Johnny's prodding his foot continued stammering for words..."Why can't we..."

"I understand dètective, your impatience," continues Blaisè. However, we have things under control. We want him brought to justice even though he will be going to New York with you. We've exhausted our investigation to keep him here. We would rather acquiesce than have him on the loose. If at any time in the future, we find evidence, we would have to expedite him back to France for trial."

"We understand and totally agree," responds Johnny, getting the tension, being creating, back to a fresh start.

"Good. Let us continue, qui"?

CHAPTER 148

Blaisè's assistant opens the door carrying liquor and crackers announcing that the doctor has arrived.

"Lue envoyer en," Agent Blaisè commands.

"No need. I am here and I can show myself in. Bonjour, messieurs. I am Dr. Americ Moniquè, the psychiatrist for the I.C.P.C. No need to stand. I have been studying the complexity of Monsieur Jean-Paul Vincent and have found he is in a word, psychotic."

"I'm glad most speak English. We would be lost," states Billy.

"Qui, dètective. Americ is also a graduate of Oxford University as a Rhodes Scholar with a degree in Clinical Psychology."

"Tell me, doctor," begins Johnny. "What would make a person do such heinous atrocities to other human beings"?

"Qui, the mind is difficult to master. I believe we all have to capacity and many times the will to take someone's life. However, most of us don't, won't or can't. In Jean-Paul's case, his father, an overzealous Christian martyr in his teaching, reached a point of destroying everything around him in the name of God, like how many wars are fought. Jean-Paul and his mother were abused mentally and sometimes physically having a profound effect on his family pushing his wife to suicide by hanging herself using three nylon stockings tied together for strength. I understand the three tied together is for some biblical reference of two in a marriage and the third being God. However, this is not the correct Hebrew interpretation...."

"Her note said the third cord was the Devil," Johnny comments, interrupting.

"Heh, heh, heh," Chuckles, Moniquè. "Perhaps in her case, it was. Winding three pieces of string will support a heavier weight with all relationships as with marriage, friendships, and business making them stronger. That is what Solomon meant speaking for all relationships, not just marriage. The third string has no meaning to being God. But of course, a string will always break in the end if the weight is too heavy. The weight of Madame Vincent's torment resulted in disappointment and her death. This is Jean-Paul re-enacting his mother's suicide each time by using the women's nylon stocking to strangle them."

"Why, then did he cut off one of their heads," asks Billy?

"Jean-Paul feels abandoned by his mother's suicide and is emotionally hurt feeling he got the short end of the stick, sort of speak. He decapitated the victims head and faces it toward the bed where the body is so she (his mother) can see herself and what she did, devastating the family. His father must have used controlling methods to blame Jean-Paul for her death due to his lack of adhering to the scriptures and his demands. A psychopath needs to have his story told so people understand what he has been through and why he does what he does... kill people. And, as in war....'To the victors, goes the spoil'. When we find him, he will tell you basically the same thing."

"What ever happened to the human recipe of love and happiness," asks Johnny?

"In his case, he had none. He has no moral compass. He may tell you he killed his father, but I feel he will not. He developed such a hate for his father, it would take years of deep psycho hypnotic therapy and that may not work. He can be cunning and charming one moment and kill you in the next. Jean-Paul is a dangerous man who needs to be stopped. We will stop him shortly."

"Come, let us go," commands Laurent.

CHAPTER 149

The caravan of vehicles came to an abrupt stop jousting Johnny and Billy forward, banging into each other like two knights on horseback attempting to unhorse the other.

"Allez, allez, allez, allez," shouts Inpector Laurent over the radio system to all the other vehicles. Johnny and Billy see dozens of police jump from their vehicles charging the door leading to the theater.

"C'mon, Billy, let's go," Johnny yells opening the door to join busting into where they pinpointed Jean-Paul Vincent.

"Stay close," commands Inspector Laurent," I should have issued you weapons."

Johnny's head turns side to side viewing all the police yelling as the stage door is busted open with this huge battering ram, thinking....*It's the same all over the world. We all do the same tactic, and it works every time!*

Inspector Laurent, yelling in French, giving orders and directions, became like a nest of cockroaches scattering when a light is turned on in a darkened room.

"Stay with me dètectives was Laurent's orders as he heard yelling from the second level.

"Arrètez! Ne pas dèplacer ou nous allons tire."

"Non Non! Ne tirez pas," screams Laurent, hearing the gun shot he ordered not to do.

As they approached where all the commotion was coming from, there lay in a puddle of blood, a man as a woman impersonator. Standing was another man already in handcuffs.

"Expliquer, reapdement," demands Laurent.

"What's going on," Johnny asks nervously, hoping it's not Jean-Paul Vincent lying in all that blood rapidly flowing from the man's head.

"Here is Jean-Paul Vincent, dètective," grabbing the man in handcuffs, turning him around.

"Ah, it is you! Julian Moreau from 'the Jewel Box Review in New York.

A sigh of relief comes from both Johnny and Billy, as they both asked in harmony;

"Who is that, on the floor?"

"Il atteint pour une arme à feu quand il nous a vus. Il doit être l'amant de protection de votre crimanal," states the lieutenant to Laurent.

"Qui. He reached for a gun when he saw my men. He must be your criminal's protective lover. My men have already told Jean-Paul why he is under arrest," continuing to give his men instructions to handle the situation at hand and to close the Theater.

"Well, what about Jean-Paul," asks Johnny?

"He will be processed, fingerprinted and photographed. My men will take him. Processing may take a few days. You know all the paperwork for us and for extradition to the United States. Let us return to I.C.P.C. for the formalities, and may I add, a drink to celebrate."

CHAPTER 150

Upon leaving a long arduous meeting with Blaisè, Moniquè, and Laurent, Johnny and Billy head to the one place they know they can unwind now, peacefully, knowing they can rest assure that their serial killer will face his recompense...The Lè Chesterfield lounge appeared like an oasis.

Marcel catches their attention with a greeting; "Bonsoir, Messieurs."

"Bonjour Marcel," both in harmony nodding their heads.

"Non...no, no. It is evening. It is bonsoir, not bonjour for a day greeting."

"Qui, merci," states Johnny.

"Ah, very good inspector."

"Non, no, no. Dètective."

"Excusez-moi, dètective," tilting and moving his head twice in the direction he wanted Johnny and Billy to look showing them who was sitting in a booth.

"Two 'Pepa' cocktails," inquires Marcel, grinning widely?

"Qui, and keep them coming. Be sure you put extra of that secret ingredient," Billy quickly responds as they pick up their cocktails and stroll toward Charlotte and Yvonne who give them both a warm and embracing greeting.

CHAPTER 151

Three days and one night have passed that either Johnny or Billy left their rooms. Empty pitches from Marcel that were once filled with his 'Pepa' cocktail, left over food and dirty dishes from room service and a sign that hung on the door handle for the housekeeping staff not to disturb.

NE PAS DÉRANGER

CHAPTER 152

Despite the **NE PAS DÉRANGER** sign hanging on the door knob, Johnny hears a knocking which seems to be getting heavier with more intensity, almost like a rhythmic drum beat.

Boom-boom
Boom-boom-boom
Boom-boom
Boom-boom-boom

Johnny pushing the shower curtain to the side, calling out; "Charlotte; please get room service. There is some franc's on the dresser to give him."

Wrapped loosely in the bed sheet with not much left to the imagination, Charlotte grabs the franc's and opens the door with a punishing tone; " Qu'est-ce qui ne va pas. Vous ne voyez pas le signe pas de déranger?"

The Young Belloy sheepishly tried not to stare at the half naked beautiful woman as he handed her a folded piece of paper.

His voice quivered as she handed him the money with her hand that was holding the sheet, *hoping it would expose her breasts completely,* as she quickly took the folded paper with her other hand.

"Merci," he stammers, standing frozen until the door closed abruptly, realizing his boyish wish is now nothing more than another cold shower using his imagination.

"I did not order room service," claims Charlotte.

"What's wrong with him," drying himself coming from the shower. "Doesn't he understand the 'DO NOT DISTURB SIGN'?

"It is for you, Monsieur Johnny," as she hand him the folded note.

Unfolding the paper, it reads:

It is time, dètective. Your prisoner is ready for you. I will send for a car to bring you to I.C.P.C.

Opening the door that connected to Billy's room, just enough for Billy to hear;

"Billy, we can go home now. We have three hours before Laurent sends a car for us to get picked up."

Without hesitation, Charlotte drops the sheet the Bell-Boy was wishing for as she softly lays herself down on the bed, extending her hand to Johnny.

"J'aime ce que vous faites pour moi.[1]"

---

[1] I love what you do to me.

CHAPTER 153

Detectives Vero, Bradshaw and criminal, Jean-Paul Vincent were surrounded with Inspector Laurent and his heavily armed policemen.

Paris Orly Airport is an international airport located partially in Orly and partially in Villeneuve-le-Roi of Paris.

"This is not the airport we flew into," implies Billy as the police guard un-cuff Jean-Paul and proceed to re-cuff Jean-Paul's left hand to Billy's right hand and Jean-Paul's right hand to Johnny's left hand.

"That is correct détective. Your flight will be non-stop to New York from this location on a United States Air Force plane. These arrangements made with our I.C.P.C. and your New York office for added security with Air Force personnel to assist you if necessary. Your luggage is on board and my men have assured me that your prisoner has relieved himself most satisfactorily. I suggest you not fall for any trickery, as you know; he is a master in deception. I would not let him out of your sight. Please sign here, Détective Vero stating that Jean-Paul Vincent is now in your custody and is now the responsibility of you and the New York City Police Department. Détectives, au revoir. Peut-être que nous allons rencontrer à nouveau. Ce fut un plaisir de travailler avec vous. Bonne chance.[1] Good Luck."

Johnny and Billy Shaked Laurent's hand with their free hands leaving Laurent in the distance being escorted with the police entourage right onto the waiting airplane.

Being comfortably seated, Billy turns to Jean-Claude saying; "You can shit your pants for all I care. You're not getting these cuffs off and I'm not taking you into the toilet to hold your dick," at which moment three armed uniformed soldiers approached Johnny and Billy.

"Excuse us detectives; we are Untied States Air Force Special Emergency Team traveling with the aircraft and will be escorting you and your prisoner to New York. This aircraft has a cage for your prisoner. The military has their problems as well. I'm sure you both are aware of this since, I assume, you both have served. You can release him for us. Relax and enjoy your long flight. It gets a little rough sometimes."

Johnny and Billy quizzically turn to look at each other leaning forward in front of Jean-Paul looking for each other's approval as the Air Force Sergeant noticing their discomfort…"Let me help you to feel more comfortable. This is a United States Air Force aircraft. You, being on this aircraft means, you are under my command since this is property of the United States government. This is how we do this. My men will attach shackles to his ankles (which they started as the sergeant was speaking) and as you un-cuff one of his hands with yours, we will put our cuffs on him and then the other. Then you will be able to attach him to you again when we land."

---

[1] Goodbye Detectives. Perhaps we'll meet again. It was a pleasure working with you.

Letting out a sigh, Johnny reluctantly says; "Do as they say, Billy. It does take a relief off us sergeant, thank you."

"Yes sir. Thank you. It is a long flight. Try to get some rest. Our team will be available if either of you need us. We will be having refreshments a little later on."

CHAPTER 154

After a restless 17 hours and 30 minutes of a burdensome, challenging flight, the captain announces over the speaker: "This is Captain Wilson. We are approaching New York International Airport and will be landing in 15 minutes. Stay seated as we start our decent and be sure your safety harness is on."

CHAPTER 155

Back to United States Soil

The aircraft came to an uneasy stop with an unsuspected jolt, most like Inspector Laurent's car; however, this huge avian is being gently directed by the flagman to the awaiting gate for those to depart. Once the exit door opened, a barrage of policemen encompassed the interior of the plane, armed and masked awaiting the Air Force personnel to open the cage housing Jean-Paul.

"What is all this," asks Billy with much uncertainty?

"Sit tight detectives, we have our instructions," insists the leader of the U.S. Air Force team.

"We are New York City's SABSO. We are here to assist in your prisoner's transfer," answers the officer being in charge.

"What the hell is SABSO," Billy asks as their prisoner is being un-shackled.

"They're the Saber Blue Society within the police department," quickens Johnny.

"No shit! I heard of them, always thought it was a myth," Billy responds being overheard by the officer in charge.

"We are real, detective. Our motto is; *'It is useless for thou to deny and impossible for thou to conceal.'* We do special secret assignments. Only those within know who we are. Yes, we are an integral part of New York City's Police Department. May the Knight that holds your saber have nothing to deny or conceal so that we may never again meet, unless either of you would like to appertain to these Lordly perks? Your reputations supersede you. We have an armored vehicle waiting. Unfortunately, word got out and there is a herd of reporters and camera's awaiting you and your prisoner. We will now cuff him back to you both so you may walk off having him in custody for the world to see that you single handedly made the city safe again. Good luck."

"So much for secrets," Johnny ascertains.

CHAPTER 156

Cuffed together, Johnny, Billy, and Jean-Paul made their way through the gangway to the waiting crowd of reporters, Mayor Bernhard, Police Chief O'Brian, The Commissioner, and Molly. Amongst the commotion, dozens of people gathered having to be restrained by police realizing something or someone important was going to come through the doors, many stretching their necks while some rocked up and down on their tip toes in hopes of seeing a Hollywood Star. Flash bulbs were flashing as the rare Blue Moon illuminates the night with the explosive popping noises, reminiscent of a pack of firecrackers, crackling their tiny explosives in sequence.

"Oh, no, exclaims Johnny!"

"We're heroes, Johnny. You're on your way to a Lieutenant' promo-tion."

"And you, to Detective Sergeant."

The dignitaries quickly positioned themselves around the three that were handcuffed for the photographers to snap a photo that will live in infamy.

Reporters starting shouting almost in unison;

> *"Raise your hands so we can see Jean-Paul cuffed to you both,"* shouts one reporter.
> *"Jean-Paul, why did you target these innocent women?"*
> *"Did he put up a fight detective's?"*
> *"Jean-Paul, how many people did you kill?"*
> *"Jean-Paul, are you innocent?"*
> *"Did you do what they say?"*
> *"What do you have to say for yourself, Jean-Paul?"*
> *"Are there bodies buried in France?"*
> *"Jean-Paul, Jean-Paul, look over here!"*

Molly made her way next to Johnny, grabbing his free hand to pull him toward her so she could whisper in his ear; "Someone leaked out his real name. I didn't want to take any chances. That's why I sent in SABSO at the last minute."

"You, you sent SABSO," with a surprising lilt to his voice.

"Yes, my father before he was injured serving with SABO, having to resign and continue as a court bailiff. Welcome home," squeezing his hand a little tighter.

"I'm so glad to see you too, Molly. You're a sight for sore eyes. You and Angie are the first people I was hoping to see."

"Look over there, Johnny, to your far left."

Looking into the crowd, Johnny sees Angie mouthing the words; *I love you, Daddy.* Standing at the other end of the crowd Billy eyes Nancy smiling as tears stream from her eyes, blowing Billy a kiss as he knows the only thing he can do in response is smile and nod happily

CHAPTER 157

Every morning newspaper had the picture of Detectives Vero and Bradshaw holding the handcuffed Jean-Paul Vincent high in the air with the headline in bold print....

BUDAPEST HOTEL SERIAL KILLER FOUND IN FRANCE- BROUGHT TO JUSTICE BY NEW YORK CITY DETECTIVES. MAYOR TO BE RE-ELECTED!
A Speedy Trial Anticipated Beginning Soon. Full story page six

CHAPTER 158

The police commissioner ordered Johnny and Billy to take the few days off pre-ceding the week-end with pay, that would not go against their regular time off or vacation. They were told to enjoy the time before the tedious task that faced them. There were boxes filled with all the evidence that would have to be presented in court for Jean-Paul Vincent's trial, including all they had from France and the I.P.C.P.

Johnny could not sleep as he usually does even after having his 'Old Crow' bourbon and listening to the classical music he cherished most. He had a lot on his mind knowing that there were boxes upon boxes of information that he, Billy and Molly would have to cipher through. They had to dot all their I's and cross all their *T's*.

Now, he had to get ready for tonight's celebration that was being held in honor of himself, Billy, the D.A.'s office, the Mayor's office and the police staff at the Budapest Hotel. A black-tie dinner in the main ball room all provided for by the Budapest. Johnny knew it was going to be a packed house with all the dignitaries form the city. Angie was just walking in the door with the new dress she bought for the occasion, giving Johnny a hug and kiss; "Thank you Daddy for the dress. I'm so proud of you, and you didn't even need my professor and class to give you their thoughts. I spoke to Orma and told her. She is anxious to speak with you and said Grandpa is looking down from heaven knowing your work is for him..." starting to cry, not being able to finish her sentence.

Consoling Angie; "It's O.K. Angie. He was a good man, father and husband. It's too bad you didn't have a chance to know him. He always said he would love to have grandchildren to take to the park and read stories to. He would have adored you and would have done anything for you. I will call Orma in the morning, I promise. Now, you better start to get ready. You'll have to help me with my bow-tie."

CHAPTER 159

The long black limousine came to a stop to the entrance of the Budapest Hotel, to a waiting crowd of reporters, photographers, and hundreds of onlookers that required a police barrier to help keep control.

Before Billy reached to open the door, comments; "I can't believe Mayor Bernhard paid for this limo out of his own pocket."

"You and Johnny are top news. The mayor wants the entire world to see this. Don't forget, this is going to confirm his re-election. I'm proud of you both."

"Thank you Nancy," Billy answers just before giving her a quick kiss. "You realize, you are going to be seen in all the papers. You know your divorce and all."

"I'll handle it."

"I'm proud of you both, too," touts Angie. "Don't mess up Nancy's make-up Billy."

One by one, stepping out of the limousine, the photographers were snapping away, changing the flash bulbs as fast as they could, dropping the used ones to the floor. People were holding out paper and pens wanting Johnny and Billy's autographs as reporters were shouting questions being ignored by the entourage walking on the blue carpet with the New York City Police Department's logo specially made for the occasion by the hotel. Smiling, they continued to the glass doors being slowly opened by the doorman as if this was rehearsed a thousand times. In the lobby were others to greet the hero detectives; Mayor Bernhard, Police Chief O'Brian, Police Captain Sullivan, the Police Commissioner, Molly, Budapest Hotel's Executive Manager, Chester Riley, Walter Thomas, Irving Cohen, and Richard Lewis, along with a mob of hotel dignitaries.

Angie, Nancy and Molly were presented with three dozen roses each. Mayor Bernhard steps forward to position himself in-between Johnny and Billy with Angie on the other side of her father and Nancy on the other side of Billy while all the others squeezed together for the photo that will be shown to the world.

CHAPTER 160

The orchestra that was faintly heard while in the lobby as background music became louder once the doors opened to the main ball room. The guests of honor and dignitaries shuffle in to the applause of two hundred and fifty people. None other than the famed Benny Goodman, known as, 'The King of Swing' and his orchestra are playing, 'Sing, Sing, Sing'. The moment the doors swung open, the drums captivated and cajolingly persuaded your foot to start tapping with an upbeat followed by the trumpets, then the entire orchestra with such a tempo, it brought the entire audience to its feet, whistling, shouting accompanied with a continuous thunderous applause. The entourage lead by Mayor Bernhard moved toward the dais and continued standing until all were in place. The orchestra is so inspiring that the applause continued giving the guests of honor their due. The orchestra continued playing following the maestro's command performance keeping on eye on his movements as the music emanates from the players as he brings to life the written musical score. The art of conducting is more than just conveying information by means of visual signals. It is a two step, between body and soul, between physical gesture and musical personality. The most mysterious, unfathomable stick waver from the maestro can go far beyond ordinary limits, something as lovers do while dancing the Tango.

Mayor Bernhard turns to his right and then to his left motioning to the guests of honor on the dais to be seated. Giving his attention to the audience raising his hand covering his lips for the shush sign quickly sticking his hand palms in a downward position waving them repeatedly, trying to quiet the room, without success. The audience continued a relentless appreciation toward those seated. Turning to Maestro Goodman for help, Benny gives the drummer a wave of the wand as a magician expecting a rabbit to pop out his top hat and WHALA!, a tremendous drum roll lasting over two minutes topped with the one tap of the cymbal subduing the crowd in anticipation of Mayor Bernhard standing at the podium.

CHAPTER 161

"Thank you, thank you all for being part of such a momentous occasion honoring our guests of honor, (*gesturing to his right and to his left respectfully*) Detectives Johnny Vero, Billy Bradshaw, and our District Attorney, Molly Penett." The crowd again rose to their feet applauding again until the mayor continues to speak with a deep exhale; "This evening is a great evening for the city of New York. These individuals gave of themselves tirelessly traveling around the globe (*at which point Johnny and Billy lean forward to catch the others eye with grins of 'the cat that ate the canary*), devoting their time off to the capture of very bad mentally disturbed individual who was killing innocent women. They have made this city safe once again for all of us. It gives me great pleasure to present these three with the key to the city."

Again, the audience rose to its feet applauding frantically.

Mayor Bernhard pauses momentarily to collect his thoughts. "Ladies first, as usual. Molly assembled a team I could not be more proud of with the help of our Police Commissioner. I have immense appreciation for the extraordinary work that all the members of our police force have done to make this happen. It is an honor and privilege to present this key to the city to you, our District Attorney, Molly Penett."

Applause.

"Mayor Bernhard, Commissioner, Chief O'Brian, Captain Sullivan, Ladies and Gentleman. I am honored to accept this key to the city and what it represents. It evokes medieval walled cities whose gates were guarded during the day and locked at night. This key represents the freedom to enter and leave the city at will as a trusted friend of city residents. I view myself more than a friend."

Applause.

"Literally, we are fighting for the soul of our city, New York City to be sure that all that is great and wonderful stays that way…"

Applause.

"To keep up with the ever-changing ways that people commit crimes, we can't just react to crimes as they happen, so I pledge to do more to reduce violent crime. I began with the idea that the District Attorney's office has to play a role to drive crime lower. In order to further progress, we must be made to make changes to keep up with the times we are living in. I consider myself as a superhero as Detectives Vero and Bradshaw consider themselves as superhero's. I am 'The Blonde Phantom,' Detective Vero can be considered 'Johnny Thunder,' and Detective Bradshaw as 'The Shadow'…"

Applause… with everyone rising to their feet again.

"Thank you for this privilege. Mayor, if you don't mind, let me pass the torch to Detective Vero."

"Thank you, Molly. It also gives me great pleasure to be here with this honor bestowed upon me. As Molly mentioned, we want this city to be a great and best city, not only within the 22 square miles of Manhattan, but the safest city in all America. I would like to quote from Walt Whitman;

I dream'd in a dream, I saw a city invincible to the
Attacks of the whole of the rest of the earth;
I dream'd that was the new city of Friends;
Nothing was greater there that the quality of robust
Love-it led the rest;
It was seen every hour in the actions of the men of that city.
And in all their looks and words.

The *"city"* symbolizes an ideal condition in an ideal society where human relationships are harmonious applying the Golden Rule. It may seem old to say this, but this is the heart of what Walt Whitman is saying when he states that *"I saw a city invincible to the attacks of the whole of the rest of the earth.* The *"city"* symbolizes ideal conditions in an ideal society where human relationships are harmonious. We are striving for this. We all are, aren't we?" Exhaling, with deep relief.

The audience with great admiration rise to their feet applauding.

"Please give your kind reception as I pass once again our torch, to my partner and friend, Detective Billy Bradshaw."

Applause.

"Thank you all. I cannot say or add anything to Detective Vero, or District Attorney, Molly Penett. That's why I'm the Super Hero, 'The Shadow.' Thank you for this honor."

Laughter and Applause.

Mayor Bernhard resumes his position at the podium, gesturing to maestro Goodman to strike up the band as he encourages everyone..."Thank you all, the dance floor is yours."

CHAPTER 162

The next few weeks were just as the Police Commissioner said they would be, hard, tedious, and very little sleep preparing for the trial of the century. All the boxes of evidence that was gathered from the crime scenes, transcripts, depositions, interviews, tape recordings, and photographs including all from France and the I.C.P.C. had to be put in a semblance that could be easily explained by the prosecution... Molly. All the information had to be in order for the defense, and given as disclosure, and visa versa. The hours dragged late into the night or early morning, many nights to 2 or 3 in the morning. Bleary eyed, with containers of Chinese food empty or partially eaten left on the conference table in Molly's office. Often Billy, Molly, or Johnny would lay their head down on the table falling asleep while someone ultimately fell asleep on the leather couch.

"Jury selection is starting in five days. I have to prepare the questions and get copies to the defense and the court. We have fifty prospective jurors to choose from. This venire is going to take a few days in itself since I am seeking the death penalty and being a capital punishment case, the jury must be composed of those who:

> *One)* Are not categorically opposed to the imposition of capital punishment and;
> *Two)* Are not of the belief that the death penalty must be imposed in all instances of capital murder—that is, they would consider life imprisonment as a possible penalty. The creation of such a jury requires the striking during voir dire of jurors who express opposition to the death penalty such that they are unable or unwilling to set aside personal, moral, or emotional objections toward the supporting of a death sentence, and is designed to produce a fair and impartial jury of which the members will fairly consider all options, including the death penalty and life imprisonment."

"And if the juror opposes the death penalty, as was in my father's jury and would not give the death verdict to that piece of shit," Johnny angrily states?

"It works both ways, Johnny. Expressing opposition to the death penalty does not automatically disqualify a juror. A party may attempt to rehabilitate the juror by asking questions as to whether, personal convictions notwithstanding, they might consider the death penalty. A juror who expresses exorbitant support for the death penalty who would thus otherwise be struck may be rehabilitated should they state a willingness to consider life imprisonment. I don't want any open doors from the defense. I got word this morning from Judge Roberts that he has dismissed all the evidence from France and the I.C.P.C."

"What the hell is up with that," Johnny explodes?

"Why did we go all the way to France," Billy adds with exasperation!

"We took a chance. In reality, there is no evidence. It's all conjecture. It didn't work with all your excellent police work. I can't take a chance any more from here on out. I can always throw something in from those records and information from Dr. Amiric Moniquè when I have Jean-Paul on the stand. The defense will object, and I will withdraw. It plants the thought in the jury's head even though the judge will tell them to disregard my statement. It's a ploy all criminal attorneys' use, both prosecutors and defense. We're in good shape here. Go, get refreshed and be back here in three hours, we have some finishing touches to cover. You both will be called to the witness stand. We have to review some questions and talk about what you will wear, and how to answer both from me and the defense attorney Jean-Paul hired. Apparently, he is quite wealthy and has hired defense attorney, Melvin Rosenthal."

"So," Billy asks. "Who is this Melvin guy? Are we supposed to be, what by him, shaking in our boots? Besides, what kind of scumbag would defend this piece of shit, Jean-Paul?"

"I agree with you. I wouldn't defend him for all the tea in China. However, our system allows that we are innocent until proven guilty and Jean-Paul is entitled to representation. He will be paid a handsome sum. I know he as put a lien on all the property Jean-Paul owns. It adds up to a lot of dough-ray-me. Mr. Rosenthal served as assistant district attorney in the Bronx and as an assistant Attorney General for New York State. During his tenure in the Bronx, he developed a reputation and went into private practice becoming a formidable defense attorney knowing all the ins and outs of the prosecutor's office. He defended reputed organized crime figures developing a style that brought him recognition from within the legal community because of his acquittal rate. He is a force to reckon with."

"We're the super-heroes of the city Molly, remember? Billy trying to re-assure himself"

CHAPTER 163

"Did you see the fucking headlines," could be heard as Mayor Bernhard yells so hard into the phone, Johnny and Billy sitting at Molly's conference table both could hear due to the fact, Molly had to hold the phone away from her ear.?

"Yes, Mr. Mayor. I have a copy here we are reading," staring at the headline…

THE DAILY HERALD

50 TO BE INTERVIEWED FOR SERIAL KILLER TRIAL
SECRET JURY SELECTION in SECRET LOCATION!
Story, page six…

"Who, who is this we"?

"Detectives Vero and Bradshaw. We are finishing up what we have to prepare. I am putting you on the speaker box, Mr. Mayor," shrugging her shoulders turning her free hand palm up, not knowing how to answer him.

"Good morning, Mr. Mayor."

"Which one of you is this one"?

Furrowing his brow answering, "Detective Vero, your Honor. I see this is another article from page six which is Vincent Razzo's crime column."

"Is that bastard back"?

"No, Mr. Mayor. He is still in rehabilitation and has more surgeries. However, he has a lot of contacts that are his informants. He pays them, on the cuff. But the uniformed men that are with him guarding him said he only gave them each $2.00 for Christmas."

"That cheap son-of-a-bitch. Doesn't even show appreciation for where it counts. Maybe I should pull the detail…."

Johnny, interrupting…"That would not be wise Mr. Mayor. We're all upset that his informants sold him the information. It just means that Internal Affairs needs to get to work. We have a mole."

"I don't want any fuck-ups. This better go well."

"Yes, sir. We are confident," assures Molly.

"What about the defense, Melvin Rosenthal"?

"We are on it, Mr. Mayor."

Click.

CHAPTER 164

The prospective jurors had to be bused to the Yonkers courthouse for the secret location, because of the exposure from Vincent Razzo's page six crime columns. The defendant, Jean-Paul Vincent, has a right to be present during jury selection and would have a police escort in an armored truck, similar to those used for transporting money at the banks.

Sitting at one of the tables are defense attorney, Melvin Rosenthal, and of course the accused, Jean-Paul Vincent who has a right to be there during voir dire and Rosenthal's assistants. At the other table sits, District Attorney, Molly Penett who is the prosecuting attorney and her staff of assistants.

Baliff: "Order in the court. All rise. Court is now is session, (once the judge is seated), please be seated. The Honorable Judge Roberts now presiding."

Judge Roberts addressing the court:

"Ladies and Gentlemen, as informal as this may seem, this is still a court of law and you've been summoned as prospective jurors in this criminal case that will be before us. The first thing we do in a trial is to select twelve jurors and in this case, three alternate jurors from among you. I am Judge Roberts in charge of the courtroom. Each of you is qualified to serve as a juror of this court and is part of your obligation for your citizenship in the state and country. No one should avoid this obligation and privilege except under the most dire and pressing circumstances. To help you with the process, I will introduce you to each of the parties seated at the table and what their role is during this trial and will ask them to stand as I do so. This location is only temporary and the trial will be held in the city of New York in lower Manhattan. The state of New York is the plaintiff in this action. The attorney representing the state is Miss Amollia Penett, who is the prosecuting attorney (standing as instructed to face the jurists). There will be many associates from her office at the table when the trial begins. The defendant in this action is Jean-Paul Vincent. The lawyer representing Mr. Vincent is Mr. Melvin Rosenthal."

Judge Roberts, turning his attention to the table;

"Counselor Rosenthal, instruct your client to stand next to you as I have introduced him."

Once standing, Mr. Vincent stood neatly dressed wearing a double breasted suit with a pocket square, white starched shirt, subtle tie, wearing horn rimmed glasses giving the impression of a meek, timid man who would not harm a cockroach.

Judge Roberts Continues....

"Be seated now, Mr. Vincent. At trial, he will be sitting with his attorney and staff, such as you see here today. As part of the jury selection, you will be asked questions to qualify you as a juror in this particular case. This part is known as the voir dire examination. The object here is to choose twelve jurors and three alternates who will impartially try the issues upon the evidence presented without being influenced by other factors. These questions are not for the purpose of prying into your personal lives, but only for the purpose of obtaining an impartial jury.

The attorney's may challenge you, which means you will be dismissed providing both sides agree to the challenge. Understand the state has the burden of proving the defendant guilty and must prove the alleged crime beyond a reasonable doubt. A doubt is based on reason and common sense. The defendant is never required to prove his innocence. The obligation of the jury is to determine the facts and apply the law set forth in my instructions regardless of your opinion of what the law is or should be.

I am going to read you now the charges being brought to you against the defendant, Jean-Paul Vincent by the People of the State of New York as follows;

Indictment number one charges the defendant, Jean-Paul Vincent with four counts of homicide in the first degree. Indictment number two charges the defendant, Jean-Paul Vincent with dismemberment of a human, by decapitation. To these charges, Mr. Vincent has pled not guilty. This being a Capital Murder case, it carries with it the death penalty. During the course of this trial, it is most likely you will be sequestered. You have heard the charge made in the information against the defendant. Other than what I have told you, do any of you know anything about this case, either through your own personal knowledge or any other discussion with anyone or from the newspapers or radio?"

Three people raised their hand. One woman juror of the three, stood replying in a loud voice; "I'm going to be sick," as she began to wobble on her legs. Quickly, she was held up by two court officers and helped out in a separate direction from the others.

"Bailiff, please escort the other two jurors to the jury conference room. I will be there within a moment to question you. Miss Penett, Mr. Rosenthal, please come with me. Officers, please remove Mr. Vincent to the holding area."

CHAPTER 165

Upon returning into the courtroom with the attorneys and not the three jurors, Judge Roberts again gives instructions:

"Officers, please bring Mr. Vincent back. In this process we will determine if you are not categorically opposed to the imposition of capital punishment and are not of the belief that the death penalty must be imposed in all instances of capital murder—that is, you would consider life imprisonment as a possible penalty. I ask that the remaining prospective jurors rise. The Court Clerk will now swear the entire jury panel for voir dire examination. When he is done, he will read your name. Please take a seat in the juror's box to begin questioning and elimination process."

CHAPTER 166

"Hello, Detective Vero," is the usual way Johnny answers the telephone on the desk. "Hey Nancy. Sure, he's here. Hold on. Billy, its Nancy."

A pale cold countenance came over Billy instantly as his eyes widened with shock to what he was hearing coming from Nancy. Billy's eyes closed shaking his head from side to side in disbelief of the words that were running through his head. Johnny's immediate thought was; *Nancy was going to stop the relationship with Billy and try to work things out with her crippled husband, feeling sorry for him.*

Billy hung up the phone, staring at Johnny with a blank look as Billy dropped his gaze.

"What the fuck, Billy"?

"Johnny, Nancy's husband, Staff Sergeant Roger Enwright is…"

"Is What?"

"Dead! He's dead!"

"What the fuck happened?"

"He was found in the therapy pool with his chair a few feet away from him. Nancy thinks he committed suicide but made it look like an accident so she would collect his insurance money and military benefits."

"I thought they were getting a divorce and she didn't care that her picture would be in the papers?"

"Yes, however, she was going to serve him with the divorce papers after she spoke to her in-laws. Nancy thinks he knew from the day I met him at his house when we stopped there and I was going to give her the necklace, and, he might have seen her picture in the newspaper with us thinking his parents sent it to him, putting two and two together."

"Billy, I'm…."

"I know. I'll call you, I need to go."

"Go, I'll take care of what needs to be done here."

CHAPTER 167

The court room located at One Federal Plaza is in a frenzy trying to conduct business as usual, only it's not. The crowds have gathered to witness the opening trial for Jean-Paul Vincent. Police barricades and those manning them had to keep the crowds under control even though the trial would not begin for another two hours. The press set up at the bottom of the court house steps since the sides were all cordoned off with police guards. Only a select few were chosen to be allowed to enter the court room which was heavily guarded.

There were many from all the female impersonators shows dressed in their theater pretentiousness waving signs, chanting, what was on them, stating;

Jean-Paul Innocent
Free Jean-Paul
Different Does Not Make You Guilty
God Loves Us All
Don't Judge Us
We Are Human, Like You!
We Pay Our Taxes

On the other side of the barrier were those in opposition, having nothing to do with Jean-Paul yelling to Jean-Paul's supporters;

Kill Him
He's a freak
Cut off His Balls
Death Penalty
Let Him Fry in the Chair
God hates Homosexuals
Don't Bend Over for the Soap
Rot in Hell

The police had their hands full keeping everyone at bay. At the ready, mounted police on horseback lined up side by side creating a solid wall of muscle in front of each separate group of dissidents keeping an open space between them. The dark black steel eyes of these magnificent beasts stared down into the faces of those yelling at each other trying to stir each to excitement, including the horses. These well trained stallions would not be spooked keeping calm and controlled by their commands given by their riders. The exhaling, and snorting thru their noses, neighing, raising their heads and nostrils flaring like the dragon spewing fire confronted by its enemy, The Ispolini, created a flutter sound that could be heard ten yards away. Riders gave commands to turn sideways into the crowd taking one step in, forcing the crowd back a few feet. At this point no-one could not see over the 14 hands high steed bringing fear into those staring into those cold eyes who once thought, they were in control. Their loud cries fainted into the background.

CHAPTER 168

Trial-Day 1

The courthouse hallways are clear and guarded. Outside the courtroom doors are those seated, waiting to be called as material witnesses for both the prosecution and the defense. The courtroom is already crowded with family, extra police staff for the Police Commissioner, Captain Sullivan, Police Chief O'Brian, and Mayor Bernhard. The judge allowed sketch artists, and some with special interests as authors searching for a new best seller. However all newspaper reporters were not allowed to bring camera's. Some spectators were able to get in through privileged contacts as to who they knew. There came to be standing room only. Those eagerly waiting in the hallway for an inside view, and are no part of the trial, were directed to leave the hallway.

Opening of Trial:
Bailiff: "All rise. Hear Ye, hear Ye. The United States District Court, Southern District of New York, City of New York, is now is session. The Honorable Judge Roberts presiding. Please be seated and come to order."

Judge Roberts: "Please read the case"

Clerk: "Today's case Your Honor is No. # 10328-34986. The People of New York State versus Jean-Paul Vincent, defendant charged with four counts of New York Penal Law code 125.27... murder in the first degree with intent to kill purposely, Victoria Morrow, Ruth Silvan, Ethel Cummings, and Beverly Hart. The defendant is also charged with first degree abuse of a corpse with dismemberment and decapitation of a human, Beverly Hart, and disrupting a crime scene, all of which took place at the Budapest Hotel. With regard to all charges, Your Honor, the defendant, Jean-Paul Vincent has entered a plea of Not Guilty."

Judge Roberts, exhaling with a deep sigh; "Is the prosecution ready"?

"Yes Your Honor."

"Is the defense ready?"

"Yes Your Honor."

"Miss Penett, you're up."

Opening Statements:
"Your Honor, Ladies and Gentlemen of the Jury (consisting of five women and seven male jurors along with three alternates, two men and one woman). Defendant, Jean-Paul Vincent, is charged with four counts of first degree murder of four young innocent women who are Victoria Morrow, Ruth Silvan, Ethel Cummings, and Beverly Hart. In the course of his heinous action of murder and without regard to anything but his own selfish abhorrent, abominable, barbaric, demonic self, cut off the head of his last victim, Beverly Hart placing her head on the night table next to the bed where the rest of her body way lying. (The

sniffling, crying and sighs could be heard from those seated). All of these women worked hard and had ambition and dreams, just like yourselves. Each had dreams of becoming wives and mothers caring for their families. Some, like your selves, may have had other dreams of maybe someday becoming a movie star like Cary Grant and Lana Turner, or singers like Judy Garland or Billie Holiday. We all have dreams that never go away. Dreams we hold for a lifetime. I want you to think about what your dream is. You don't give up hope, do you? Neither did Victoria Morrow, Ruth Silvan, Ethel Cummings, and Beverly Hart, who was not only murdered, and remember, Beverly had her head cut off and placed on the night table. Their dreams will never ever come true because of one person sitting at that table (*turning and walking over to the defendant to stand in front of him, staring, pointing to Jean-Paul Vincent*). This man did this to these poor innocent young women, all in their twenty's.

(Returning to stand in front of the jury continues) I want you to think of when you were twenty, twenty two, twenty three years old until now and what you would have missed out on... love, family, the touch of a caress, a kiss that meant true love, holding your son or daughter, seeing your mother or father growing old. Victoria, Ruth, Ethel, and Beverly will *NEVER* be able to have this, all because of this man (once again, moving to stand in front of Jean-Paul Vincent, pointing at him). I will be calling witnesses to his character, his deception, his background, evidence that he committed these horrific atrocities on these victims who are not hear to testify. However, we are here for them. We will speak for them and bring them to life for you to realize what the defendant has taken away from all of us... lives that only God has the right to do! I will ask you, if it were your daughter, sister, cousin, niece, mother, aunt, or even a grandchild, what would you want of this man? I want the death penalty! You, you, you, and you (pointing to some of the jurors) and all of you (making a swooping gesture with her hand) will be the voice of Victoria, Ruth, Ethel, and Beverly. I will share with you how this man (again turning and pointing), Jean-Paul Vincent used the Holy Scriptures to twist and turn them to fit his evil heart to murder and mutilate. I will ask you to have the mental capability to be courageous and strong as God commissioned Joshua saying; 'Have not I commanded thee? Be strong and of good courage; be not afraid, neither be thou dismayed; for the Lord your God is with you wherever you go.' Molly turns away from the jury, walks to stand in front of Jean-Paul, staring eye to eye raising one finger each time she loudly resided a name; *VICTORIA-RUTH-ETHEL*-BEVERLY, and quietly returns to her seat.

Judge Roberts: "Mr. Rosenthal, I believe you have the floor."

Rising to address the court; "Thank you, Your Honor, Ladies and Gentlemen of the Jury, I will be defending my client, Jean-Paul Vincent who has been accused of murder. When you go to the library or book store and you pick up a book, how do you know what it's about? The cover may tell you a bit and you well know the expression; you can never tell a book by its cover, now can you? I'll bet that you, as I do, read the dust jacket which tells you in one or two paragraphs the high points of the story. It's something that you just read that wants you to know more. If the hook works, you buy it. Some books don't have a synopsis and you've been disappointed after reading it because you bought it based on the cover. Miss Penett's dust cover of her story is not very clear and has accumulated a lot of dust itself. Mr. Vincent is innocent. Her hook is to have you believe how my client used the Holy Scriptures as a basis for these murders. What Miss Penett failed to tell you is this is only a theory and not fact and is the dust on her cover. Her book will never reach the best sellers list. As a matter of fact, it may never get published. Why? Because there's too many pages of jibber-jabber that the publishers (pointing to the jurors themselves) you, you are the publishers can't understand and become quite confused as you are editing this book.

So, you decide to put it on the shelf and it accumulates all this dust until one day, another editor finds it and brings it to your attention. After you blow the dust off the cover and you open it to read it again in hopes it magically changed the words on the pages for you to understand. To your disappointment, the words are the same and you just can't get past the introduction. So is the case the prosecution is trying to present. The introduction to this case has no substance or meaning and is based on, well, theory and theory is nothing more than a paradigm containing the basic assumptions of nothing more that dust. I will explain to you how none of the so called evidence being presented against my client has any substance or truth to it. There are no witnesses to my client committing such crimes or witnesses to seeing him before or after the murders as to where they took place. I don't want you to be frightened by what you will hear or see. I want you to strong and courageous as the prosecution asked you to be. However, to be strong and courageous as God told the Israelites; 'Have nothing to do with a false charge and do not put an innocent or honest person to death, for I will not acquit the guilty.' Miss Penett said that only God should have the right to take a life, not you, not me, nor anyone else. Passing judgment on my client will make you as God, taking a life that does not belong to you. Thank you."

Judge Roberts: "It is much later than anticipated getting a very late start. I like to start my courtroom early. We will recess until Monday morning at 9 A.M. I will not have going forward, my courtroom over flowing. I will only allow entry for seating capacity. No more standing," rapping his gavel.

Baliff: "All rise."

CHAPTER 169

"Billy, I'm so sorry about Nancy's husband. It hit you and Nancy like a ton of bricks falling from the sky. It must be a heavy load she's carrying particularly since she said for you not to be there until the dust settles with his family and all the papers and crap she has to deal with from the Army. We can get her into the courtroom with Angie since Angie is using this in her psychology classes as her thesis. At least you two can see each other while we are not meeting with Molly and her team."

"I know, I've got to get my head straight for what's coming. I spoke with Nancy and she said how proud everyone is of Roger and what he sacrificed. There was a military ceremony held with honors at Woodlawn National Cemetery, upstate, Elmira, New York. I didn't know one existed here. She was telling me that the grounds started as a marshalling center for Union soldiers during the Civil War and eventually became a cemetery. She told me that the ceremony was beautiful giving Roger a full honorable burial for his sacrifice and service. There was only Nancy and his parents along with Roger's friends from the hospital rehabilitation center. Roger got the full ceremony with a 21 Gun Salute and of course, Nancy received the flag from his coffin. She thought his parents should have it and gave it to them."

"Billy, Roger is going to be part of her life forever. It just is. It will never go away."

"I know. I accept that. I want to build our life together now. There are a lot of complications. Roger's parents have no idea about us. Nancy inherited the house and now his parents want her to take an active part in their business that Roger would have had. They want Nancy to be part of their lives and eventually take over the business. Nancy is confused and feeling pressure from them and some guilt since she really never loved him."

"Suggest to Nancy to tell her in-laws just that, not that she didn't love him, but feeling over-whelmed. She has to go away for a while and get herself together. Tell her to tell them she is going to visit and stay with her sister, you know the one you told me about that lives in London and of course just stay with you for that time."

"She doesn't have a sister."

"They don't know that. You both need to be together to work through this."

"You know, Johnny... that may just work. I'm going to talk with Nancy. Here's Molly. Roberts starts on time. We better get downstairs."

CHAPTER 170

Trial-Day 2

Bailiff: "All rise. Hear Ye, hear Ye. The United States District Court, Southern District of New York, City of New York, is now is session. Come to order. The Honorable Judge Roberts presiding... Please be seated."

Judge Roberts: "Members of the jury, I want to apologize for any inconveniences you have experienced this week-end being sequestered. I can imagine being away from your family is not easy and may cause some discomfort. However, I want to assure you, I will do everything in my power to make this experience as convenient and comfortable as possible. I was told that the hotel, food and any accommodations such as going to church with your escorts has not been totally unpleasant. If any of you have any special requests, please let the clerk know and I will be sure to accommodate you. Let's begin. Is the prosecution ready"?

"Yes, your honor."

"Is the defense ready?"

"Yes, your honor."

"Call your first witness, Miss Penett."

"The state calls Detective Johnny Vero."

Bailiff: "Please state your name and address for the court."

Detective Vero gives his name, rank and his address as the police precinct he is associated with, as all police do as well as officers of the court, giving their address as the court house, never giving out their 'real' addresses for obvious reasons which are an accepted practice.

Bailiff: "Please place your left hand on the Bible and raise your right hand. Do you solemnly swear that the testimony you are about to give shall be the truth, the whole truth, and nothing but the truth, so help you God"?

Of course, everyone says, 'yes, I do.' No one has ever heard someone say;

'I'll do my best,'

'I will try,'

'Count me in,'

'I guess so.'

Even though some have been known to lie, it is always; *'I do.'*

Detective Vero; "I do."

CHAPTER 171

Molly "Detective, How long have you been a New York City Detective?"

Vero "I've been a homicide detective nine years and three years as a uniformed officer."

Molly "In all of your twelve years, have you ever seen such horrific, gruesome, heinous, grisly murders as the four victims...

Mr. Rosenthal jumps up, interrupting Molly, upon hearing her question, loudly states; "Objection your honor, inflammatory!"

Molly "With-drawn."

Judge Roberts; Miss Penett, we've just begun. Try to refrain yourself from such questioning. Please re-phrase."

Molly; "Yes your honor," (Sighing). "Detective, please describe the crime scenes, in your own words, as to the execrable conditions you found?"

Vero: "Execrable, I don't know what that means?"

Molly; "It means, horrible, sickening, repulsive, and monstrous."

Mr. Rosenthal; "Your honor!"

Judge Roberts; "I'll allow it. It sounds like a Webster's dictionary definition to me, so Detective Vero can understand the question?

"Yes, Your Honor."

"Continue."

Mr. Rosenthal (Exhaling heavily) sits down.

Molly; "Thank you, your honor. Detective, in your own words, please tell the court how you found the four victims: Victoria Morrow, Ruth Silvan, Ethel Cummings, and Beverly Hart."?

Vero; "Of course, these sights will never leave me. I've seen plenty during my time on the force. Not this. Each victim was young, pretty and had a lifetime to enjoy. Instead, each one was lying on the bed, nude, having had sexual intercourse and strangled with their own nylon stockings and a dance ticket from the Flamingo Room."

Molly; "What is the Flamingo Room and where did you find those dance tickets, detective"?

Vero; "The Flamingo Room is a refined dance hall featuring a society orchestra where men go to dance by buying tickets for ten cents and pay the girls that work there to dance with them by giving the girls a ticket for each dance. The tickets we found were put into their vigina's."

Subdued gasps were heard from the jury and throughout the courtroom.

Molly "Tell us detective, what was familiar with the knots that were tied from the nylon stockings used to strangled these four victims?"

Vero; "They were all the same knot butchers use to tie roasts with. It's an easy knot that tightens easily and quickly. It has an advantage to other knots, which means that once you tie them, you can adjust them very easily without needing an extra finger to hold the knot in place as you tighten it. Butchers use this

TEN CENTS A DANCE

because it grips the meat neatly. A butcher's knot is more of a noose than a slipknot, in that it tightens under the load and a slipknot doesn't."

Molly "Your Honor, I submit exhibits A-B-C-D and E, photos, showing the victims with the same knot Detective Vero just mentioned. They are all the same, precise in size and shape. I would like to pass these among the jurors."

Molly hands them to the Bailiff, who in turn hands them to Judge Roberts. Giving them a quick look returns them to the bailiff, instructing him to let the jurors pass them among themselves, commenting...

"You, are about to view some pictures that are part of this trial. They must be seen to help you make a determination as to the evidence being presented. I know this may be hard; however, it is your duty to stay steadfast and keep in mind as to why you were chosen and why you are here.

The jurors passed each photo, slowly, analyzing every one, shaking their heads side to side, hearing terrible low grunts and tsks. The entire court room became painfully quiet having their eyes glued on each juror as each one stared at the photo in disbelief before passing it to the next juror and the next and the next until all were finished circling back to the bailiff. Two of the female jurors were crying, particularly after viewing Exhibit 'E,' a photo of Beverly Harts head sitting on the night table with eyes bulging and mouth open wide. Their sniffling was the only sound echoing within the court room walls.

Judge Roberts; "Madame Forman, does the jury need a moment to refresh?"

Turning to her left to catch the juror's opinion, a few nodded, yes.

"Yes, Your Honor, thank you.

Judge Roberts; "It is already 4P.M. We will resume tomorrow morning at 9A.M."

Mr. Rosenthal; "Objection your Honor. The jury will fester on those photo's the rest of the day and night and nothing else."

Judge Roberts; "Over-ruled. Court adjourned," rapping his gavel as the last authoritative statement, just like putting the cherry atop a cake.

Bailiff; "All rise."

CHAPTER 172

As the court room emptied, Molly gets hold of Detectives Vero and Bradshaw with her two assistants; "You know that your days and nights belong to me until this trial is over. We are going to dinner to discuss some points we must cover in the next few days."

"Okay, Molly. Nancy is waiting in the hall. Let me tell her and I'll meet you in the lobby."

"Don't dilly dally Billy. I will only be a minute to check with the Bailiff where the jury will be dining. We can't be at the same restaurant."

"Dilly dally Billy. That could replace 'Billy the Kid," quips Johnny, everyone nodding with a chuckle.

"Believe me, Billy doesn't dilly dally when (hesitating)....never mind, I'll hurry."

CHAPTER 173

Trial-Day 3

Bailiff: "All rise. Hear Ye, hear Ye..." continuing to recite the court room formal introduction through rote memorization.

Detective Vero, being reminded that he is still under oath, takes the witness stand to continue being questioned.

Molly; "Detective, you found...let me rephrase. There were woman's clothing and shoes that were hanging in the closet in room number forty where victim #2, Ruth Silvan's body was found?

Vero; "Correct."

Molly; "Were they the clothes and shoes that belonged to Miss Silvan?"

Vero; 'No, they were...."

Rosenthal; "Objection! "Calls for speculation, your honor."

Judge Roberts; "Sustained."

Molly "Detective, how do you know that the clothes and shoes found in the closet in *room number forty did not belong to Miss Silvan?*"

Vero; "The size of the dress, the length, and the shoe size were too big for the victim."

Molly; Please, continue.

Vero; They are exactly the size, length and shoe size that would fit the defendant, Mr. Vincent, perfectly. We measured him, had him try on the shoes and dress. It was a perfect fit. Jean-Paul Vincent is a cross dresser and is in shows dressed as a woman. He is a known for his impersonations of women.

Molly "Your Honor, I present exhibit 'F', a photo of Mr. Jean-Paul Vincent wearing the clothes found hanging in the closet in room #40 where victim number two, Ruth Silvan was found. It shows how these clothes fit Mr. Vincent perfectly," handing the photo to the Bailiff, in turn to the judge.

Judge Roberts; "Any objection, Mr. Rosenthal?"

"No, your Honor."

Judge Roberts;" Bailiff, pass this to the jurors."

Each time a piece of evidence was submitted and passed among the jurors; silence fell upon the court room. No questions were asked of the witness until every juror viewed the evidence, like shades pulled down before going to bed to quiet the room, and once morning arrived, the shades were lifted, everything came to life when the evidence was handed back to the bailiff. The shades were lifted and the questioning sprang into motion like the sun rising in the east each day to awaken all for another day.

Molly "Detective, in your own words, how did you and detective Bradshaw come to investigate Mr. Vincent?

Vero; "We came to the conclusion that our killer was a cross dresser which led us to the shows and shops that are frequented and performed in by female impersonators. We had to investigate all the information we gathered and we considered many individuals that would fit the profile of a man who would dress as a woman."

Molly; "How so, what were you looking for?"

Vero; "As you saw in the photo of Mr. Vincent dressed as a woman with the clothes we found in the closet, fit perfectly. I went through each article of clothing and shoes we found at the scene. The sizes did not co-inside with victim number two, Ruth Silvan. She was too small for the clothes. So we knew it was a larger person, not too much larger, perhaps a man who would have a slight build. A person with fine features that he would pass for a woman. That's how we decided to start looking in the places I mentioned."

Molly; "How many places and how many people did you consider that may fit the description you described?"

Vero; "Both Detective Bradshaw and myself visited every woman impersonator show consisting of at least one hundred men, all specialty shops that cater to woman and their employees with special requests including wig shops, and bath houses that are known to frequented by the men who are in the shows and in the entertainment business. We found strands of hair on the bed that did not match victim number two hair, but rather turns out to be hair from a wig. We visited all the wig shops in the area and found that Mr. Vincent purchased wigs from The Vanity Hair Emporium where Mr. Vincent has a card on file of all his wig purchases."

Mr. Rosenthal; "Objection Your Honor. There must be hundreds of cards on file of who purchases wigs from men who perform."

Judge Roberts; "I'll allow it. However, Miss Penett, get to your point quickly."

Molly; "Yes Your Honor. Did you look through the card file?"

Vero: "My partner, Detective Bradshaw did and there were not hundreds. These were card files on only a few who purchased more expensive wigs with natural hair in them. We checked everyone who had a card on file."

Molly; "Why then did you concentrate on Mr. Vincent?"

Vero: "All the others were not in show business any longer or were deceased. Some were older and would not fit the description we had in mind for the clothes we found."

Judge Roberts: "Let's stop here. It is four thirty. I want the jury to have a good night's rest after their evening dinner. I hope you enjoy the restaurant I've chosen for you tonight. Court is adjourned until tomorrow morning at 9A.M."

Bailiff; "All rise."

CHAPTER 174

Trial-Day 4

It is 9A.M. sharp and the bailiff has not called the court to order and is nowhere in sight. A buzz starts among those already seated waiting for the bailiff to announce his opening dialogue. "This is highly unusual, particularly for Judge Roberts," Molly whispers to Detective Vero and Bradshaw sitting in the first row in the gallery behind the railing known as 'the bar,' separating where the attorney's, their staff and plaintiffs sit, known as 'the well.'

The bailiff calls the attention of the court stating a brief announcement that *court will be delayed until 10A.M. due to the court stenographer having to make adjustments to yesterday's transcripts to be ready for council.*

"We have an hour. Let's go upstairs to my office and do more briefing and have coffee, which I missed this morning."

CHAPTER 175

"Louise, we don't have time for you to be sappy or intoxicated with admiration. Please bring us coffee. We have until 10A.M. to be back in court."

"Yes, Miss Penett. Good morning detectives," thinking *of how Detective Vero would be naked lying next to her. Would he kiss the way she dreamt of? Would he hold her gently in his arms and make love to her as she often thought of, making night desires day dreams.*

"I don't know why Rosenthal hasn't objected more than he has. I threw some 'things' out to test him, and he just sat there. I can't figure him," states Molly.

"Maybe he realizes the evidence so far can't be disputed and is waiting to cross examine," Billy mentions.

"You haven't ever been up against him," questions Johnny?

"No and I called many of my colleagues to ask about him. Most said he has a great track record defending a lot of the slug clients he represents. Okay, let's cover some points I want to throw at you Johnny..."

CHAPTER 176

Trial-Day 4 continues...

Bailiff: "All rise...."

Judge Roberts; "I apologize for the delay. I wanted to read through yesterday's transcript before giving copies to council. Bailiff, if you will, please hand these to Miss Penett and Mr. Rosenthal."

Molly; "Your Honor, I recall once again, Detective Vero to the stand and he has been briefed...."

Mr. Rosenthal; "Your Honor, I request to know as to what Detective Vero was briefed on?"

Molly; "I didn't finish my sentence, Your Honor. I was about to say Detective Vero has been briefed that he is still under oath. Is that okay with you, Your Honor?"

"Yes, Miss Penett, continue."

Molly; "I submit into evidence these gold crosses on chains found in Mr. Vincent's apartment. Exhibit 'G'".

Mr. Rosenthal; "Objection, Your Honor. These are crosses that can be from anywhere and anyone, not necessarily from these murder victims. They can be from Mr. Vincent's mother, grandmother, aunt or girlfriend."

Judge Roberts; "Over ruled Mr. Rosenthal, I'll allow them into evidence. Make your point quickly, Miss Penett before I change my mind.

"These are similar to what some of our victims wore as seen in this photo taken from the Flamingo Room, which I submit as Exhibit 'H', also showing Mr. Jean-Paul Vincent standing next to victim Ruth Silvan who is also wearing a gold cross. Victim's number one, Victoria Morrow wore a gold cross. Her roommate, Susan Fleming asked Detectives Vero and Bradshaw if she could have it when the trial is over. Also, victim number four, Beverly Hart's brother asked the detectives if he could have the gold cross his sister, Beverly wore. This is proof that these gold crosses belonged to our victims that were found in Mr. Vincent's residence. They are proof that these were taken from the victims and kept as souvenirs."

Molly; "Tell us, Detective. Was there fingerprints found in any of the victim's rooms?"

Vero "Only partial prints with the exception of one latent print that was found in victim number three's room, that of Doris Zollermann also known as, Clara Blum."

Molly; Detective, please tell the jury what a latent print is."

Vero; "Latent prints are impressions produced by the ridged skin, known as friction ridges, on human fingers. Our finger print specialist, Kevin Kowalski, analyzed this print to known prints of individuals in an effort to make identifications or exclusions. Officer Kowalski concluded the print belonged to, as I said, Doris Zollermann also known as Clara Blum who works at the Flamingo Room as the bookkeeper."

Molly; "Why is this important, Detective?"

Vero; "It shows that Miss Zollermann was in the room. She has been identified as the person by the hotel clerks as the guest who requested and signed for each of the rooms, numbers, 18, 40, 70-6, and room number 30-6.

Molly; "Why was Officer Kowalski able to find Miss Zollermann's finger print as a match to the finger print in room number 70-6?"

Vero; Miss Zollermann has an arrest record for prostitution and illegal gun possession. She has admitted to securing those rooms for these women who worked at the Flamingo Room as dancers and where she is employed as the bookkeeper. She would have the dancers; only a select few, give their phone numbers to men who would pay for prostitution. The phone number was the same number that the men would call. It led to an answering service. The men were instructed to leave a message and Clara would call them back with instructions of paying and time and day to be at the hotel. They would have to pay first through a Western Union wire to the Western Union office on Forty Eighth Street and Lexington Ave. Clara would collect the money and set up instructions for the men with the answering service as to meeting at the Budapest Hotel and when to meet the women. Clara would then sign for the rooms herself using the victims' names, pay for the room and leave, except for one time when she went to room 70-6 where her finger print was found. Clara said there was always one man that requested certain room numbers. She never met them or even knows if they showed up. It didn't matter, they were paid in advanced."

Molly; "Why did Miss Zollermann go to room number 70-6?"

Vero; "Clara told us that she thought of taking the place of victim number three, Ethel Cummings and decided not to. She felt she was not attractive enough and Ethel came to the door, so she left after giving Ethel the key."

Judge Roberts; "Miss Penett, do you have much more of Detective Vero?"

Molly; "A few more points, Your Honor, before calling others to the stand."

Judge Roberts: "Okay, let's end here for today. Court is adjourned until tomorrow morning, 10A.M, not 9A.M." rapping his gavel.

Bailiff: "All rise."

CHAPTER 177

Trial- Day 5

Day five is a bit offbeat throwing many off due to starting a bit late. The jury decided to ask the judge some questions in the jury room, which took more time bringing everyone together two hours later than usual.

Molly continued to question Detective Vero pointing out in her questioning why it's important to know:

Mr. Vincent spoke French.

Why did he choose women with the same color hair as each other?

How did Mr. Vincent know how and where to cut off victim number four, Beverly Hart's head?

How does the bible found at Mr. Vincent's office located in his theater tie in with the investigation?

Why are the specific room numbers significant?

Detective Vero being a seasoned detective was able to fulfill each without hesitation, with confidence and determination to convict Jean-Paul Vincent of four ruthless cold blooded murders.

Vero; "Mr. Vincent is French. He was born in France. I would like to read what the tribute poster that was hanging in the lobby of Mr. Vincent's theater says about him."

Judge Roberts;" Go ahead, Detective."

Vero; "'Julian Moreau is skilled at female impersonations being graceful with femininity. His rise to stardom began in regular appearances in vaudeville and several completed successful tours of the United States and Europe. He began his performances at an early age in France where he was born and raised performing at the famous Moulin Rouge Theater in Paris. Monsieur Moreau (meaning little dark) refuses to be a caricature of women which he feels would not be true. Rather, his dark side reveals a true woman, not just imitating one. Although, Monsieur Moreau served in the French Foreign Legion with a professional fighting unit, he strives to present the illusion of actually being a woman which he considers his real side.' Julian Moreau is Jean-Paul Vincent. He was born and raised in France and is most comfortable there. So he chose to flee there to hide amongst the French not to stick out as a foreigner. His father and mother ran a farm slaughtering animals than selling them in their butcher shop. This is where Mr. Vincent learned how to cut meat, cut through bone, flesh sinew, fat and where joints were to separate them. This is how Mr. Vincent was able to cut off Beverly Hart's head. All the nylons found on the other victims had knots butchers use to tie a roast with. All the women had the same color hair which matched Mr. Vincent's mother hair color.

Mr. Vincent's mother committed suicide. Her suicide letter explained that her husband was a religious fanatic and that she and Jean-Paul were constantly subject to his abuse and misuse of the scriptures as he interpreted them. Both

Jean-Paul and his mother went through much suffering at the hands of Mr. Vincent. So, each victim that Jean-Paul killed was to symbolize his mother's death in essence by his father's hand represented by the knot used with the nylon stockings. The same knot used every day by his father, a butcher's knot."

Mr. Rosenthal; "Objection, Your Honor. Hear-say."

Molly: "This is proved by Dr. Americ Moniquè, a French psychiatrist who works for The International Criminal Police Commission, located in France, Your Honor. He will be testifying in the upcoming days with the actual letter found next to Mrs. Vincent's body."

Judge Roberts: "Umm," keeping his gaze on Molly, protruding his bottom lip over his top lip, and furrowing his eyebrows, giving indication of uncertainty. "I am instructing the jury to hold the thought of the suicide letter until the court hears from Dr. Moniquè directly and for the court reporter to strike that from the record. Go ahead, Miss Penett, tread lightly."

Molly; "Thank you, Your Honor. Continue Detective."

Vero; "The bible we found in Jean-Paul's office had markings and notes to coincide with the room numbers the victims were found in at the Budapest Hotel. Jean-Paul was raised well versed in the scriptures from his father which Mr. Vincent did not deny when we arrested and questioned him. When we crossed referenced the scriptures with each of the room numbers the victims were found in, there were certain meanings to the room numbers and why Jean-Paul requested those rooms when he called the answering service Doris Zollermann hired for setting up her little prostitution ring."

Mr. Rosenthal; "Objection, Your Honor. A prostitution ring run by Doris Zollermann has not been established."

Judge Roberts; "Sustained. Detective, do not add anything that has not been presented to the court."

Vero; "Yes, Your Honor.

Molly; "Tell us, detective, what drew you to that theory and to the room numbers the victims were found in and what the bible meaning is for these numbers?"

Vero; "Strangely, Walter Thomas, a private investigator for the Geneva Insurance Group was frequently at the Budapest Hotel to survey security and the valuable oil paintings they insured hanging in the Budapest Hotel. When we questioned him as to why he was in the lobby so often, his story checked out. He heard of the murders and certain room numbers. Being a bible scholar of sorts, he volunteered his theory as to why certain room numbers were requested, which was correct."

Molly; "Your Honor, I submit exhibit 'I' which depicts the room numbers each victim was found in and the bible meaning of the numbers belonging to each room."

Mr. Rosenthal; "I object, Your Honor. I viewed this in disclosure. It is nothing but a theory and proves nothing."

Molly; "Your Honor, if the court allows, I can prove that there is a significant meaning to the room numbers and what they represent in the bible and how the four innocent victims actually had a part in Mr. Vincent fulfilling what he thought he was chosen to do, and that is to send a message to the world."

Judge Roberts; "Miss Penett, if there is any hocus-pocus, I will stop this immediately and strike it all from the record. Do you understand?"

"I do Your Honor. Thank you. Detective Vero, you can step down for now. I have this exhibit as submitted made larger for the jury to see and understand. Let's look at the first poster keeping in mind why these room numbers were chosen for their biblical references. I call to the stand, Professor Peter Von Gusssen who is sworn in by the bailiff.

Molly; Please identify yourself to the court and your position and qualifications.

"My name is Professor Peter Von Gussen. I was head of the Center for Theology, Religion and Culture at King's College, London. I am presently Professor of Religion and Theology at New York University where I direct the institute on Religion in the World."

Molly; "Professor, in your understanding of the scriptures, can you please explain the meaning behind the numbers of the rooms where the victims were found. Let's start with;

Number 18:
Professor; "The significance of this number comes from its symbolic meaning for bondage, both oppression and spiritual. The children of Israel were in bondage to several nations for eighteen years. Number one denotes singleness and eight denotes new beginnings. Eight survived the flood; circumcision took place on the eighth day symbolizing a circumcision of the heart. Jesus showed himself alive eight times after his resurrection from the dead." He takes his victims into bondage and abuses them, killing them because he is giving them a new beginning, somewhere, somehow."

Molly; "This was victim number one, Victoria Morrow's room number."

Number 40:
Professor; "This number symbolizes a period of testing. The Jews wondered the desert for forty years. Jesus was tested during his forty days of fasting by the Devil. The flood... it rained for forty days and forty nights. Being that the number four is used in forty, we see on the fourth day of creation, God separated the night from day, light from dark. Now the number zero, visually, resembles a circle. We're dealing here with meanings of cycles, time, like what comes around, goes around. As a numerical value, the zero can be interpreted as a void, a representation of non-existence, like death. When we begin to contemplate zero, we soon find ourselves on an endless adventure. So, testing. He is testing himself, us, how many he can kill before he is caught? Separation of night and day, light and dark. Maybe good and evil? He is creating a void of non-existence by death and he is going to lead us on an endless adventure."

Molly; "This was victim number two, Ruth Silvan's room number."

Number 70-6
Professor; "Moses after breaking the Tablets because of his anger with his people because of their idolatry had to face God. His anger and frustration had

become replaced with love and compassion. When he returned to the Lord, in the book of Exodus, said; 'Oh, this people have sinned a great sin, and have made themselves gods of gold. Yet now, if thou wilt forgive their sin-; and if not, blot me out of thy book.' That dash is found nowhere else in the bible. Contained in this little punctuation mark are all the emotions of a man who had given every fiber of his being to these people. He loved them, cared for them and patiently led them when others would have given up. But Moses consumed by love and overcome with emotion, pauses as indicated by the dash and then pleads for God to take his own life rather than the lives of the people. The number seventy denotes possible judgment. There were seventy elders by Moses and Israel spent seventy years in Babylonian captivity. The number six denotes the number of man and the cities that were given as cities of refuge where the manslayer was permitted to flee. So, the killer is passing judgment on his victims but yet shows love and compassion toward them even though they have committed sins against God by killing them and wants his self to be free. He knows he can't plead to God for them, so he is helping both God and his victims in his mind, thinking he will flee to wherever the city of refuge is in his mind. Only he knows where that may be."

Molly; "This was victim number three, Ethel Cumming's room number. Mr. Vincent chose France as his city of refuge."

Number 30-6

Professor "The number thirty denotes mourning and sorrow. Both Aaron and Moses' death were mourned thirty days and again the number six, man's number, cities of refuge. So, he is mourning his victims and yet is looking for an escape to the city of refuge.

Molly; "This was victim number four, Beverly Hart's room. Thank you Professor. Ladies and Gentlemen of the Jury, this is concrete proof that the room numbers coincide with the defendant, Mr. Vincent's plan to fulfill the meaning to these scriptural references using innocent women who are the victims we must speak for. No more questions for Professor Von Gussen."

Judge Roberts; "You may step down, Professor. Thank you. You may be recalled as you know. I would like to rap this up for today. Are there any objections, Miss Penett, Mr. Rosenthal.?"

"No, Your Honor,"

"No, Your Honor."

Judge Roberts: "May I remind the Jury that there is no discussing this trial among yourselves, but only during deliberations. Court adjourned," rapping his gavel.

Bailiff: "All rise."

CHAPTER 178

The trial continued for days, turning into weeks. Both the prosecution and the defense brought in witnesses to the stand including:

The I.P.C.P. Personnel flown in from France. Detective Bradshaw, and the finger print specialist. The Budapest Hotel housekeepers and the desk clerks. The maintenance man, along with the hotel detective The Flamingo Room owner, his attorney and Doris Zollermann. Relatives and friends of the victims as character witnesses as well as the private investigator for the insurance company that insured the paintings at The Budapest Hotel. Some days, the chanting of the protestors and supporters could be heard from the street to the point of Judge Roberts having to issue an order to remove them to over one thousand feet away from the court house. The jury was tired of being sequestered and wanted this to end and return to their families and routine mundane lives they so came to appreciate.

Closing arguments from the defense and the prosecution came to an end, making the claim; *they rest their case,* which really became the real beginning to an end for the jury.

Judge Roberts: "Ladies and Gentlemen of the Jury, I must remind you as you go into deliberations form all that you heard and viewed, this is a first degree murder trial of four women. It carries with it, the death penalty. You may not categorically be opposed to the imposition of capital punishment and you may or may not be of the belief that the death penalty must be imposed in all instances of capital murder—that is, you would consider life imprisonment as a possible penalty. That would be a life sentence for each victim, with a total of four life sentences. We know that would be impossible. However, it would mean the defendant; Jean-Paul Vincent, would never be released from prison and would ultimately die there. That in itself is a death penalty. We've come this far. Do not rush to decisions unless you yourself believe the decision you came to are yours alone without being coerced by anyone else. Listen to one another. The individual in this case as well as the victims deserve your complete attention and thoughtful consideration. Therefore, I release you to your deliberations," giving a hard rap to his gavel.

Bailiff; "All rise for the Jury," as they are escorted out.

CHAPTER 179

Jury Deliberations-Day 1

Bailiff;. "Okay Jurors, here is where you will deliberate among yourselves. I or another bailiff will be right outside that door. Bathroom, only one at a time and will be escorted by either a male or female bailiff. You have your notebooks, be seated anywhere you like and you may begin."

Juror: "Wait! How do we start?"

Bailiff: "You heard what the judge instructed you. Follow the judge's instructions to the law. Respect each other's opinions and value the different viewpoints you each being to the case. Listen to one another. Get to know one another. Talk about your feelings and what you think about the case. Talk about how you want to go ahead with the deliberations and lay out some rules to guide you. Talk about how to handle voting. And, of course, you must decide on the Presiding Juror. This person should be a good discussion leader, is fair and a good listener and organized to put everyone's' thoughts together. Here is a black board with caulk and eraser to help you.

Madame Foreman; "Aren't I the lead Juror as Madame Foreman?"

Bailiff: "Only if the majority wants to keep you as such."

Juror: "What are the responsibilities of the Jury Foreman?"

Bailiff; "Encourage discussions, keep focused on the evidence, let the court know if there are any questions or problems, and tell the court when a verdict has been reached."

Juror; "Are there any rules on how to deliberate?"

Bailiff; "No! Now review the judge's instructions on the law that defines the charges, review the evidence, both the exhibits and testimony which there is a lot of. Once you have reached a verdict, fill out the form given to you by the judge, which I am handing to you now."

Juror; "What if someone is not following instructions or refuses to deliberate?"

Bailiff; "This is a violation of your oath and the court should be notified immediately for further action. Are there any other questions?"

Jurors shaking their head side to side for a no.

Bailiff: "I'll be right outside that door."

CHAPTER 180

Jury Deliberations-Day 2

The door to the jury room hadn't shut when the jurist starting talking all at once about picking a lead juror.

Madame Foreman; "Look, I have been Madame Foreman since the beginning as thought by most of you and......

Juror1;"Oh, hogwash and bullshit." Interrupting. "You have done nothing except sit in the first chair. From what I have observed, I think Mr. King should be foreman. He has leadership experience being a naval officer for twenty years and knows how to run a tight ship. Mr. King also is working at the Brooklyn Naval Yard as a civilian foreman. Isn't that right, Mr. King?"

"Yes, it is. I would be glad to be Jury Foreman. I know I would do the right thing and keep everyone organized and on point."

Juror 2; "Let's vote then. If there isn't any other suggestions?"

Madame Foreman; "I want myself to be nominated."

Mr. King: "Okay. We all have paper and pen. Write down who you want, any name on the jury, fold it and pass it forward."

Madame Forman; "Pass them to me and I will lay them out on the table."

Juror; "Mr. King, are you okay with that"?

Mr. King; "I am. Madame Foreman will unfold them and lay them out according to whose name is written down.

Madame Forman; "Quickly, pass them forward. Here we go," carefully unfolding them one at a time...

1 for Mr. King
1 for Mr. King
1 for Mr. King
1 for me, Ah ha!
1 for Mr. King
1 for Mr. King
1 for me,
1 for Mr. King
1 for Mr. King
1 for Mr. King"

Juror; "Madame Foreman. Is it really necessary to go on? Its obvious Mr. King has the majority of the votes.

Mr. King; "Yes, it is. Please Continue Madame Foreman. All the votes need to be recorded so there can't be any concern of misconduct."

Juror: "See, that's why Mr. King would be best chosen, as he just exemplified."

Madame Foreman; 1 for Mr. King

1 for Mr. King, so Mr. King, you have ten votes and I have two. Congratulations," as she continued with indistinct mumbling.

Mr. King; "First things, first. Again, paper and pen in front of you, we are going to take a straw poll. We've all heard the same evidence and testimony. From what we came into this room with, and that is weeks of hearing and seeing what was presented. No name, just place a G or a N, fold it and pass it forward."

Juror; "What does this mean, we're voting?"

Mr. King; "No! It means we are taking a consensus to see how we feel and if we need to, open it up to discussion. If all the ballots are in agreement, then we know where we stand. Are we ready to write and pass?"

CHAPTER 181

Jury Deliberation-Day 3

Molly, Johnny, and Billy sat in Molly's office, paced the hallways, made telephone calls, had lunch delivered (not to miss the call from the court that a verdict has been reached) discussed what they could have said differently and pondered the verdict.

"I really feel that we presented evidence and testimony that could only bring a guilty conviction," Molly concludes.

"What the hell is taking them so long to reach a verdict? I don't like this. The jury should have walked into that room, voted and turned around and said they're ready. " Billy comments.

"There was a lot of doubt brought out by Rosenthal; particularly there were no witnesses and only circumstantial evidence, theory, and conjection. We could not bring out anything that the French felt about Jean-Paul killing his father and feeding him to the pigs. It was only another theory and Roberts would not allow it. We know that Jean-Paul is guilty as sin and needs to be put to death," states Johnny.

CHAPTER 182

Jury Deliberations-Day 3

Judge Roberts; Asking the Court Clerk; "Any word as yet?"
"No, Your Honor, not yet."

CHAPTER 183

Jury Deliberations-Day 4

Judge Roberts; "Any word yet?" calling to his court clerk.
"No, Your Honor, not yet."

CHAPTER 184

Jury Deliberation-Day 5

Court Clerk; "Your Honor, verdict is in."
Judge Roberts; "Put the call out Court will reconvene in two hours."

CHAPTER 185

The court room gallery filled quickly with the victims' families and friends from the Flamingo Room, witnesses, Detectives Vero and Bradshaw, Mayor Bernhard, Captain Sullivan, the Police Commissioner, and well as those from the Budapest Hotel who previously took the stand. The reporters were eagerly waiting out in the hallway for word to rush to a phone to get the verdict to their editor for a front page release that would get them a raise.

Molly, her staff and Mr. Rosenthal with his staff and Jean-Paul Vincent entered the area known as the Well. The Court Clerk leaves his position to summon Judge Roberts to inform him the court room is filled and the jury is ready. Leaving his chambers, Judge Roberts enters the court room.

Bailiff: "All rise..." Reciting his rhetoric.

Judge Roberts; "Has the jury reached a verdict?"

Jury Foreman, Mr. King; "Yes, we have Your Honor."

Judge Roberts; "Bailiff, bring me the verdict."

He opened the form that contained the verdict signed by the juror's. He always read it himself first before handing it back to the Bailiff to return it to the Jury Foreman.

As the bailiff is walking toward the jury to return the verdict to the Jury Foreman, Clara Blum, A/K/A Doris Zollermann, jumped from her seat in the gallery charging to the front of the court room busting through the gate that swung in to the Well area. All on-lookers were too shocked to realize what was happening as Clara pulled a .38 caliber pistol from her handbag pointed it at Jean-Paul Vincent, yelling; "You killed my Vickie. She was like my daughter, I declare you guilty..."

Blam! Blam! Blam! Three shots were fired into Jean-Paul Vincent causing him to slump in his chair. People put their fingers in their ears to stop the piercing ring from the gun shots. Blood from his head and chest splattered hitting everyone around him. There was chaos within the first few seconds until what was happening was absorbed in the mind. One Bailiff covered Judge Roberts getting him to safety. The jury was scurried out of the court room. Clara dropped her weapon while two police officers standing in the back of the court room ran to throw Clara to the ground, handcuffing her and securing the weapon she used.

Johnny ran to Molly; "Are you okay? Molly, Molly, are you hit?"

Shocked at what she just witnessed inches from her, covered with blood and what looked like brain matter, grabs Johnny, pulling him toward her, holding him, sobbing; "Yes, yes. I'm okay. Just shook up, that's all. Did I just see what I think I saw? Oh my God!"

CHAPTER 186

Three days have passed. The newspapers were having a field day with their headlines. They did not care if they were inaccurate, as long as they sold newspapers:

CONVICTED PROSTITUE KILLS DAUGHTERS MURDERER IN COURT ROOM.

JURY FOR BUDAPEST HOTEL SERIAL KILLER SHOT IN COURT ROOM

JUDGE ROBERTS WOUNDED AS SHOTS FIRED IN HIS COURT ROOM

ACCUSED KILLER AND HIS ATTORNEY KILLED IN COURT ROOM GUN BATTLE

CHAPTER 187

Johnny, Billy, and Molly are sitting in her office reading the headlines of all the newspapers that are being sent up to her from the newsstand in the lobby.

Molly calling to Louise on the intercom, "Louise, don't bring me any more newspapers. I've seen enough."

"We don't know what's going to happen to Clara," states Billy.

"No we don't. And we'll never know what the verdict was," continues Molly.

"Why?' Billy asks.

"Because it was never read by the Jury Foreman and it can never be put into the record. "Where do we go from here," asks Molly?

Billy quickly stands stating: "I'm going to go see Nancy. Have a good night," not able to get through the door fast enough.

Johnny turns to Molly; "Let's go get dinner…"

Thank you, I look forward to your review on Amazon.com
fred berri

CAST OF CHARACTERS

Main:
Johnny Vero: Lead Homicide Detective (Sergeant).
Billy Bradshaw: Homicide Detective. Johnny Vero's partner.
Amollia (Molly) Penett: District Attorney elected after Marin Bernstein
Clara Blum, A/K/A, Doris Zollermann,
Jean-Paul Vincent A.K.A: Monsieur Moreau: Owner and female impersonator in the show; 'French Cabaret' and serial killer.

Murder Victims:
Victoria (Vicky) Morrow: First murder victim, room #18
Ruth Silvan: Murder victim #2 found in room #40.
Ethel Cummings: Budapest Hotel, Victim #3, room #70-6.
Beverly Hart: Victim #4 at Budapest Hotel in room # 30-6

Sub-Characters:
Angie: Johnny and Simone's daughter.
Judge Roberts: Presiding judge.
Inspector Laurent: Inspector with the International Criminal Police Commission, known as the I.C.P.C.
Nancy: Works at Chantal's and Billy Bradshaw's girlfriend.
Melvin Rosenthal: Jean-Paul Vincent's defense attorney.

Budapest Hotel Employees:
Greta: Budapest housekeeper found Victoria Morrow.
Chester Riley: Budapest Hotel house detective.
Halina Elzbeta: Budapest Hotel housekeeper found victim #2.
Herb Glickman: Budapest Hotel Maintenance man.
Pamela and Arthur: Budapest Desk clerks.
Jeannette: Deceased Budapest Hotel Clerk

Cameo Appearances:
Simone: Johnny's Ex-wife, living in France.
Norma (Orma): Johnny's mother
Officer Vero: Johnny's father
Freddy Redken: Angie's boyfriend.
Philip Bernhard: New York City Mayor.
Patrick O'Brian: Police Chief.
Martin Bernstein: Retired District Attorney.
Staff Sergeant Roger Enwright: Nancy's husband.
Gwendolyn Wright: Owner of Vanity Hair Emporium wig shop.

Captain Wilson: Airline pilot transporting Detective Vero, Bradshaw, and Jean-Paul Vincent from France to the U.S.

Flash: Police photographer.

Kevin Kowalski: Finger print specialist.

Howard Sneider, M.D: Medical Examiner

Antonine Chavrolet, M.D: Assistant Medical Examiner.

Louise: District Attorney, Molly Penett's Gal Friday.

Mary Webb: Victoria Morrow's mother.

Irving Cohen (Poco): Owner, The Flamingo Room.

Ronnie Ramer: Committed suicide, jumping off roof-top.

Margaret Matthews: Ruth Silvan, victim #2's mother.

Richard Lewis: Attorney for the Flamingo Room.

Charlie Goodman: Announcer, Yankee Stadium.

Vincent Razzo: Newspaper crime columnist.

Johnny's some time girl friends:

Audrey:

Grace:

Marlene:

Richard Lewis: The Flamingo Room's attorney.

Rizzuto (Phil): New York Yankee baseball player, short-stop.

DiMaggio (Joe): New York Yankee baseball player, outfield.

Susan Fleming: Victim #1, Victoria Morrow's room-mate.

Theodoros Stamos: Owner of Dorothee's specialty shop.

Andre: Owner of Andre's specialty shop.

Collete: Concierge at Chantal's.

Henry: Elevator operator at Chantal's.

Monsieur Chantal: Owner of Chantal's specialty shop.

Doris: Bookkeeper at the Flamingo Room.

Maurice Warren: Greeter at the Savoy Bath House.

William Short: Fictitious name used by Billy Bradshaw at the Savoy Bath House.

Jonathan Wadsworth: Fictitious name used by Johnny Vero at the Savoy Bath House.

Monaca: Madame at the 'The Nostalgia Hideaway.'

Lilly: Prostitute the 'The Nostalgia Hideaway.'

Walter Thomas: Insurance Agent for the Geneva Insurance Group insuring the oil paintings hanging in the Budapest Hotel.

Sylvester: Beverly Hart's Brother.

Tony: Butcher

Hoffstra and Bullock: Policemen mentioned in a morning briefing

Phil: Owner of candy store who ran gambling ring.

Gerogie: Clara Blum, A/K/A, Doris Zollermann's boyfriend.

Johnson: Detective in squad room.

Marcel: Bartender at the Hôtel de Ville.

Charlotte and Yvonne: Prostitutes at The Lè Chesterfield bar and lounge in the Hôtel de Ville.

Agent Antoine Blaisè: Agent with International Criminal Police Commission.

Dr. Americ Moniquè: The psychiatrist for the I.C.P.C.

Mr. King: Jury Foreman.

Un-Named:

Bank manager, assistant manager, secretary, bank tellers, and customers.

Murderer of officer Vero.

Police Commissioner: Un-named.

Hutchison River Parkway stranded couple: un-named.

New York Municipal Airport hooker: un-named..

Molly's father: Un-named.

Budapest Hotel Elevator Operator: Un-name. .

Robber at Crosstown diner: un-named

Police Officers who arrested the would be robber at the Crosstown Diner: un-named.

Prostitute with Johnny at the Nostalgia Cafe': Un- named.

Clara Blum, A/K/A, Doris Zollermann, (Mother; un-named)

SABSO officer in charge: un-named.

Jurors: Un-named.

Court Clerk and Bailiff: Un-named.

Super-Heros:

The Blonde Phantom: D.A. Molly Penett

Johnny Thunder: Detective Johnny Vero

The Shadow: Detective Billy Bradshaw

REFERENCES

Poems:
Splendor in the Grass
William Wordsworth

Dream'd in a Dream
Walt Whitman

109 Dunston Avenue, Yonkers, N.Y. One time residence of author fred berri

Songs:
Take Me Out to the Ball Game: The original music and 1908 lyrics of the song by Jack Norworth and Albert Von Tilzer has become the unofficial anthem of North American baseball and are now in the public domain in the United States and the United Kingdom.
The Star-Spangled Banner: The national anthem for the United States was originally a poem written in 1814 by amateur poet Francis Scott Key. Key gave the poem to his brother-in-law Judge Joseph H. Nicholson who saw that the words fit the popular melody "The Anacreontic Song", by English composer John Stafford Smith. Thomas Carr of the Carr Music Store in Baltimore published the words and music together under the title "The Star Spangled Banner", although it was originally called "Defence of Fort M'Henry". It is now in the public domain.
I'm going to sit right down and write myself a letter: 1935 popular song with music by Fred E. Ahlert and lyrics by Joe Young, now public domain.
Nancy with the laughing face: Music and lyrics by Jimmy Van Heusen and Johnny Burke.
Sing, Sing, Sing: 1936 written and composed by Louis Prima. It was recorded by Benny Goodman and arranged by Jimmy Mundy.

Translation: Google

Jury selection information: Wikepedia

ABOUT THE AUTHOR

Thank you for reading my novel.
I hope you enjoyed it and I look forward
to seeing you in my next adventure.
fred berri

Berri was born in the Bronx. After some years, his family moved to Yonkers, N.Y. where he finished his high school education. After graduating from High School, he relocated back to the Bronx where his mother found an apartment in a two family house on Arthur Avenue in a section known as Fordham and 'Little Italy.'

Early on, he learned to work different jobs, too many to mention, each one teaching him something different, starting with shining shoes. Each job brought him closer to being my own boss. He started a one man business in New York, which he sold after many years, employing over 100 individuals.

Berri relocated his family to Florida where he retired after many years as a *Financial Specialist* and a top producer for one of the largest banking institutions in the U.S.

Berri graduated Columbia State University with a business degree.

During his career, he has been interviewed by *newspaper reporters* for his business, written many *articles* for trade publications as well as *articles published for* web based sites. Berri has done public speaking and has had the opportunity to be in a few T.V. commercials, including voice-overs.

He believes the mind can imagine and create what you let it, using the children's story we are all familiar with as an example... 'Humpty Dumpty' was pushed!

Published works:
Cousins' Bad Blood (novel)
E-zine.com (Online magazine)
ArticlesBase.com (Online article library website)
GoArticles.com (Online article directory)
Services (Trade magazine by Building Services International)

Website creator and founder:
www.retirementusa.com

Radio Interviews;YouTube:
https://www.youtube.com/watch?v=dpZhhdG7RnQ
https://www.youtube.com/watch?v=v1csJDLTiiQ

fredberri@gmail.com